THE
JAGUAR CONSPIRACY

ᴍMᴍ

A Michael McAllister Mystery

PAUL McNABB

MITCHELL MORRIS

Published by
Mitchell Morris December/2012
A Division of Celeris Publishing Group, Inc.
Port Richey, FL

Mitchell Morris is a registered trademark
of
Celeris Publishing Group, Inc.

ISBN-13 9781937629458
ISBN-10: 1937629457
Library of Congress Control Number: 2012952441

Dedication
In Memory of
Vic Mroszczak

This book is dedicated to my fellow adventurer on two and four wheeled machines, Vic Mroszczak. I met Vic when I began working in Calgary in 1997. We shared an interest in vintage British motorcycles and rode them across California, Oregon, Montana, British Columbia and Alberta for many years.

When he bought a trailer in Scottsdale, Arizona for a winter escape we extended the scope of our investigations into classic cars, attending the automobile auctions each January.

When my wife and I bought a townhouse in California he was a regular visitor, showing up with a truck and trailer full of oily British motorcycles. He was with me the day I came up with the idea for this book. I continued to bounce ideas off him as a manuscript took shape.

Always upbeat, he firmly believed I would get the book published even when the manuscript was in very rough form.

Vic passed away unexpectedly on May 27, 2012. I wish he had lived to see the book published, but I still feel him looking over my shoulder each time I fire up the old Jag for a ride up the coast.

ACKNOWLEDGEMENTS

In 2006, I was asked by Philip Porter to begin writing a monthly column in E-type Magazine (www.e-typeclub.com), aptly named The McNabb Report. My assignment was to write about owners, cars and events in North America.

One of the very first interviews I managed to set up was with a restorer named Terry Larson, who lived in Mesa, Arizona. His specialty was restoring C- and D-type Jaguars, racing cars from the fifties, as well as other significant Jags. I visited various auctions in Scottsdale during the week then arrived at his home and shop on Saturday morning. He warned me he was very busy so I'd have to be quick. He'd excavated down a level, built a large shop and garage then covered it over in dirt when he was finished, an ingenious way of keeping the work area cool in the summer and warm in the winter.

At the time he owned a Jaguar team D-type raced by Stirling Moss at Le Mans and a C-type with a California racing history. He raced both of the classic Jags in the vintage racing series on the west coast. It was the first time I had seen a real C- or D-type Jaguar and I guess seeing the cars and shop made quite an impression. On the flight home, I started dreaming up a story about a C-type Jaguar in an underground garage.

Chapter 1

His teenaged daughter pounced on the phone when it rang, but after a brief, perfunctory greeting, she quickly handed it to him. Sheriff McDougall had accepted the offer to head the office in San Mateo County, leaving behind his detective job with the San Francisco PD, specifically to avoid receiving phone calls like this one.

"Jake, you better get over here quick." Craig Johnson's voice wavered slightly as he spoke.

He tried to calm his deputy for a minute before he proceeded with orders.

"Tape off the area around the doorway. Don't let anyone, especially Slim, near the apartment. Block off the parking lot. Don't let anyone out before I get there."

He gulped down a sandwich made from his hastily converted dinner, while speeding toward the location. Upon arrival at the two-story apartment complex twenty minutes later, he was relieved to see his orders had been followed explicitly. Patrol cars, lights flashing, guarded the entrance. One of the cars quickly backed up, to allow the sheriff in, then resumed its spot. Yellow tape blocked an apartment door near the top of the stairs. The second he was out of the car, he was surrounded. He raised his hand to silence his three deputies, who all started talking at once. He wanted to have a look at the scene himself first, then draw his own conclusions, before hearing their take on it.

Snatching a pair of rubber gloves from a deputy, he hurried up the stairs. When he opened the door of the apartment, the smell of death hit him like a wave of heat from a blast furnace. Entering the residence suddenly didn't seem quite as necessary as it had just seconds before. From the doorway, he could see a severely bloated, most likely female corpse lying on its side, facing him. With her long hair, she might have been lovely a few weeks ago. Now, two holes replaced her eyes. Loose skin hung from jaws mocking him with a toothy smile. The corpse was fully clothed, but the feet were bare. A large pool of dark brown liquid surrounded the torso. The scene looked like a murder, maybe a stabbing or a shooting, but he couldn't see any damage to the blouse from his vantage point. The biggest problem was the ants. A long line streamed from the slightly open kitchen window, down the counter top and across the floor to the victim, compromising the scene more every second. He pulled the door back by the side but did not shut it.

Back on the street, he barked orders to the deputies. "CSI will be here for a long time. I want you to split up and knock on every door in the complex. Somebody must have seen or heard something. Link the residents to the cars in the parking lot. Don't let anyone in or out for the time being. Find out if there's a car parked here that doesn't belong."

An hour later, McDougall watched in carefully concealed fascination from the parking lot as Bobbi Clayton, head of CSI, began the investigation. Using a kind of robot-remote control machine with a video camera strapped to its metal arm, images of the corpse were recorded from all angles while a vacuum normally used to collect hair and other trace evidence was employed to collect the ants. With the investigation radiating outward from the position of the corpse to all corners of the apartment, the whole scene was systematically combed for evidence.

According to the deputies, residents hadn't seen or heard anything. All of the cars in the parking lot checked out. The sun was rising over the mountain range to the east when the corpse finally began its trip to the lab. As she secured the body in the back of the cadaver van, Bobbi was brisk, efficient, and mildly anti-social as always. "Don't bug me on this one. The bench will give up her secrets. I'll call you as soon as I know something."

McDougall nodded, not saying a word. He had already deduced that the victim was undoubtedly a resident, Susan Thompson, a student at nearby Stanford University in Palo Alto.

A few days later, Bobbi laid out her findings in her typical, no-holds-barred fashion.

"She'd been dead about three weeks based on the amount and date of mail in her mailbox, which was packed, and the state of decomp. No gunshot or stab wounds. The brown fluids around the corpse you mentioned were from the body draining. We couldn't find any blood spatter, even microscopic, on the walls or the floor. As far as a possible rape, the bed was made but contained some semen residue. I sent it out for DNA analysis, but I wouldn't hold my breath waiting for the results because it will take forever. I also recovered some pubic hair that could lead to DNA as well, but ditto on how long it will take to get the results. I couldn't find anything under her fingernails which leads me to believe she wasn't attacked. If she was, she certainly didn't put up a fight. The stomach exploded into the genital area sometime during the second week most likely. Finding any DNA evidence inside the corpse was not possible. The ants would have probably finished off anything that existed, anyway. Dirty dishes and food in the sink attracted the ants. Although she was a bit of a slob, in my professional unquoted opinion, the apartment had not been ransacked. She was wearing a semi-expensive necklace and bracelet, so I think robbery is out."

She paused a few seconds to allow McDougall's brain to filter out enough of the gruesome mental pictures her words had evoked so the information could sink in. When she saw his eyes un-glaze, she continued.

"Cause of death was a broken neck, but not in the manner of a manual strangulation. The only thing I found was a little bit of human tissue on the side of the coffee table. Between you and me, if I had to guess, I'd say she tripped on the leg of a chair while walking across the room, hit her head on the side of the table and kind of spun to the position at death. Don't quote me on that to anybody else, because it's a little wacky, even for me. My guess is the death will be labeled undetermined. More power to you if you can make it into a murder. It's either the dumbest accidental death I've seen in my career or a perfect crime. The place wasn't wiped down or sanitized in any way I could find, which leads me away from the perfect crime idea."

Months later, multiple DNA hits were reported from the samples taken from the sheets of the bed. A couple of boyfriends were linked, but not a shred of evidence pointed to a crime. The pubic hair yielded a good DNA sample but it didn't match any of the known boyfriends. The victim turned out to be quite active sexually. Eventually, McDougall's attention was called to other cases; leaving Susan's to grow cold.

Chapter 2

McAllister jolted awake from a familiar nightmare: children running for their lives, screaming for him to save them from a madman. An aching back told him he'd fallen asleep crumpled in the chair in front of the computer again. Orange digital numbers glaring at him from across the room assembled themselves blurrily into the shape of two o'clock. He wasn't surprised. An hour or two of sleep was about the best he could hope for in one stretch these days. A quick shake of the mouse revealed a strange e-mail message:

Mr. McAllister: You don't know me so I am sending this e-mail in order to explain myself in advance. I own four classic Jaguars once owned by a WWII RAF pilot named Jack Waldorf. It came to my attention some time ago a fifth car was part of his collection but the car disappeared around 1960. After years of searching, one of my associates stumbled onto a link identifying your father's old Jag as the missing car. I tracked you down via the magazine articles you write. I was able to see a sample of your column on-line and notice you call the car Lucille. The reason I am contacting you is as follows: the Pebble Beach Concours d'Elegance has decided to honor the cars of Jack Waldorf in a special display on the eighteenth fairway this year. Considering it is already May we're in quite a rush to get ready. I would be honored to pay for the shipping of your car to San Francisco as soon as possible. A nice party is planned in late July for the private unveiling of the cars and I would also like you to attend. Pebble Beach would like to perform a professional photo shoot of the five cars together for an article that will appear in the concours program. Late July is the absolute latest they can wait for the photos and still meet the publishing deadline. I would be pleased to take care of your accommodations from July until the show a few weeks later. Perhaps you would like to do some sight-seeing? I know this is a lot of information to digest so consider my offer and then call me at your earliest convenience. My cell phone number is on the mast head.

Best regards, Peter Stafford

He'd been writing a little column in a classic sports car magazine since his first career had gone down the toilet. A Pebble Beach story would be a vast improvement over the local shows he had been covering. He immediately agreed, with one stipulation. A few weeks later, he set out on his hair-brained, mid-life-crisis-induced adventure, driving his father's fifty-year-old jag to San Francisco. As an added bonus, he had some unfinished business in California, and the trip would allow him to deal with it.

The trip covering the northwest to the first stop took a full week. Avoiding the main highways gave Michael the chance to enjoy the smaller towns found only off the beaten path. The combination of his personality and the shiny classic car, made it impossible to stop for gas without making a new friend. A Jaguar-only show in Bend, Oregon, presented an opportunity for a compelling story and pictures before heading south to the bay area. A couple of days later, while driving across the Golden Gate Bridge, he flipped open his cell phone to notify Peter that he would arrive at his Baker Street address in a few minutes. After some colorful curses spouted while carefully navigating the maze of the marina district and many prayers as the Jag fought for every inch of the steep incline leading to their final destination, he finally spotted a man standing in the middle of the street, motioning him into an open garage. The outside was rather plain, blending in with the others on the street, and in no way prepared him for the grandeur he carefully rolled into. A tiled entry began just outside the door and continued through the entire room, grey and rough, giving a texture to the floor. A circular room capped in a dome gleamed in white like a vision of heaven or a Hollywood movie set. The rotunda of the congress building in Washington was slightly larger, but not nearly as exquisite. Panels in rich, bold colors leaped from the sharp contrast of the walls depicting vintage racing scenes, possibly from Le Mans, and classic cars posed like models in a fashion magazine. He realized he had just driven into a whole new world. This one celebrated classic automobiles, or more correctly, Jaguars, and his father's old car was his admittance ticket.

The rather distinguished looking gentleman guided him to the center of a circular metal disc in the floor and then motioned for him to cut the engine. A quick glance yielded a good deal of information, a talent learned over a twenty-year period of training. Six feet tall, thin as a rail and impeccably dressed in a custom-fit blue and white pin-striped shirt, khakis, tasseled loafers and a navy sport coat, the man was the epitome of class. His perfectly trimmed beard and mustache were a shade lighter than his noticeably pale face. This man was either ill, distraught, suffering from allergies or just didn't get out enough. Mentally reminding himself of the basic etiquette his mother had drilled into him as a child, Michael gave him a friendly smile as he shook his hand.

"Mr. McAllister, I'm Peter Stafford, so good to meet you. Thank you so much for coming. I commend you for driving all the way out here. It's the way these cars are supposed to be driven."

"Let's make it Michael, and Peter, the pleasure's all mine. If you hadn't invited me, I'd never have tried." Michael unobtrusively kept his eyes on Peter, whose greeting contained a genuine passion for the cars, belying any hidden illness.

Peter walked around the old Jaguar and gave her a detailed inspection. "She's magnificent. I can't believe the cars are finally together again. Would you like to see the others?"

"Certainly." A pristine E-type convertible lounged on the other side of the garage, menacing in black on black. "Surely this E-type is one of the group."

"Actually, no. It's a nice one, and restored to a very high level, but it's not a significant car. I'll show you the others. Stay there beside your car." Michael did his best to make his lounge against the Jag appear casual and not tense or unsure.

Peter walked to the wall and pushed a button, then he hurried back and stood beside Michael on the disc. Suddenly, they felt a small jolt as they began to descend, car and all. As they dropped to a lower level, a room emerged that he would never forget. A twinkling art gallery presented itself, decorated by recessed lights. At the same time, it had the appearance of a bank vault, because no windows existed in the underground room and it did, indeed, hold treasures. Four cars stood on grand display on the far side of the room. Two years of writing his column about classic Jaguars had prepared Michael to appreciate the jewels illuminated before him. First in line stood an XK120 roadster. The second and third cars were the stars, a C-type and next its cousin, a D-type. A story came to mind he had read a few months back about a man in Arizona who specialized in restoring these types of cars. The article contained a short history of the Le Mans champions but he'd never seen one in person. A large saloon touring car painted boldly in red with white accented fenders completed the collection. The restored cars, polished to a level of brilliance, dazzled like rock stars under floodlights during a concert. He'd never seen paint glisten so brightly. Each car was flawless. Peter offered a brief tour and commentary. The XK120 turned out to be a very early aluminum-bodied car, probably worth more than Michael's house. The restorations were of the highest quality. The skills employed by father and son upon Lucille were no match for the work done on these cars.

"I feel like I should apologize for all the road dirt on my car. I guess you're going to have to give me a bucket and sponge so I can get to work."

Peter laughed. "Nonsense. I have an expert coming over in a few minutes to clean and polish your car. I plan to display all five tonight at the party for my special guests and trust me, Lucille will be just as shiny as the others." With that, he turned to head back to the disc. "Let's get your bags up to your room."

Michael bent his knees straining for one final look as he ascended, still in awe of the perfection of the cars on display. When he arrived back on the street level, Peter showed him through a side door entrance into the house. The residence was even more spectacular than the showroom for the cars below. An alcove with a stairway led up a level then opened to a small dining room with a simple table set for six. Such a small setup didn't seem like it could work for the party he expected that night. The rug had such a thick pile that it felt like quicksand.

"Drop your bags by the stairs here, Michael, and come with me to the kitchen for coffee. Maria can make anything you like. I'm going to have my own special mix."

"Please make my mine the same as yours."

Maria turned out to be the Latino woman he'd spoken to on the phone the first time he had called. It quickly became apparent that nothing happened within these walls without her knowledge and approval. She effortlessly prepared the refreshments while continuing to direct a team of caterers.

"Have you visited San Francisco before?" Peter asked as he held his cup with a careless ease Michael tried to mimic.

"No. It's my first time. It seems like quite an interesting city with a bit of a European feel."

"I'm going to take a walk down to the marina in a few minutes. It's the best I can do for exercise these days. It's pretty steep coming back up, but you're welcome to join me if you like."

"I've been sitting in that car seat for days. A walk sounds good. I need to change my shoes, though."

"Come with me then. I'll show you to your room."

A grand curving stairway led to the second floor answering his earlier question. An immense central room was lavishly prepared with a table set for possibly thirty or more guests. Each place-setting gleamed with butter-colored stoneware, polished flatware, glass goblets, and colorful splashes of cut flowers. The house was built just at the top of the hill, and they were only now one level up from the street at the front entrance. A journey to yet another level and then down a long hallway finally yielded his temporary home. Peter opened the door for him, to a small, tidy room with an attached en suite. Michael discovered that his bags had mysteriously made the trip on their own.

"Come down when you're ready. I'll be in the kitchen."

Michael hurriedly stashed his clothes in a dresser. A French door curved at the top in a Mexican style caught his attention. Further investigation yielded a balcony providing a panoramic view of San Francisco Bay. The Golden Gate Bridge was barely visible on his far left through some trees on the hill. Out in the center of the bay a fortress dominated an island that could only be Alcatraz. A small table and chair offered an invitation for coffee in the morning. Michael decided that the man who owned this house knew something about how to live.

The trip back down to the kitchen through the maze of hallways and stairs required full concentration. When he got to the street-level floor, he found Peter wearing a wide-brimmed, safari-type hat, mentioning something about protecting his face from the sun. Michael thought the man needed more sun rather than less but given that he was a guest in the man's magnificent home, he kept his mouth shut.

The walk ended up lasting a couple of hours, during which Michael felt that he was grilled. The questions might have been a test. Possibly Peter wanted to know more about the man who owned the one car missing from his magnificent collection. Of course the encounter wasn't entirely one-sided. Michael learned a few details during their conversation concerning the previous owner.

"The Jags were owned by a British fighter pilot who immigrated to the United States after the war, making his home in Los Gatos." Michael hadn't heard of the town and wasn't sure where it was located. "He died mysteriously in a plane crash, flying a restored version of his Spitfire. The cars were locked away by his mother, who was living with him on an estate at the time of his death."

Michael waited for him to explain how the cars were acquired, but Peter paused, as if he wasn't ready to share that information.

"I know you gave me a short explanation on the phone, but I'm afraid I still can't quite understand how you found me?"

"I'd been searching for your car for several years in an effort to reunite the five cars. I knew the serial number by heart, S-eight-three-eight-eight-five-seven. There's a website for the cars called XK Data dot com. I'd look for the number every once in a while and some of my friends did as well. It was our last hope. I think it was Tanya who found it one day. She checked online after I complained about the lack of leads. She looked on the Web site just as your car mysteriously appeared."

"I never put anything about my car on a Web site."

"No, but you attended some shows or possibly it was in the course of doing your interviews. Somehow, someone looked under the hood, wrote down the chassis number, took some pictures and entered it on the Web site, with you listed as the owner. I'll show you the pictures that were posted of your car when it was registered. You might recognize the venue."

The explanation still didn't make sense to Michael so he pushed on. "How did you figure out I was in Oklahoma?"

"It was noted under one picture you were a writer for the *XK Gazette*. I looked up the magazine on the Web, found an e-mail address and asked how to contact you. It was a long shot but somehow it all worked out."

Michael nodded and decided to let the issue drop for the moment. The explanation was plausible, but something about it just didn't ring true to his ears. It might bother him a bit but he also knew now was not the time to ferret out the truth. He knew better than to chase it. Eventually it would just come to him. He would not only learn how Peter had really found him, he would also find out how his father had ended up with one of the famous five cars. In Michael's business, the truth always came out.

During the walk, Peter regaled Michael with interesting commentary about the history of the marina, which he was surprised that he enjoyed hearing just as much he enjoyed hearing about the cars. Peter pointed out areas that had been utterly devastated by a massive earthquake in the late eighties. Overall, that part of the walk was thoroughly pleasant. However, the endless stairs leading back to the Stafford house made them both suffer. Michael was relieved when Stafford stopped to catch his breath a couple of times. Although much younger, Michael certainly wasn't in any shape for the hill, and it made him feel better that Peter wasn't either. The last three blocks were quite challenging.

Drenched with sweat, Michael reached the open garage back at the house to find Lucille had already been carefully bathed and was in the process of being polished to perfection. He watched for a moment as a young man expertly applied wax to the hood. If Lucille was to be black tie for the evening, then perhaps he should do his best to clean up as well. After a brief moment, he excused himself and found his way back to his room. Michael mentally chided himself for not packing a formal suit and tie. He had always thought that any event requiring a penguin suit would be the one event he would never get an invitation to. Yet here it was, the moment he had said would never come, and it was upon him. After a shower and shave, he did the best he could with the clothes he brought to look as presentable as possible for Peter's guests. At exactly half six in the evening Michael headed downstairs. He might not be black-tie-ready but that didn't mean he couldn't be punctual.

―――――――――――•❈•―――――――――――

Although she was rushing around like a madwoman trying to make sure the guests were well cared for, Tanya noticed a dark figure descend the stairs. Lean, not too tall, nice broad shoulders and longish dark brown hair tucked over his ears and falling down his neck, with black jeans and matching leather jacket completing a rather sinister look. When the stranger turned the corner, she managed to catch a look at his face, a rather nice one, with a bushy mustache to match the hair, but otherwise clean shaven. "Yum-yum." She whispered under her breath. She guessed him to be in his forties, fair game. He wore rich, black, alligator boots, and she was impressed. She always noticed shoes. She also knew every detail of this night's festivities and this guy wasn't on the guest list, *unless. . .the writer, of course.* She followed him at a discreet distance as he made his way toward Peter. He spoke in a pleasant voice, slower than most Californians but with just the slightest southern twang. *Delicious.* She moved in for the kill.

─────────────────❖─────────────────

Since Peter was the only person at the party he knew, Michael maneuvered his way through a group of about thirty to his side and joined in a conversation with a few other guests, totally unprepared for what was headed his way.

"Michael, I'd like to introduce my niece, Tanya."

Slowly, Michael turned. When his eyes landed on her, he froze. The moment shook him to his foundations. The elegant room faded around them, the bold colorful pictures lost their brilliant hues and even the cars appeared to rust. Nothing compared to the beautiful treasure that stood before him. Skin, a pearlescent white, almost shimmered against the fancy cut strawberry blonde hair that lay gracefully against her shoulders. Freckles covered her face, but they didn't distract from her slate blue eyes that peered into his very soul. A beauty glowed about her, even with the evil smile that broadened her pink, shiny lips.

"So you're the writer from Oklahoma."

"Pleased to meet you." The breath caught in his throat, making it difficult to concentrate on a clever reply.

"Peter, I'm going to steal this gentleman away from you for a while. You can have him back when I get through with him." With that, she put her arm through his and led him away. He was quite willing to be stolen.

"Is there a lot of money in writing?"

A tough opening line. "I guess some journalists do well. I don't."

"Are you famous? Do you have lots of writing groupies?"

"I've been recognized once so far, at a small show last week as a matter of fact. Apparently writing about Jaguars doesn't automatically pull groupies."

"I think Peter tracked down a few back issues after he figured out who you were. I remember some sarcasm in the story I read."

"I hope I don't come off like I'm making fun of my subjects because I find most of them quite charming."

"No. I didn't mean it that way. You do a nice job of making fun of yourself, but in a subtle sort of way. I liked your commentaries on style. You went to great lengths to describe your Ray-Ban sunglasses, Tommy Bahama shirts, ball caps and other paraphernalia necessary for the club drives. Thank God you didn't include those silly little European driving gloves with the half fingers."

"I'll make a note to get downstairs and throw them in the trash before you see the car."

"Do you mind me asking why you're dressed like a cowboy? Do you live on a ranch? Who's taking care of the horses?"

Her attack was like machine gun fire. Michael smiled as he replied. "I was pretty good at roping and riding when I was twelve. I'm not sure I'd do very well now. I guess I just feel comfortable in these clothes. I'm afraid they're all I have. There isn't much room for suitcases in the Jag."

"You have quite a bushy mustache. I don't believe I've ever kissed a man with a mustache, or a cowboy for that matter."

"I could take that as a challenge."

"You could. It might be the toughest one you've ever come up against, though." She turned before he could attempt a reply and gave a sweeping motion with her arm across the walls to the ceiling. "What do you think of the house?"

"Although I've only been to Europe a couple of times, it has the same feel, but in an unpretentious way. I guess what I'm saying is, it's pretty fancy but still feels like home."

"I'll take that as a compliment. Peter already told you that I did the decorating, right?"

He was surprised. "Honestly, no. I had no idea."

"I own an interior design shop. When I graduated from university, Peter's home was my first assignment. The finished product made a name for me in San Francisco, and I've been on the fast track ever since."

Determining her age was difficult, late thirties, he guessed. The maturity and composure she put forth when she spoke made her sound slightly older. He found her self-assurance sexy.

"I can certainly see why you're in demand." *At last, a good line.* Judging from the look that she gave him, she understood exactly what he meant.

"This house has quite a history. It was owned by a drug dealer."

"I'll bet that went over well with the neighbors." He scooped a couple glasses of wine from a server who passed by and steered her toward a quiet corner so she could continue talking to him.

"He bought the house in the sixties and immediately covered it with giant tarps, telling everyone that he was renovating it. What he was really doing was building the underground garage with the turntable."

"I have to say Peter has the coolest garage I've ever seen."

"When it was finished, the neighbors thought the turntable was so his big limo could drive in and then turn around inside and be pointed back out. No one knew a secret basement had been built. The underground room was used as a drug lab. A chain of flower shops around town were used for selling the drugs. I think he was Colombian. The shops were a big success. Of course, it was all just a front for a drug operation."

"I assume he finally got caught. Was it how Peter acquired the house?"

"He got caught all right, but it wasn't quite like that. I think one of his men finally informed on him. The city of San Francisco confiscated everything in a drug bust. A big interdivisional squabble ensued about who would get the money if the house were to be auctioned. It was deadlocked 'til the eighties. The neighbors were furious, but no one in the local government would budge. It was lucky for Peter, though."

"Why do you say lucky?"

"Peter didn't have any money when the drug bust occurred in the early seventies. He'd started his company with my dad called BSI, Brothers Software Incorporated. They wrote software code like crazy. When they went public the stock increased in value and split, over and over. In the late eighties, they were pushed out of the corporation. However, they made a huge amount of money when they sold their shares."

"Why would the corporation push them out? It doesn't seem to make sense."

"I guess you could say Peter didn't play well with others. He was great when it was a small company, but he couldn't deal with the bureaucracy. It turned out to be the best thing that could have happened to him. So there he was, having all the money in the world and suddenly nothing to do. That's when he made some good decisions."

"It would seem hard to make bad ones in that situation." That comment earned him a saucy smile that made his heart skip a beat.

"Oh, he could have made some seriously bad decisions. He had an addiction problem. Please don't say anything to him about it. He used to pop pills and stay up for days at a time when he was a young man writing code. It got out of control."

When she took a sip of her drink he noticed she wasn't wearing a wedding ring; the best news of the evening. His brain strained for ideas to keep this enchanting creature talking.

"So tell me about the good decisions."

"He'd always wanted a Jaguar. He finally got around to buying one and having it restored, the black E-type you saw in the upper garage. The project kept him busy. Every day he'd be down at the shop first thing so he could watch and learn while they restored his car. It took over six months."

"What was the other decision?"

"He bought this house."

"I thought you said the city wouldn't stop arguing over who'd get the money."

"The big earthquake in nineteen eighty-eight changed everything."

"I forgot about that. Peter told me about it while we were walking earlier. I think I remember seeing some pictures on television about it, too."

"The epicenter was right here. Down by the marina the land turned to quicksand because it used to be an old landfill. Many of the homes in this area were total losses. The city needed some good news. Peter had been wandering the area for weeks looking for a home. He started down by the marina, but eventually moved up the hill because of the view. When he found the house, it was still boarded up. He forced his way in and fell in love with the place. By then, he had the money to renovate it. So it all fell into place at just the right time."

"Plus he had a Jaguar collection that would fit perfectly in the basement."

"No. The Waldorf Jags came a few months later, just as I was hired to do the complete renovation. That's a great story but too long to tell now. Listen, I've enjoyed talking with you, but I have to circulate and be a good hostess. I've got you beside me at dinner. We can continue then."

"Of course. Sorry to monopolize your time. I'll see you at dinner."

He watched her join the other guests and expertly greet the crowd. She wore a pair of stylish black silk pants with a red, oriental-style blouse. About halfway across the room she glanced back, just for a moment, as she took a call on her cell phone. Maybe she was checking to see if he was assessing her from a posterior point of view. She needn't have wondered. He wasn't trying to hide it.

Conversations with the other guests over the next twenty minutes proved futile because a blond named Tanya had a strangle hold on his mind. Relationships with women had been a game he'd played fairly successfully up to this point in his life. Instinct told him that she was used to getting what she wanted. If Peter was rich and Tanya's father was his partner, then she was rich, too. Michael was comfortable financially but exponentially less-so than the Staffords. The only way to have any chance with her was to appear uninterested, and he wasn't entirely sure he could pull it off. She obviously already had his number. Blinking eyes and a pouty smile had been all it took to get what she wanted. When the dinner bell rang, everyone adjourned to the massive central dining room. He found his name, with some difficulty, written in calligraphic script on a neatly folded piece of vellum that was easily worth the same as a Buick. He had been placed strategically between Peter on the end and Tanya on the left. He held her chair and she flashed her wicked smile again, the one that heated the room a few degrees. *Time for round two.*

Peter busied himself with the other guests during much of the meal. Questions concerning a broad range of topics including the mansion and the cars were deftly volleyed, and he was careful to show attention to all in attendance. Michael admired his social skills but was mostly thankful that Peter's monopolization of the conversation with the other guests allowed Michael to use the time to focus on Tanya. However, he was disappointed to find that she had a nasty habit. A smart phone had become her personal assistant, one who required frequent attention. The proficiency she displayed in reading a text and responding was astonishing, especially the speed of her fingers racing over the microscopic keyboard. What he considered bad manners, she dispensed with the smile, the one he was sure had gotten her out of trouble every day of her life up to this point. One glance and all was forgiven.

An extremely fit-looking gentleman across the table seemed to be vying for her attention as well. She finally leaned over to Michael, and whispered, "That's Phil Roberts. You might have heard of him. He's a racing car driver. We were an item for a short period of time quite a while back."

"He still seems to be interested."

"Not Phil. He's got plenty of girls. He's not about to settle down with anyone." She put her hand up over her mouth and leaned a little closer. "He's like a prize poodle, nice to look at but a bit too much inbreeding. He's a talented driver but a little on the thick side, if you ask me. I found him boring."

Useful information. A racing car driver wasn't exciting enough to keep her attention. Had he met his match with this one? She remained encouraging, igniting a new topic every time their conversation lagged.

As dessert arrived, Peter tapped his glass with a spoon. Everyone quieted down.

He stood to address the gathering. "I'd like to take a moment and introduce our guest of honor." A tug on his sleeve signaled Michael it was time for him to stand as well. "This is Michael McAllister." He looked at him again. "Michael, the people here are quite knowledgeable about the Waldorf legacy. We'd be most interested if you could tell us a little about 'Lucille', as you call her." He sat down.

So it appeared that the price of admission to dinner and the Pebble Beach show was an extemporaneous speech; a small price, all things considered.

"I've heard some of the story from my father and a few other tidbits from his friends. I'll tell it the best I can. My dad took a business trip to California from our home near Tulsa, Oklahoma, in the early sixties. I don't know exactly how he met my mother, but she made quite an impression. However, the feeling was not mutual. She was a bit of a free spirit, maybe even what was considered a flower child at the time. A second trip a few months later didn't help much. He dreamed up an excuse for a third trip. I suppose he knew it was his last chance. My mom lived in Malibu, while he rented a room in Pacific Palisades. After taking a walk the first evening he arrived after a long plane ride, he happened to pass the big Brentwood Motors dealership and spotted the Jag. The shop was closed so he returned first thing in the morning and bought it. I think he paid nine hundred and fifty dollars. It was out of character for him because he owned an accounting firm, not exactly the background for making rash decisions. I guess he believed becoming more spontaneous would give him a better chance. Apparently the Jag did the trick." Muffled laughter erupted by the group at his illicit comment.

A silver-haired man at the other end of the table surprisingly interrupted Michael. "That was it, Peter. The condition was we had to sell the car to someone far away because Emma never wanted to see it again. We shipped it down to Brentwood Motors and let them sell it for us. McAllister bought the car and gave his hotel in LA as his address. We had the original records of the sale, but there was no way to track down the owner."

This was Michael's first glimpse into the mystery of how one of the Waldorf Jags had come into his father's possession. He wanted to ask more questions but decided to wait until he could talk to Stafford privately. He continued, "Apparently my mother wasn't very happy on the ranch where we lived. It could be lonely because the location was a bit secluded. I'm afraid she divorced my father when I was about three. One condition of the divorce was that I would remain with him. My father immediately parked the Jag in one of our barns and covered it with sheets. He said many times over the years that he never wanted to see the car again. However, I think it was linked to the love of his life so he couldn't bring himself to sell it. Finally, he seemed to have a change of heart. He asked me to help him with a complete restoration of the car. Unfortunately, he died not long after the restoration had been completed. The car belongs to me now. I treasure it as a remembrance of my father and mother. I plan to keep it forever.

"I stumbled into this writing job fairly recently. I'm only beginning to learn the history of the cars. I'd like to thank Peter for his gracious offer to include me in the event at Pebble Beach. It's quite exciting to learn about the first owner." He looked around the room not knowing exactly what to do next. "I think that's all."

The guests were intrigued by the story, but didn't let him off that easily. Someone in the back called out, "Tell us about the restoration of the Jag."

Michael, unsure whether he should stand again or remain sitting, glanced at Tanya, who waved him on. He took to his feet again and adjusted his jacket. "My dad called me one evening and said he needed to talk to me. I thought it might be something serious. I'd owned my own place in town for some time at that point. When I drove out to the ranch, he led me to the barn, and he pointed to the Jag. He said we needed to do a project together. He could be a little distant at times, so I was excited. He had a very high IQ. If he had an instruction book, he could figure out anything. He wasn't one to ask for help from others, so this was a very special event and I was happy to be included in it. Somehow we found out about a local Jag club. A member pointed us to a shop that specialized in rebuilding Jaguar engines so we pulled the motor and took it over to them. The car still had the original Moss gearbox, but another club member suggested we should upgrade it to a modern five speed with overdrive. A new transmission would make it cruise better on the highway. We decided it was a good idea. Another shop wanted to paint the car, but the owner warned us that we would need to build a frame for the body when we brought it in; a jig, I think it's called. Well, next thing I knew my dad bought a welder and a friend of his showed him how to use it. He welded the jig together himself. We managed to get the body off and bolt it to the jig. The paint shop came and hauled it away on a trailer. We ordered modern four-pot disc brakes from Wilwood and installed them on all four wheels. The wire wheels were rusted, so we bought new ones and mounted modern tires. Dad bought a sandblaster, handed it to me and pointed at the frame. We painted it with a rust retardant primer and then a final black coating. The speedometer and tachometer didn't work so we had to mail them to a guy in Reseda, California, for refurbishing. Eventually, everything started coming back, and we reassembled the car as best we could. We called pretty frequently for help from the Jag club and someone always seemed to know what to do when we got stuck. The interior and the top were impossible for us to handle. We found kits on the Internet, but thank God, dad didn't think we could do it." Everyone laughed politely.

"A specialty shop in town agreed to install the top and interior so when the car was drivable, I sat on a five-gallon paint can and drove it over. My dad demanded Italian leather. The top was so complex, I'm still not sure how they managed to get it redone. I guess the framework was still functional."

Another question from the back, "How was the drive out?"

"My friends thought I was pretty foolish to think I could drive a fifty-year-old car out to California and not expect trouble on the way. I think they had a pool on how far I would make it. In reality, the car did fantastically well. I cruised at seventy miles an hour most of the way only turning about two thousand RPMs. I think I got about twenty-five miles to the gallon. The five-speed with a tall fifth gear paid off. The car's comfortable and surprisingly roomy. I brought my clothes, a computer, even a guitar along. Everything seemed to fit."

Tanya caught his attention. "How did you come up with the name Lucille?"

"I forgot about that. Thank you for reminding me. I play a mean blues guitar as a hobby. When I say mean, take that literally. If you heard me, you wouldn't like it much. One of my favorite musicians is B.B. King. He named his guitar Lucille, a big, bold, black Gibson guitar. I thought it was a good name for the Jag as well." He returned to his seat before any more questions could be asked.

Tanya continued to tease him. "I guess I should apologize. You really are a cowboy."

"I used to be. Now I just pretend."

After dessert Peter adjourned everyone to the garage and the room below. It took a couple of trips as the silver disc could only take ten or so people at a time. Tanya showed him a curved metal stairway in the corner. It must have served an escape exit in case the lift malfunctioned. After everyone assembled in the basement garage, Peter gave a short talk. The five cars dazzled under the artificial lights. Lucille was now on the end next to the sedan. Michael had never seen her clean up so nicely. The spokes on the wire wheels were even polished to a luster that gleamed like the chrome on the bumpers. The racing memorabilia contained in cases along the wall distracted him from the cars for a few moments. Checkered flags hung in a line above the cases, testimony to the racing career of Jack Waldorf. After thirty minutes, the lights flickered, signaling the showing was over.

The guests returned upstairs, as cars arrived to take them back home. Tanya threw a monkey wrench into the evening when she appeared to engage Phil Roberts in a close conversation, one that made Michael question her previous statement about the two of them being former lovers rather than current ones.

A stroll for some fresh air seemed in order, not down the hill this time because he didn't want to make the climb back up, but parallel, across the crest. The street was only a short block long and dead-ended in some kind of park, a large one, with a viewing deck. The lights of the city and marina sparkled in the panoramic view.

As he returned to the main house, a sports car screeched away, the twelve-cylinder song unmistakable. Several young men ran to retrieve the cars for the guests, undoubtedly some neighbor boys trying to make a little extra cash. Peter's E-type, parked regally in the center of the garage, begged for attention. Even though this was a city car, Peter probably experienced the same fanfare as Michael with Lucille. A second dark metallic blue colored modern Jaguar crouched ominously next to the classic, probably Tanya's ride.

A woman's alarmed voice suddenly broke the silence. A quick search of the garage led him toward the stairs leading down to the basement. He heard the sound again, slightly louder than before. At first, he thought perhaps a couple had sneaked down for some illicit sex near the cars. However, something didn't seem quite right. Quietly descending the stairs proved to be a challenge due to his shiny boots, worn for the party. The tiny glow from the trophy case provided just enough light to maneuver around the room. When his eyes adjusted, it was clear they weren't making love. The couple was locked in a death grip, a man choking a woman. His instincts kicked in before his thought process.

"Stop! Let her go!"

The stranger released his grip on the woman's throat, and she collapsed to the floor. It suddenly occurred to Michael that he was unarmed and facing an assailant, but it was too late to stop. As soon as he grabbed the assassin, he was suddenly thrown across the room. The attacker seemed to have tremendous strength, like no man he'd dealt with previously. A row of hooks snagged his jacket as he hit the wall. The pegboard on the wall, meant to hold tools, grabbed hold of his jacket, keeping him from escaping. He tried to slip out of it, but it was too late. The last image of the evening was an arm bearing a hammer descending towards his head in slow motion, turning out the lights.

The D-type Jaguar provided just enough ground clearance for Tanya to roll underneath near one of the rear wheels. A burning throat didn't stop the air from tasting sweet, but she was still in danger. Her rescuer lay motionless across the floor, possibly dead. She heard footsteps. They sounded panicked and frantic as they rushed around the room. The most essential thing in her life now was to control her breathing and remain quiet. An expletive exploded and then echoed across the room. The footsteps made one more lap then seemed to give up, disappearing up the stairs. Or did they? Maybe it was a trick to get her to show herself. An eternity passed before she summoned the nerve to act. The exit seemed a thousand miles away, but she had to try and make it, not only for herself but also for her rescuer. Metal steps clawed at her knees as she painfully ascended. The rail at the top allowed her to pull herself to her feet as she struggled to the street level.

One of the parking boys came by and froze in mid step when he noticed her. In an attempt to call for help, she raised her hand toward him.

"Help me." She could only mouth the words before she fell to the ground.

Chapter 3

The moon was distant and cold, but not as distant and cold as his wife's heart. The pairing had seemed ideal at first, because his wife came from an extremely wealthy family back east. Five years after they were married, her mother died, and she shared a fortune with a single sister. Exactly how much money was involved was held secret, as all money issues were kept strictly private between his wife and her attorney. That was fine with him. Their relationship started slipping when she was unable to conceive children. During the last ten years, they had been acting out a fantasy for their friends, but when they were home alone, his wife was tough and domineering. Her life centered on charity events, frequently held in the evenings. During the past year it seemed she had even increased her involvement. He owned a machine shop, quite profitable but not ideal for her high society friends. When he arrived home at the end of a workday the last thing on his mind was trying to clean the grease under his fingernails so he could choke himself into a tux for some lame event. His only goal now was a way out of the marriage, a way that included some serious cash. The prenuptial agreement he had signed was his only obstacle.

Restoring Jaguars, namely E-types or XKEs as they were known in the States, provided a safety net while he plotted his escape. This British sports car had set the world on end when it debuted in Geneva in 1961, offering one of the most beautiful designs ever, but with great performance and at an affordable price to boot. His latest challenge was a classic British car show coming up in Palo Alto. This last week, every evening, dinner to midnight was required to get his latest car in top condition.

Cars were different from people. They could be made perfect. No task was too small to be ignored, and he meticulously labored over the minutest details, striving for perfection with each mechanism. The day of each show was nothing less than a military operation. Like clockwork, he rose before the sun and loaded all the necessary cleaning materials into a special case that would fit into the fairly small and flat trunk area. A variety of towels and brushes were packed for the last minute touches. Trailering the car to the show would have been easier, but he enjoyed the challenge of driving it over, giving it a last minute cleaning and still winning. The other contestants would never be allowed to refer to his cars as "trailer queens."

A space had already been reserved for his entry on the field when he arrived around nine. The deep green rye grass of the manicured grounds of Stanford University backed by the calm reflecting ponds provided a splendid venue. Only a few traces of misbehaving white, streaked clouds marred the otherwise flawless blue sky. A few quick conversations with the other owners delayed the last minute details of cleaning the Jag but only for a few moments. At eleven, the order for all to put their rags down blared from a hand-held megaphone. A group of judges toured the lines of cars and carefully deducted points for various crimes against the nature of Jaguars. At four, the winners were announced. A gleaming chromed trophy sat on the rich leather seat of his classic as he prepared for the trip home.

A student strolled near as he closed up the last bag of supplies. Most of the younger generation were not aware of the history of Jaguar, but still appreciated the beauty of the fantastic sports car.

"I don't suppose there's any way I could talk you into giving me a ride in this beautiful car?"

An attractive redhead leaned over the passenger's door, her blouse unbuttoned one lower than it should have been. Her bulging breasts glared at him over the top of a black lace bra.

"Well, I have a bit of a drive home, and I don't want to get back after dark."

"It doesn't have to be a long ride. I've always admired these cars. I'd like to see just once what it's like to ride in one. Is that so much to ask?"

"I guess we could take a little spin around the area." He finished up, and as they got in the car, he cautioned her. "Don't slam the door. It's quite delicate. Just get it close and give a short, firm pull."

The door latched with a pleasant thump that spoke to the exquisite fit and condition of the car.

As he drove away from the campus, she said, "Let's go over the hills to the Pacific Coast Highway. This car must be driven by the ocean."

He wasn't the first, nor would he be the last older gentleman to behave like an idiot in the presence of a beautiful young woman. He revved the Jag a bit higher than normal as he went through the gears and climbed the hill. The motor growled ominously as the car sped effortlessly over one summit after another. The panoramic view of the ocean at the crest was what had driven men to work harder and longer than needed at their various jobs since the war in order to live in this small bit of heaven on earth. Her thick red hair cascaded in the wind. A fair share of male pedestrians couldn't help but notice her. Some even whistled as the car passed by, winding its way along the road.

As the ocean appeared dead ahead he lamented, "I really must head back. I don't want to have to drive home in the dark."

"If you'll turn north I just live a couple of miles up in Half Moon Bay. You can drop me off and be on your way."

As a strand of the open road appeared, she challenged him, "I want to go fast!"

Instinctively he pushed down hard on the gas pedal, his IQ still challenged by the beautiful young woman, and watched the needle on the speedometer rise swiftly to 110 mph. The trees were a blur as they whizzed by.

When they arrived, she turned to him, "Why don't you come up for a quick coffee for the road?"

His answer sealed their fates. "Sure. It's been a long day."

Her apartment was at the top of a rusty set of stairs scarred by the ever present salt air. Inside, she dropped her purse by the door and headed back to her bedroom. After a minute, she reappeared at the door, naked from the waist up.

"Wanna join me in the bedroom?"

The challenge was to remove his slacks without taking his eyes off her supple, young body as it was revealed. The sex that followed over the next twenty minutes or so was a dream he had never allowed himself to imagine. The sex was rough, even including positions his wife would have never allowed. Her commands were followed enthusiastically. When they were finished, he dressed, and she promptly walked him to the door.

He paused, then turned around to face her. "Do you suppose I could get your number, so we could do this again sometime?"

"Look, you gave me a ride, and I gave you a ride. Let's just leave it at that." She closed the door abruptly in his face.

As he left, he noted her name on the mailbox at the bottom of the stairs: Susan Thompson.

A few weeks later, a clumsy attempt to use one of the maneuvers he had learned from Susan on his wife landed him in the spare bedroom, possibly permanently. As far as he was concerned, humiliation was the last straw. The local bars offered no solace during his first few attempts to find women to satisfy him outside his marriage. The social skills necessary for seduction did not seem to be part of his tool kit. Every day, failures like these increased his frustrations.

A plan began to take shape, slowly at first, but growing steadily stronger. Step one involved a drive up the coast one day for lunch. The road was not one that could be driven quickly. An hour later, he arrived at a burger shop located directly across the street from Susan's apartment providing a convenient opportunity to case her complex. The door to her unit hypnotized him while he munched on a burger and fries. Just as he was about to leave, she miraculously appeared, crossing the street to the bus stop, wearing a pair of dangerously low cut jeans that showed the darkly tanned skin of her lower back with tiny reddish blonde hairs catching the sunlight. The sight of her skin so close he could almost touch it melted his last shred of decency. On the drive back to work, he had the plan finalized.

Friday morning he called out to a seemingly disinterested wife as he descended the stairs to the garage, "I'll be late tonight. I can't leave the shop until I have our project out the door and the paperwork finished."

His plan began in the parking lot of a giant discount store. He stashed his work truck indiscriminately among a dozen SUVs and walked to a nearby neighborhood. On the third block, he found an older Chevrolet truck, an ideal candidate. Computer searches had provided instructions on how to steal a vehicle. He had practiced on his own truck until he could break in with a Slim Jim and hot wire the ignition. In less than a minute, he could perform the entire process perfectly.

A few miles down the road, he stopped to switch the license plates with a set he'd stolen the day before. Susan's apartment complex appeared an hour later, but he parked a few blocks away. A firm knock yielded the results he had expected. When she opened the door, he easily pushed his way inside.

"We're going to have another party, you and me, just like before. If you scream or fight, I promise you'll be sorry."

Perhaps fear caused her to freeze, but she seemed resigned to do what was necessary to survive the ordeal. A smarter woman would have expected a man to return after their wild earlier encounter. His plan was to recreate their previous sexual act, nothing more and nothing less. He even brought a condom, not only for protection, but also to avoid leaving behind any evidence.

Eagerly, he followed her back to the bedroom, where she stripped down and lay lifeless, giving him none of the commands that had driven him so wild during their previous encounter. She gave him less than nothing, she might as well have not even been there. The situation was so awkward that he eventually gave up, and they both dressed in silence.

As he prepared to leave, he turned to her. "What was wrong this time? I mean, you do find me attractive, don't you?"

"Attractive? What do you mean by that?"

"Well, the last time we were in bed a few minutes after we met. You must have found me attractive."

She sighed. "Look, I'm going to tell you the honest truth because I don't want this to happen again. I was flunking Business Law. I decided I had to seduce my professor to get a passing grade. He was about your age, so I used you for a practice run."

The pain her words caused him screamed through his body like an electrical current. A recurring nightmare unfolded. As a child, he was frequently the butt of cruel jokes from the other kids due to his pimply face and pudgy body. The girls were the worst offenders. He thought that, as an adult, his life had finally changed.

Years of carefully buried frustration suddenly consumed him. Humiliation, rejection, and anger combined and turned into a blind rage. Without thinking, he put all of his frustrations into a back handed slap to her face. A coffee table on the far side of the room broke her fall. Her body slid to the floor, where she laid motionless on the cheap carpet. It was over almost before it had begun. He was spent, she was on the floor and he felt empty.

"Okay. Cut the dramatics. I shouldn't have done that. I won't bother you again." He seethed from humiliation.

When she didn't respond, he walked over to her body and stooped down. Gently, he moved her on her side, and looked into her heavy-laden eyes that pleaded silently for help. Each breath she drew grew more labored than the last until they finally stopped. A gurgling sound signaled the end. Her eyes continued to hold him transfixed as they dilated and then glazed over. Reality caused him to jump to his feet and back away. Murder wasn't supposed to be part of the plan.

No one knew I was coming here. This girl probably didn't even know my name. There's no link to me in any way. All I have to do is clean this place up and make sure I don't leave any evidence.

The scene of the murder was the first challenge. Should he clean it thoroughly or leave everything just as it was? The bed certainly had to be remade because he didn't want to leave any signs of the rape. Was it possible to make this look like an accident? The apartment was a mess with dirty plates and scraps of food in the sink. The rest of the rooms were no cleaner. Maybe it would provide a perfect cover. There would be so many fingerprints, the police would never suspect foul play.

Fifteen minutes later the apartment was arranged the best way to conceal the crime. As he prepared to exit, a pickup truck full of construction workers pulled in just below the apartment window. They opened up a six-pack of beer and laughed, telling stories to celebrate the start of the weekend. He wondered if they'd ever leave. Finally, after what seemed an eternity, the group broke up and went separate ways. He took one last look at the student. She seemed almost more beautiful dead than alive, and it took all his self-control to resist the urge to have sex with her again.

The stolen truck had to be returned to the discount store and discarded among a maze of shoppers. The young girl's pleading eyes haunted his thoughts on the last leg of the drive home. The evidence that he'd been with her also consumed his thoughts, and he had to get rid of it. When he heard the safety of the garage door close behind him, he started at the utility sink briskly scrubbing his hands and arms with Gojo hand cleaner dispensed from a container. He stripped off his clothes, which might also contain evidence, and moved to the indoor drain. He continued the washing process with a bar of soap stolen from the sink and a hose extended from the wall. The water sent a chill through his body the first instant it touched his skin. He continued to wash thoroughly, allowing the water to drain through his illegal system down to the stream in the back. If his wife poked her nose downstairs, he would simply say he was filthy from work and wanted to clean up as much as possible before coming inside.

The surgically clean shop was almost identical in design to the professional version at work. Every tool necessary for working on his intricate classic cars was strategically stored in modern cabinets. An hydraulic lift, stereo system, and television completed the state-of-the-art workspace. The crowning touch, a large Jaguar emblem professionally painted in acrylic located in the center of the floor. The drain directed water down a pipe that led to the stream behind his house, allowing him to wash his cars inside the garage. He made sure city inspectors never got the chance to check his property after it was installed. He browsed rows of chemicals and selected one he knew would destroy any living cells. A half a gallon chased the pure water down the drain to destroy any living evidence.

When he finally felt clean, mentally and physically, he walked up the stairs, threw his clothes in the laundry hamper, walked confidently to his bedroom and breathed a sigh of relief. His wife snored audibly as he passed her bedroom. He made a big show of taking a shower, just in case she awoke.

The excitement of the death kept him awake long into the night. Scenes of her pleading eyes ran through his mind a thousand times. DNA at the crime scene didn't seem to be a possibility. No criminal record existed anywhere to match it to, anyway. His fingerprints were on file due to his Navy service so they could be a problem. But none of it really mattered, because he was high on the experience. Taking a life made him feel powerful. For the first time, he felt proud of himself.

The *San Jose Sentinel* yielded nothing about the woman's death for several weeks. Finally, he caught a report on the television newscast announcing the death as possibly a freak accident, because the authorities could find no evidence of foul play. The examiners thought she might have tripped, and hit her head. After questioning several boyfriends, nothing sinister came to light, and just like that, he was free of all worry. Perhaps he'd committed the perfect crime.

In the weeks that followed, an urge began to grow inside, an urge to do it again. Taking a woman against her will was the strongest high he'd ever felt. Could he really do it? Did he have the nerve? Could he do it without being caught? Workdays started to be filled with computer searches devoted to crime. Each day his fantasy grew stronger. Eventually it controlled almost every minute of his life.

Chapter 4

*C*hildren *screamed. A bad man chased them. Their pleading eyes begged him to save them. This time he caught up with the man but his arms weighed a thousand pounds, preventing him from throwing a punch.* As the dream faded, he grew conscious of the fact that someone was slapping his face. He pushed the hand away, and looked up to see several people towering over him like skyscrapers. There he lay, back flat against the cold floor as the noise and confusion assaulted his senses from every angle.

A man's voice barked orders forcefully. Some kind of stretcher appeared from nowhere and gobbled him up. A rough journey up several flights of stairs followed, and then concluded with an unceremonious arrival on a bed. The same voice barked again.

"You and I are going to have a conversation. You're going to tell me the truth. Why did you try to kill Tanya?"

"Could I bother you for a glass of water?" Michael carefully pulled his legs over the side of the bed and sat up. Identifying his location as his bedroom in the Stafford mansion was slightly reassuring, though painful. A powerful ache pulsed in his head, and his ears were ringing. Careful exploration of his forehead with his shaking fingertips revealed sticky blood. Then he remembered the blow from his attacker.

The man standing before him motioned for one of the cops to bring a glass of water. Cautiously, Michael eyed the man, assessing him, determining that he might be the one in charge.

"That was Tanya in the basement? Is she all right?" Michael asked as he graciously took the glass from the cop.

"Okay. Let's start over. My name's Detective Clark. I'm with the San Francisco PD. I'm investigating the attempted murder of Tanya Stafford. I'm going to ask the questions and you're going to answer. Are we clear?" Michael nodded slowly and carefully. "Tell me what happened."

Clark had the look of a man who could take care of himself. As if the thick, bulging muscles pressing tightly against his shirt wasn't intimidating enough, his overall height and body mass were. Large hands, rough and gnarled, gave the impression they could tear a man to pieces in a minute.

Michael took a long, slow drink of the water, composing himself to remain as professional as possible. After a moment, he gave the detective a concise and detailed report of the events prior to the attack.

After he finished the initial statement, Clark lifted his brows and tapped the pen against his notepad. Perhaps the detective looked surprised, or maybe even suspicious, but either way, it didn't stop the onslaught of more questions, which Michael answered to the best of his ability, while trying hard not to vomit all over the man's shoes.

Clark took a deep breath, and nodded his head. Apparently, he seemed satisfied after the lengthy questioning. "Excuse me a moment." He politely stated, then went out in the hall.

"Stay here by the door and don't let him leave. Look in on him from time to time. I thought we had an open and shut case, but now I'm not sure. His story has a ring of truth to it. I don't want to take him to the hospital, at least not now. I need a few more questions answered. Keep an eye on him and be careful." Clark might have been talking to another policeman, but Michael got the impression that he was meant to hear every word.

The door opened again. This time it was Maria. "I only haf some aspirins."

"I'll take whatever you have." He swallowed a couple with a single gulp of water. He looked back at her. "I didn't try to hurt Tanya."

"I know."

Chapter 5

S usan Thompson's "accidental" death created a domination addiction. A new plan slowly evolved over the next six months. Find a woman, incapacitate, rape and then release her. Bars appeared to be the best place to find a victim, especially if he could find one that was a little drunk to begin with. Date rape drugs seemed ideal for incapacitating a potential victim. Finding a local underground source for GHB, or gamma hydroxybutyrate didn't prove difficult. The drug was expensive, but luckily, money was not an issue. Computer searches revealed additional important information, tips to help him accomplish his chosen crime. The crux of the plan was to bring the victim back to his garage where he could exert complete control over the situation. Disposing of the victim afterward would be easy.

After what seemed like an eternity, his wife decided to visit her sister for a long weekend, something she did every few months or so, the exact something he had been waiting for. Others observed the same calm demeanor they expected to see in him, but just underneath the surface lurked the dark soul of a psychopath. The shop would have to run itself on Friday afternoon; he had more important matters to attend to.

A bus stop near his home offered a ride to San Jose. A neighborhood near the stop led to an acceptable Ford Explorer. New computer reports stated that Ford Explorers were the easiest and most available vehicles to steal, and for once, the reports were true. After slipping on a pair of rubber gloves from his shop to avoid leaving fingerprints, he broke into the truck in under a minute. A few miles down the road, he pulled over, opened a briefcase containing the stolen license plate from a few weeks ago. The briefcase looked business-like, just in case a police officer pulled him over. It only required a minute to replace the plate on the Ford and toss it down a sewer drain.

Excitement tingled through his veins as he arrived in front of a bar that he felt was promising. After stepping out of the vehicle, he shoved the gloves in his pockets and casually entered through the front door. It was time to hunt. Nervousness caused his hands to shake almost uncontrollably as he took a stool at the bar. The lights were as lazy as the bartender in the second-class sports bar. The elevated chair proved ideal for casing the lay out. Customers yakked out meaningless stories at volumes directly related to their blood alcohol content.

The ideal victim would be a hot babe already a little tipsy. A perky blond wearing a tight sweater was at the top of his list but she was with a girlfriend sitting at a low table just a few feet away. After a beer, his courage strengthened enough to make his move, but by then another man had moved first. Anger pulsed through his blood stream for the next hour while the newcomer laid on his best BS. Two rounds later, he scored with her friend, leaving his choice target alone. When she made eye contact, he moved in.

"I'm a good listener. You look like you could blow off some steam. Can I buy you a drink?"

A year earlier, his lack of self-confidence would never have allowed him to smooth talk a hottie like this one. With little encouragement, she launched into a story about a failed office romance with a salesman.

At eleven, he finally got up his courage. "Listen, would you be interested in continuing this conversation at your place?"

Her gaze went from the wedding ring on his finger to his eyes. "You're married. That was the whole problem with Bill. I can't go home with you."

"Okay." He laughed. "Can't blame a guy for trying." When she turned away, he poured the entire tiny vile into her drink. He was only supposed to use half, a very small amount, but it needed to work quickly. A few minutes later, he tested her, "Listen I've got to get home. It's been nice talking to you. Maybe I'll bump into you again."

"You know, I'm not feeling so good."

"Maybe you better get home, too. Let me help you to your car."

She became faint almost immediately after they stepped outside the bar. Rolling her into the back of the Explorer proved to be easy. He retrieved the gloves from his pocket for the drive home. They were a damn nuisance, but he didn't want to leave fingerprints. A few blocks away, he pulled over on a dark side street to tape his victim's wrists and ankles tightly for the ride home. The automatic door opener he'd transferred to his pocket commanded entry to his fantasy zone.

Now, the scene he'd endlessly rehearsed in his mind over the past few weeks became a reality. The zombie-like victim didn't resist the transfer from the truck to a device he used for straightening bent frames. After he carefully secured each wrist to a corner, he strolled over to the Budweiser refrigerator and selected a can of his favorite beer. Slowly, he strolled back to assess his victim. Her body felt good, at least through her dress. However, even if he tried, nothing would revive her from the drug-induced state, not even a short session with a blowtorch. Now that was a naughty idea. He retrieved a pair of shears from his workbench, taking his time and offering a little peek of skin here and there. The original scene with the college student proved impossible to recreate. The sex wasn't the same. After an hour, he grew tired of her.

A large screwdriver had been part of the recurring fantasy. He retrieved it from the toolbox and waved it in front of his victim hoping for the same fear and pleading he'd seen in his first victim, but she was barely conscious. Why didn't she plead for her life? That was the next part and it was important to him. A jab to the stomach should get her attention. Dark red blood gushed out, and splatted onto his shirt. The sudden gasp from her lips drew his attention to her vacant eyes. Again, he thrust the weapon into her, but she refused to plea for her life. A long moan followed, barely perceptible before her body slumped against the restraints. He paused.

This wasn't going the way he had planned. With one quick motion, he wrapped his fingers into her hair and yanked her head up to watch as her eyes glazed over in death. He leaned closer, to savor her last breath against his skin.

What went wrong with the plan? Had he over-dosed her? He had known for the plan to work, it had to be precisely followed. Now, the best part was ruined. He wouldn't make the same mistake next time. Only total control, the power of life and death over these helpless women, would satiate his masochistic urge. The victim had to beg for her life, just before death. Nothing else would do.

Cleaning up the crime scene was just as important a part of the process as the killing. The sheer amount of blood covering the garage floor shocked him. The next step was to place the victim in the back of the Explorer for transport away from the kill zone. He removed the tape from her wrists, which undoubtedly contained his fingerprints, and disposed of it. The next step in the cleaning ritual involved washing down his body over the drain with soap and water to remove any incriminating evidence. The final step, flushing the drain with one of his painting chemicals, he completed quickly.

Daylight peaked in the upstairs windows, bathing his napping body with a gentle light. Undisturbed by his wife, his nap lasted late into the afternoon, where he awoke and groggily made his way into the kitchen for a cup of coffee. The caffeine would clear his mind, allowing him to handle all the after dark work. He would wipe down the truck, removing any possible fingerprints, and then drive it towards San Francisco where he would abandon it in Chinatown. He would then take a bus to complete the trek home.

Two days later, the story hit the newspaper's front page. The stench emanating from the truck attracted the attention of a nearby storeowner the next afternoon, who immediately called the police. A flatbed moved the putrid vehicle to the forensics lab for investigation. Reporters pounced on the story as soon as word spread about the strange looking puncture wounds. Seeing that his victim had made front-page news stroked his ego. The authorities were scrambling to make sense of the crime. Headlines made him feel important for the first time in his life.

Chapter 6

Detective Clark headed toward Tanya's room like a tank, only to be blocked at the door by the attending doctor.

"Not tonight, Detective. She's sedated."

"When can I see her?"

"I'll meet you here at nine in the morning. I know you need to talk to her, but she's injured. I'll make sure she's okay and then I'll let you interview her. Deal?"

At eight forty-five the next morning, Clark leaned against the wall reading the local newspaper when the doctor arrived. The white-coated professional gave him a solemn nod before walking into Tanya's room to complete his examination. Of course, Clark's impatient pacing up and down the hall didn't make the time pass any quicker. When the door finally opened, the doctor stepped through and immediately turned to Clark with a concerned glare.

"You can go in now, but there's a problem."

Clark raised an eyebrow and waited for an explanation.

"She can't speak. Remember, she was strangled. She's sustained some kind of injury and I'll need to investigate, but not right now. The ordeal of a scope down her throat would be too much for her to endure. I'll find out exactly what's wrong soon enough but for now she can only nod a yes or no. If you need more details I guess you can see if she can write something out. I'll give you ten minutes, no more. I've given her a sedative, she needs rest."

Clark knocked and then gingerly opened the door. A small, frail woman lay in the bed. He hated interviewing physical abuse victims. As a big man, he could lift heavy objects and pulverize anyone who dared attack. But he couldn't heal the wounded, he couldn't make it better.

"Tanya, my name is Detective Clark. I'm sorry, but I need to ask you some questions. I'll be as quick as I can."

She nodded. The routine questions were simple, and the easiest to answer with a simple shake or nod of the head. The answers quickly eliminated Michael McAllister as a suspect. It seemed the cowboy interrupted the attempted murder just as he had claimed and had undoubtedly saved the woman's life. The next few questions proved more difficult because the sedative kicked in, making her groggy. Tanya struggled against the drugs to write out the answers, but for the most part, they were incomprehensible. She scribbled the name Phil Roberts. Immediately Clark recognized him from the list of attendees at the party.

Using the evidence from the victim and some serious good-ol boy charm, Clark got a warrant within a matter of hours and was shortly thereafter standing on the porch of a swank townhouse in North Beach with four officers backing him up. A classic red Ferrari sat in the driveway. Detective Clark planned to shake Roberts up a little bit to see what happened. If he refused to talk voluntarily, it would be a sure sign of his guilt. A heavy knock on the door went unanswered.

Not wanting to lose time Clark tried to peer through the windows into the front room but they were effectively blocked by wooden shutters. "You men stay here on the sidewalk. I'm going to make one trip around the building and see if I can pick up anything." A gate to the left offered little resistance and Clark followed it down the side of the structure until he came to another window, this one not covered. The room was too dark to make out much inside.

"Somebody bring me a flashlight."

He heard footsteps run to one of the patrol cars and a moment later a young officer handed him what he requested. Using the shaft of light, he carefully investigated the room from right to left, as best he could. On the far side he saw a figure slumped in a chair with the head resting on a desk. "Do you see what I see?" The officer concurred. Clark rapped on the window firmly and loudly stated his presence, as he was required to do, but elicited no movement from the figure inside.

He returned to the front door. "Break the door in." One of the other officers managed to kick the door open on his third try. "All of you wait here. I'm going to confirm we have a corpse inside. I don't want anyone disturbing evidence so I'll go alone. Get your guns ready in case I need help."

Entering through the living room he glanced to the right, at a kitchen. Nothing seemed out of place. Moving the other direction down a hallway he found the room he was seeking on the left. Even from the doorway the stench of blood was noticeable. A stream of light illuminated a corpse slumped at the desk as he had seen from the window. A gunshot wound was now visible in the side of a male's head with blood spatter clearly visible on the wall. Even from across the room it was obvious the man could not have survived the wound. Clarke retraced his steps to the front door. "Call CSI. We've got a corpse."

Five hours later Clark returned to his office. Crime scene investigators determined the corpse was indeed Phil Roberts based on identification in a wallet. Death was due to a single gunshot wound to the head. Failed murder attempt then suicide? Could it be that easy? Time and evidence would tell.

Chapter 7

His wife left to visit relatives again back East. She invited him with a tone indicating she wanted his answer to be no. He declined, using the excuse he was too busy with work at the shop to get away, the same excuse he used every time. He drove her to the airport, but then instead of driving home, he headed north over the Golden Gate Bridge to Healdsburg, about sixty miles away. A business meeting a few weeks earlier with a potential client had alerted him to the possibilities of the location. The self-control he exhibited waiting for his wife to leave town dissipated as quickly as her plane rose into the sky. A murder attempt in the sleepy little tourist village without any kind of preconceived plan would prove extremely dangerous, which only added to the appeal in his mind. A strong adrenal rush drove him on when he reached the town square.

He backtracked on foot to an apartment complex he'd seen on the way into town. Several two-story buildings angled around the parking lot with plenty of stairwells and landscaping for cover. A spot beside a tree offered the safety of darkness while he slipped on a new set of his trusty surgical gloves.

Over the course of about a half an hour, three cars entered the complex. A man drove the first so he ignored him. The second, a woman who parked at the far end of the complex, was inside the apartment before he had a chance to get a good look. A couple occupied the third. A few people left the complex during the same time so he had to be careful to stay in the shadows to remain undetected.

Just when he was about to lose his patience and leave, a young woman parked her car and walked within a few feet of him to a doorway nearby. When he heard her key click to unlock the door he was already closing on her, shoving her into the apartment. Another young woman sat in her nightgown in front of the television with a tray holding a large bowl of popcorn. If they had reacted quicker, one of them might have escaped but they seemed frozen with fear. A large knife lying innocently on the kitchen counter sealed their fate.

"If you both do exactly as I say, you'll survive this. If either of you makes a sound or tries to get away, I'll cut you to pieces."

The curtains were already closed in their tiny, shoebox of an apartment, the kind new college grads share when they're starting out in the work force. Flashing the knife near each young face proved to be all he needed to do to keep them compliant. He marched them down the hall and into the first bedroom. The girl dressed in the nightgown, he decided to save for later, shoving her into the closet.

"If you try to get away, I'll cut your girlfriend's head off!" The girl's crying caught his attention, and he turned to the other woman.

He removed his sport coat and laid it by the door, then motioned with the knife to the second victim to get undressed. When she removed her panties, he grabbed them from her hand, stuffed them in her mouth, and then shoved her hard onto the bed. Her lack of resistance made him think she was possibly in shock. Still holding the knife in his right hand, he mounted her from the front, scooped her legs up with each arm, and entered her viciously. Tears streamed down the sides of her face during the attack. As he came inside her, his arms practically forcing her knees beside her ears, he pulled her head back by the hair with his left hand. The knife moved across her throat hard and deep. A gurgling sound marked the end of her life. Her eyes fascinated him until they dilated then closed in death.

When he maneuvered himself off the corpse, he noticed a lot of blood on his shirt and arms. He stood at the door of the bedroom so he could block any attempted escape by the other girl. He wiped the knife and laid it on the foot of the bed. The blood on his clothes would be a problem. Carefully undressing, he stacked his clothes in the hall. Moving the corpse was awkward but he managed to roll it off the bed. He broke its fall to the floor so the first girl wouldn't hear what was happening. The pillow was soaked in blood so he pulled the cover up to the top to hide it as best as he could.

He tip-toed to the closet and jerked the door open, confronting the remaining girl whimpering in the corner. When he pulled her out, he could tell she'd peed her panties.

"Your roommate is okay. I've tied her up in the other bedroom. Let's get this over with as quickly as possible and then I'll leave." The knife told her to lose her nightie. This one was a little more vocal, although she uttered nothing approaching a scream for help.

"I'll do anything you say. Please don't hurt me."

She gagged when he slit her throat. The fear in her eyes was thrilling, the best so far. He staged them side by side on the bed with legs open, to shock whoever found them.

The bloody shirt was a problem. A washer/dryer combo off the hall provided a solution. During the wash cycle, a long hot shower removed the blood from his body. The phone rang halfway through the drying cycle. After the fifth ring it went to message. "Hey, Jen. Pick up. Listen I'm running late on my shift. I'll be by in about an hour. See you then. Where are you?" The wrinkle free shirt didn't look great, but his jacket covered most of it. He smiled at the thought of a boyfriend finding the bodies. Hopefully he'd use his own key to the apartment and maybe even incriminate himself. Three hours after pushing his way into the apartment, he cracked the door to make sure no one could see him exit.

The trip back to the car was deliberate, not rushed. The Golden Gate Bridge was a mess when he crossed an hour later driving his wife's Lexus. Several policemen worked an accident, trying to keep the traffic moving. He rolled down his window and asked one of the officers what was going on. The policeman just waved at him to keep moving.

The next morning's paper couldn't arrive soon enough for him, although he was careful to let the paperboy pass by before he hustled in his bathrobe to the walk to retrieve it. The San Francisco paper shouted the gory details from the front page. A boyfriend of one of the girls was being held as a person of interest. One of the reporters caught wind of the devastating injuries inflicted on the victims and coined the name "The Slasher". He was finally starting to get the kind of recognition he craved.

One story in particular held his interest. Written by a leading psychologist, the article contained a tedious analysis of personality types and motivations. The analysis was laughable. No one could possibly understand the thrill of the murders unless they, too, had experienced it. However, it did serve to get the next step of the plan to start solidifying in his mind.

Chapter 8

The next morning, Michael woke to a splitting headache. Staring at the ceiling of the Stafford house, he recounted the details of the previous day in his mind. A small cast on his arm was a big surprise when he tried to scratch his forehead. Eventually Maria popped her head in the doorway and noticed he was awake. She simply nodded and left. Soon Peter appeared.

"Michael. I'm so sorry about what happened. Are you feeling any better today?"

"I think so. I guess a good night's rest helped. I have a hell of a headache."

"It wasn't just a good night's rest. You were out all day yesterday. I asked a doctor to come by to see you and he gave you an injection. I have something to help with the pain."

He accepted two pills gladly, and washed them down with a glass of water.

"How's Tanya?"

Paul McNabb

"I'll never be able to adequately thank you as long as I live. You saved her life. The doctors said she wouldn't have survived even a few more minutes without your help. She's a bit like you, not much good yesterday. However, when I went to see her this morning, she was starting to get her spark back. She can't talk, though. She's had an injury to her throat. The bastard choked the hell out of her. It shouldn't be anything permanent but there's no telling how long it will take her to get her voice back."

"Any idea who was responsible for the attack?"

"At first it seemed it was Phil Roberts. He apparently committed suicide the same night Tanya was attacked. A note was found under the corpse saying something like if he couldn't have her, no one could."

"The man who attacked Tanya wasn't Phil Roberts. Phil was small, like a jockey. This guy was bulkier and strong as a bull. I may not look like it, but I know how to take care of myself. The attacker threw me across the room like I was a toy."

"Tanya said the same thing. Clark misinterpreted some information she gave him as identifying Phil as her attacker. She couldn't talk and I guess there was some confusion with her answers. That's why they went to his house and found him. I didn't push her about it when I visited the hospital but apparently she knew for sure it wasn't Phil."

"The police will sort it out in time."

"Yes. Let's not worry about it now. You've got to eat something. May I send Maria up with a sandwich?"

"I don't think I can hold anything down yet. Let me try to clean up a little. I'll find my way to the kitchen when I'm able."

Peter nodded and left. When Michael stood up for the first time in over a day, it left him slightly nauseated. He looked in the bathroom mirror to assess the damage. A nasty looking cut started high on his forehead and disappeared into his hairline. The finishing touch was a very black eye. He awkwardly managed to shave and shower. Still, the warm water soothed him. It felt good to be clean.

50

Almost an hour later, he wandered down to the kitchen. Maria tried to feed him but he begged off. He got a pleasant surprise when he found a Diet Dr. Pepper in the fridge. Michael wasn't sure when his addiction to the drink had started but it was certainly his favorite. At that point, carbonated beverages were necessary to settle his stomach before eating. Another stroll in the fresh air at the top of the hill seemed to be just what the doctor ordered to help clear his mind and help him feel a little better. Halfway along the block, he came to the viewing area of the city that he'd seen the first night. In the light of day, he could read a large sign he'd missed in the dark identifying the park as the Presidio. The name sounded familiar, but he couldn't place it. The Diet Dr. Pepper and the fresh air having done all they could for him, he started back to the house. The street only held six houses on each side because they were large estates. One had elegant juniper trees trained together at the top to form an archway over the front door. Another had magnificent urns at the base of the front stairs from which sprouted a plethora of ivy vines that covered the ground back up to the walls of the house, making it look like the house had been standing in that exact spot for ages. All were intricately and impressively landscaped.

As he arrived at the Stafford residence in the bright sunlight, he fully appreciated the majesty of the house. The home filled two lots but the one on the left seemed to contain a courtyard behind a full one-story wall. Upright yews guarded each side of a small arched door surrounded by ivy. The front door repeated the arched doorway but this one was two stories high and guarded by lions that looked like sculpted marble from Roman times. Two stone cherubs perched themselves on top of the archway performing some task he was unable to determine. The front of the house rose a full three stories high from street level. He backed up to the center of the intersection for a better view of the entire house and noticed the streets were Vallejo and Baker. Not too many cars had a good enough reason to visit the neighborhood, so he stood in the middle of the road without worry of being run over, observing the house from the side, studying its design as it extended a full half block down the hill. His room was on the very back of the house, so he couldn't see it clearly, but he could just glance an awning extending over a window to what he guessed was the right one. The double garage door was about as far as he could throw a palm-sized rock down the street. When he had first arrived, he thought the house was white but now in the daylight he could tell there was a slight olive tone mixed into the walls. Maybe it was white a long time ago. Had Tanya selected the exact shade?

The questions seemed too difficult for his muddled brain to solve, so he gave up and headed inside, asking Maria for a sandwich and another soft drink. He was beginning to once again feel human when Peter joined him.

"Do you think we could visit Tanya this afternoon?"

"No need. She's coming here later. The doctor just released her. Her father died some time ago and her mother lives in a townhouse nearby. I'll take her to see her mother and reassure her she's okay but I'm bringing her back here afterwards. She has a room upstairs she uses whenever she stays over. I'm going to hire extra security and turn this house into a fortress so I can protect her until the police find the man who tried to kill her. "

"Well, I'm relieved she's better but I think I need to go back upstairs to rest a little more. I did a short walk, and I'm already exhausted. I'll look forward to seeing you both later."

Two more of Peter's pills sent Michael into a deep sleep just minutes later. He finally awoke to the setting sun. The clock on the nightstand told him it was almost seven. The only attempt he made to freshen his appearance before he went downstairs was to run his hands through his hair.

Michael found Tanya and Peter sitting quietly on bar stools around the immense granite island in the kitchen. When Peter looked up at his entrance, she turned. Instantly, she hopped off the stool and rushed toward him with opened arms. Tears streaked down her beautiful face as her arms wrapped around his neck.

Instinctively, Michael slipped his arms around her, taking a moment to enjoy the short visit to paradise her embrace afforded.

She whispered in his ear, "You saved my life." She gave him a soft kiss on the cheek, then pulled back. Her trademark evil smile flickered for just a moment. "You're a mess."

"I'm trying out a new career as a punching bag."

Obviously still a little shaken, she ignored his weak attempt at humor. The catty rich-kid from the first night he had met her was gone, replaced by an emotionally defenseless young woman. Her vulnerability made her even more beautiful to him. She took his hand and led him to a seat next to Peter.

"Feeling any better?"

"Well, I'm pretty damned weak. I slept all afternoon again. The headache is starting to go away, though, so I guess a doctor would say I'm improving."

"Detective Clark's on his way over. He wants to ask some more questions."

A firm knock on the door announced his arrival, and he wasted no time with his questions, firing them at the group as soon as he was in the door. Another Diet Dr. Pepper appeared, as if by magic, in the refrigerator. Apparently, Maria had noticed it was his favorite. A lot of the stores out west didn't seem to realize how important it was to stock Diet Dr. Pepper.

Tanya had kept a hold of Michael's hand since he had first entered the room, only allowing him loose to pop the top of the can. She promptly regained control of his hand as soon as it was free. Her grip on Michael's hand slowly tightened during the interrogation that followed. One question had been nagging at Michael. How had Tanya been lured downstairs in the first place? The answer came out during the discussion that Phil had called out to Tanya from the front of the garage. When she walked over, three men with their heads covered by stockings had accosted them, one with a gun pressed to the back of Phil's head. One man grabbed Tanya and the other two left with Phil. Drawing Tanya in seemed like a cowardly thing for Phil to do in Michael's opinion, but he decided to keep that to himself.

Tanya's voice, which had started off as only a whisper, quickly gave out. Detective Clark eventually seemed satisfied, but promised he'd return soon for another session. Michael had a possible lead percolating in his head, but he wasn't quite ready to discuss it with Detective Clark, not just yet. His heart skipped a beat when, as he was leaving, Clark motioned to him.

"I forgot something, Michael. Would you walk out with me?" Michael followed him to the street. "There's one definite suspect in all of this."

"Who?"

"Peter."

"Not possible."

"Listen, I've seen a lot stranger things in this city. A lot of money is at stake. Tanya's set to inherit both her father's fortune and Peter's. He's got no children. Maybe something's changed."

"She seems to be his favorite person in the whole world."

"Just the same, be careful. You're right in the middle of all of this and you don't know these people. If you see or hear anything, I want to know about it."

Clark gave him a card with a cell number. He had to admit, the detective had a point. What did he really know about Peter or Tanya? Perhaps he should be careful of what he was getting himself into.

Chapter 9

An empty house greeted the Slasher when he arrived home from work. Expecting a note from his wife explaining her absence, he thought it a bit strange that he didn't find one. He decided she must be out shopping. Dinner turned out to be somewhat less than he had hoped for because the refrigerator was practically empty. He was just sitting down at the table with a meager sandwich and a beer when the doorbell rang.

Opening the door, he was surprised to find the visitor was Bill Thompson, his wife's family lawyer. Although Thompson was always polite to a fault and dressed impeccably, the Slasher despised him because of his secretive relationship with his wife about her finances.

"Sorry to bother you at home like this. May I come in for a quick chat?"

"Nothing has happened to...?"

"Oh no. Nothing like that."

"Come on in. Can I get you something to drink?"

"That won't be necessary. I don't think this will take long."

The den was close to the entry and this was a meeting he wanted to keep short, so he led the way. When they were seated Thompson gave him the surprise of a lifetime.

"Your wife wants a divorce."

The Slasher kept a concerned look on his face but his mind was racing. Lawyers in California didn't make house calls in divorce cases. What was really going on here?

"She says the two of you aren't engaged on any level anymore. She thinks you might be seeing someone else."

The whole scheme suddenly dawned on him. When he thought his wife was out shopping and doing charity work over the past year she'd really been seeing her lawyer, and not just to get legal advice. He'd been giving her some excellent service, all right. An opportunity had presented itself, though. This was the plan he'd been hoping for all along. If he played it right, all his dreams would come true. His next response was slow and measured, delivered perfectly, with an air of indignation.

"The only thing I'm doing is working my ass off, trying to keep my business going."

He tried his best to show the expression of a beaten man as he hung his head.

"She wants to know how difficult you're going to make this."

He paused and tried to shift to a look of surprise in a way that looked natural.

"What do you mean by how difficult?"

"I mean how much is a divorce going to cost? I've advised her that under California law she doesn't owe you a penny. She had her fortune long before she married you. However, she doesn't want to be dragged through the courts and have to endure a lot of negative publicity. She's willing to pay to make this quick and quiet."

He paused for maximum effect.

"What's she offering?"

Bill was sweating a little. It seemed like he had a lot riding on the negotiation, too.

"This house."

"What else?"

"What do you mean what else?"

Time to move in for the kill.

"I mean how much cash?"

His expression changed to a cold hard stare.

"We were thinking about five hundred thousand dollars?"

We? He thought his wife was the only one divorcing him.

"Get serious. She's worth fifty million, probably a lot more."

"What do you want?"

Although he'd rehearsed this scene many times previously, it was important to sell the idea that the divorce was something he'd never considered. If he asked for too much, he risked blowing the whole deal. He had to be careful how he bargained. After a long silence he made an offer.

"Six million. Half now, half when it's final."

"I can't go over four."

The reply was abrupt, as if it had been carefully considered for some time. Four was plenty, but he couldn't fold that easily.

"I need at least five."

"Four is as high as I am allowed to go without taking this to court. Believe me; you don't want to face me in a courtroom."

He hung his head again and mumbled.

"Four then."

"Good. I'll send the papers over by courier in the morning with a check for two million dollars."

He decided to see if he could get the lawyer to admit he'd been carrying on with his wife.

"What's she going to do?"

"That's none of your business."

"Come on, Bill. I'm not going to make any trouble for her."

"Off the record, I think she's going to live in the house in New England, near her sister. She also wanted me to point out a lot of this furniture is hers."

"Bring a truck and take whatever you want. I don't have any hard feelings toward her and I don't want any of her personal stuff."

"Very well then. I appreciate you being so civil about this."

"I've known for a while we were coming to this. I guess it's always a little bit of a shock when it actually happens."

"I'll tell her we've reached a fair agreement. I'll send the papers to your work tomorrow morning."

Good ol' Bill had been banging his wife, and in the process, solved all his problems: four million dollars and the house, which was worth another two or three easy. Now he would have all the time in the world for his new hobby. The divorce would probably take months to work its way through the courts, even if it was uncontested. A private investigator might be employed by his wife to check on his indiscretions. He would have to depend on a complete restoration of Jaguar E-type number 7 to help keep himself out of trouble until he was in the clear.

The plan had sounded simple enough at first, but after a couple of months the only thing on his mind was getting his hands on another victim.

Much greater preparation was required now that he was a wanted man. The newspapers proved to be a rich source of information concerning the police work being done behind the scenes. The police had linked victims two, three and four by his methods and victim type, not via DNA, and they still had no clue that victim one was a related case. After an analysis of everything he had learned, he decided it would be better to bring the victims back to his garage so he could control the killing zone. Luck had played a key role in Healdsburg. The police had no choice but to announce a multiple-murderer on the news after the double murder. The ensuing media frenzy delighted him. The fear among the citizens of the San Francisco Bay area was palpable. Sometimes he would walk through the city during the day just to experience it.

Tuesday night he decided to conduct some research. After consulting a map, he decided Pleasanton might be a good choice to find his next victim, because it was located far enough away from his home to confuse the police. His brand new Jaguar sedan, a divorce present he'd given himself, was perfect for transportation because it was just a practice run. Downtown Pleasanton had a lovely main street with many family-type bars and nice areas for an after dinner stroll. He knew the set-up was all wrong for him as soon as he arrived. Too many potential witnesses roamed the sidewalks for him to take a woman without anyone noticing. One bar buzzed with activity, so he decided to at least have a look. Inside, a survey of the room yielded few potential victims. Even with the windows opened out onto the street, the noise level was high. From a vantage point at the bar he sipped a beer and watched a little baseball on the big screen television until he noticed a woman take a seat at the other end of the bar. As a result of his previous victims and his forthcoming divorce, he possessed a much more relaxed and confident attitude, and was able to effortlessly move in on her for a chat. After a few minutes, he was bored, and knew the location wasn't going to work anyway. Ending the conversation was too easy.

"What would it take for a beautiful woman like you to take me home tonight?"

"I thought you'd never ask, but I want a ride in that Jaguar. I'll leave my car here and pick it up later."

Her response caught him completely off guard. Minutes later, they pulled into the driveway of a small but immaculate home only blocks from Main Street. She inanely chatted about her recent divorce. The conversation didn't interest him in the least. Likewise for the glass of wine they sipped while they sat on her sofa. However, the next idea she suggested was something completely new and exciting. A ritual ensued as she retrieved a small bag from the flour can in the kitchen, poured the white powder on the glass-topped coffee table, sliced it finely with a razor blade and then expertly snorted it through a rolled up twenty dollar bill. When it was his turn, the cocaine almost blew his head off. The reaction was almost instantaneous. The sex that followed was euphoric, as she attacked him on the sofa, ripping their clothes off and screaming while he was inside her. The orgasm at the end was the most explosive he'd ever experienced.

As they sat side by side in the aftermath of their drug crazed sex party, he considered killing her, but he decided too many people might have seen them together at the local bar. His brand new Jaguar sedan had been sitting in the drive for several hours as well. One nosy neighbor to write down the license number was all it would take to ruin his future plans. A murder at this location was just too risky.

"Can I grab a quick shower?"

"Sure. I'll join you."

One last blowjob in the shower ended their sex party. At the door she asked, "Why don't we exchange phone numbers? I'd like to get together again some time."

"I don't think so. This was great but it's not going to work out."

The gentlemanly thing to do would have been to drive her back to her car but he was irritated that he wasn't able to murder her. She served no further purpose. As far as he was concerned, she could walk back in the morning and retrieve her car.

Towns like Pleasanton were too small and open. Bigger ones like San Jose were much better suited, offering the anonymity of the writhing masses of humanity. However, San Jose was too close to home for his comfort. Still, he stopped in at a well-known sports bar for a look-see and was completely shocked when it happened again. It took minimal effort and a little small talk to move in on a lonely thirty-something woman intent on drinking herself into a stupor in the middle of the week.

This time he asked if she could score some coke. As it turned out, she knew exactly what to do. A straight-forward request for sex, and bingo, he was following her home for a night of no-holds-barred athletics. Just like the last one, she was begging him for his phone number when he left. While he liked the easy sex, the main event for him was always murder and he'd been denied twice now. The cocaine had his full attention, though, and he knew how to get it. He'd watched her carefully as she sized up the staff at the bar. One of the bartenders was the connection.

His next consideration was how to score it elsewhere. Berkeley seemed like a possibility. The town was the right size and had the complexity of the university population as well. Thursday night made sense for hunting, because a lot of the students started partying to mark the approaching weekend. Cocaine became a big part of his preparation. During a drug-induced fog a few days earlier, it seemed like a good idea to ride the bus to San Jose and steal another Explorer. He dabbled with a little DIY, painting the white vehicle red, something to throw off the police. The paint job was far from perfect, but at night, it would easily pass. A freshly stolen tag completed his kit as he headed out after work the next night. The energy level of a crowded sports bar proved irresistible. Most of the young students ignored him when he tried to chat with them at the bar when they arrived to order drinks, but he was persistent, and it paid off.

A hot babe took a seat next to him, dressed in jeans and a white tank top. Her well-tanned and strategically revealed body attracted the college boys instantly. A competition ensued, as she deftly brushed-off each come-on. The scene was amusing for a while, but he grew bored. He introduced himself with a fake name, and she probably responded with the same.

"You're in rare form tonight."

"Thanks. It's how I get my kicks. These guys don't have a chance."

He ignored her for the most part, but said something every once in a while. Finally, he saw his chance and poured a small vile into her drink. After she took a few sips, he monitored her behavior carefully. "Well, I'm not going to give you the satisfaction of rejecting this old guy. I'm heading home—Hey, are you okay?"

An unintelligible response was exactly what he was waiting for. A wad of cash took care of both of their bills. An act as if they were both drunk covered the fact he practically had to carry her outside and a half a block to his truck. The coast was clear so he threw the powerless victim into the back of the truck and sped away.

A few blocks away, he pulled to the side of the road, climbed over the seat to the back of the truck, and taped her wrists and ankles tightly. The finishing touch was the piece he put over her mouth. Endless fantasies played through his mind on the long drive back to his house. As soon as he arrived, he spent a couple of hours playing with her. First came the cocaine, then he secured her to his specially built rack. He snorted several more rows as he stripped off her clothes and slapped her around a little. When she failed to respond satisfactorily, he gave up. She just needed a little time to sleep off the drug in her system, and then he would be able to have some real fun with her.

Friday morning he showered, shaved, and readied for work. As he went down into his lair, he was greeted by the terrified screams of his victim, artfully tied to his rack, naked, shaking in fear, and covered with bruises and blood.

When he hit her full force across the mouth, he thought a tooth might have flown across the room. "Yell all you want, darling. With these heavy-duty insulated walls, no one will ever hear you. I have to go to work now. I want you to wait right here, though, because we have a big date tonight."

He tried his best to make it through the workday, but after lunch, he just couldn't contain himself anymore. A foreman he'd hired recently seemed to run the shop pretty well on his own. He found that a good raise provided plenty of incentive to keep the shop busy, and he'd even found some new customers. When he arrived home, he was about to hit the garage door opener when he caught a glimpse of the trash truck driving up the street. He stopped at the entrance of his drive, got out of his work truck and made an effort to pick up some branches and put them in the cans next to the street just before they arrived. The guys running the truck gave him a friendly wave. Only when they rounded the corner did he dare to drive around back. Entering and leaving the garage was his only risk for exposure, so he knew he had to be careful.

He used a butcher knife from the kitchen to keep her attention focused on his demands. Her eyes were as wide as her open mouth when he finally plunged the knife into her belly an hour later. Everything was perfect. Her life ended about two hours after the session started. Another two hours was spent on the clean-up operation. Under the cover of darkness, he headed to the San Francisco airport that night, parking in the short-term area. The AirTran, a sky rail used for transporting people in the airport, took him to the BART, the bus and train system for the city. He rode the train south as far as he could, and then caught the last bus to an area near his house. The walk at the end allowed him to assess his fifth victim. The plan had gone pretty well. The sex and killing were good because she had been fully awake. Her eyes had fed him her fear right up to the end. Yet, something of the satisfaction of a job well done still eluded him.

Two days later the San Jose paper announced the victim had been found. A strange aroma had caused complaints which were in turn eventually investigated by the airport police. One reporter immediately speculated that it was the work of The Slasher, which soothed him quite a bit.

Chapter 10

Michael jolted awake at three in the morning drenched in a cold sweat. The nightmares had disappeared while taking the painkillers, but as soon as he had stopped, the horrid dreams had returned. Now, it seemed his choices were either be a drug addict or deal with the nightmares. Neither option appealed to him much.

The one up-side to being awake in the pre-dawn hours was the abundance of time he had to think. The attack on Tanya compelled his full attention. Who could have done it? More importantly, why? What could he do to help? He methodically worked his way through the evidence. Most likely, someone from the party was the culprit, but who? The prime suspect would have to have a group of men helping him. Why would a killer go after Tanya and not Peter? That didn't seem to make sense. Peter was the one with the money. Adding Phil Roberts' murder to the mix only served to muddy the waters further. What did he have to do with all of it? After an hour, Michael had an idea. It was only a slim chance, but it was something that just might work.

The next afternoon, Detective Clark assembled Peter, Tanya and Michael in a garden at the side of the house beside a koi pond with extremely large lily pads, their edges turned up like saucers. Michael noticed a tiny frog sitting proudly in the middle of one of them. Calico fish cruised below like sharks. A wonderful statuette of a jaguar reclined by the pool of water; flattened almost like a modern art study but with a lifelike quality. The big cat appeared to have just taken a drink and stretched out for a rest. How could this piece of art have coincidentally found its way to the home of a Jaguar lover?

Detective Clark started. "Michael, you may not be aware of this, but we have a serial killer on the loose in the city."

Tanya gasped. "You don't think...."

"No. I don't think there's a connection. However, the fact remains you need to know our police force is stretched thin trying to catch him. Every detective in homicide has duties pertaining to this case. Christ, the press dubbed him 'The Slasher', it's gotten that bad. I have to be honest with you, if Tanya hadn't survived the attack, we might have bought the murder-suicide scenario whoever planned it was going for and not looked any closer. I'm nowhere on a motive in this case."

Michael took a deep breath. "Detective, I have an idea. You probably won't like it."

"At this point, I'll listen to just about anything."

"First, I have a confession to make. I've presented myself to you as a writer. Nothing could be further from the truth."

Tanya's mouth dropped. "We have copies of your articles."

"Maybe I should say things aren't as they seem. I want to make everything very clear to you. Yes, I've written a monthly column in a Jaguar magazine for about two years. However, my profession for the twenty years previous to that was with the Tulsa police force."

Now it was Detective Clark's turn to seem shocked. "You're going to have to explain that one."

"I'll try to give you the short version. After college, I moved back to my dad's ranch. I didn't plan on staying long, but I was trying to figure out what I was going to do for a living. One day, I saddled up my horse and rode the fence line to check on things. On the far side of the property I discovered the body of a young girl. She'd been murdered and dumped just inside the fence on our property." He had to stop and take a deep breath.

Detective Clark seemed to sense he was having difficulty. "Take your time. We're in no hurry."

Michael composed himself and continued.

"Even though it was a long time ago, I can still see her face. She looked so small and defenseless; ravaged, then thrown away like a piece of trash. I'd seen the girl in town. I knew her parents. I guess I became obsessed with finding whoever killed the little girl and bringing them to justice. As fate would have it, one of my fraternity brothers had just been hired as an assistant district attorney in Tulsa. Another friend from my high school wrestling team was a police officer. I'd earned a degree in marketing and was planning to be a sales rep with a fat expense account and a company car. Suddenly that didn't seem very important anymore. My two friends offered to vouch for me if I joined the police force. I started at the bottom but managed to make detective after six years, probably with a lot of help from my connections. A year later I got my wish and was assigned to the case of the girl I had found on our property. " He stopped and took a drink.

"How did the case turn out?"

"We solved it. The only problem was it took me fourteen years and eight more children were killed during the investigation." He paused. "I should have solved the case a lot sooner. Those children didn't have to die."

He'd been gazing at the ground as he told his story. Now he looked up and into the eyes of the others. Each sat silently in a state of shock after hearing the story.

"Are you still employed by the police force in Tulsa?"

"No. I took retirement shortly after the case was solved. I guess I got too emotionally involved. I'm sorry to bore you with these details but there's a point to my story. I felt I had to come clean so you'd understand what I'm about to propose."

"Well, let's hear it."

"I think you'd agree that most likely someone at the party is behind this murder attempt. It seems to me that each person needs to be interviewed to determine which one is the perpetrator." He lifted a hand and scratched his head. "And, since you three are the only ones who know my background as a detective, I figure I could lend a hand. I'd be ideal for investigating your suspects, because I have the perfect cover. I could ask to do a story about a car. I think all of the guests are car people. I really am writing stories about my trip out here. I think it would allow me to do some snooping without raising suspicion."

Detective Clark's brow wrinkled as he shook his head. "I just don't know. I could use the help but…"

"I think you could easily eliminate most of the people attending the dinner. There shouldn't be too many left to investigate." Michael added hopefully.

Detective Clark folded his arms across his chest and rocked back on his heels. "You of course know, we have a standard protocol to follow here. There's no way I could hire you in an official capacity. Any cooperation you offered would have to be off the record." He gave Michael a once over, then released a long sigh. "Are you licensed in any way in California for doing detective work?"

"Absolutely not."

"What about a gun permit?"

"I have a permit that's good in Oklahoma but probably not in California. Plus, I didn't bring a gun with me anyway."

"Let me think on this one and I'll get back to you." Peter took the cue and escorted Clark to the front door. When he returned he offered Michael a smile.

"I must tell you, I feel a little better with an extra trained officer in the house."

Tanya slid her arm inside of Michael's and with a glimmer of hope looked up into his eyes. "Maybe you could be my personal bodyguard."

An uncontrollable smile broadened across Michael's lips. He wasn't sure if it was the way her voice purred when said the words, or the fact that 'personal' was stressed, that made the idea tempting and appealing. His eyes followed the curve of her jaw to those kissable lips. Perhaps, she was the mystery he wanted to solve, and he had an open invitation. How could he refuse?

"Could we discuss compensation?"

The next day, Detective Clark phoned him on his cell. "I talked to your boys back home. They said you were the best detective they ever had."

"They're just hoping I'm not coming back."

"Don't give me any of that false modesty. They said you caught the killer single-handedly."

"An exaggeration, I assure you."

"They said I'd be crazy not to use you, so I am. I'm putting my ass on the line here; so don't screw this up. Why don't you and Tanya take some time to heal over the next week, and I'll get to work on the background of the guests for you. I'll meet up with you later and we'll fine-tune how we'll proceed."

Chapter 11

Michael, realizing the chance that recuperating from their injuries offered them, decided he would take advantage of the downtime and spend every possible second of it with Tanya. A competent assistant handled Tanya's affairs while she convalesced. Texting replaced her lack of a voice, at least for the time being. A straightforward project on a full house restoration would keep her crew busy for months. All in all, they had nothing but time.

Taking pictures of cars in the basement consumed the next couple of days. A professional crew arrived one of the mornings for a photo shoot of the five cars for a fancy book Pebble Beach produced each year for the show. The story was finished, but a crew had been waiting for the opportunity to photograph all five cars together. The book was going to press in a matter of days so they were under the gun. Michael used the opportunity to learn everything he could from the photographer. The pro had a fancy camera with all kinds of background lights and reflectors. The most interesting shots were taken with the cars in the dark. Using a big flash mechanism resulted in pictures of the cars leaping out of a dark back ground like chromed fighter planes. The finished product on the show in Bend, Oregon was e-mailed to England in a Word file accompanied by about twenty pictures. The magazine editor replied all was received in good order, buying another month of time from his deadlines.

Tanya offered her help on Michael's Pebble Beach story. Two days of shooting produced approximately five hundred pictures with a goal of producing five or ten outstanding ones. The story about the Waldorf legacy took shape as well.

The nervous tension prevalent in their first meeting slowly evaporated. Her voice grew a little stronger each day. His original plan of playing hard to get had long since been abandoned. He'd imagined a tough game of one-liners, like he'd grown accustomed to with other women. However, since the murder attempt, everything had changed. A truce seemed to have been drawn, refreshing, to say the least. He'd fallen in love with her within the first five minutes. Her feelings, though, were more difficult to ascertain. The situation dictated he bide his time and let things work out naturally. Since she'd grown up wealthy in a large cosmopolitan town, he knew she was more sophisticated. Did he have something to offer her? His plan morphed into full blown detective work. Find out as much about her as possible without raising suspicion. The next morning was the beginning of phase two.

After breakfast Tanya offered to help with another session downstairs by the cars.

"I'm going to bring a coffee. Can I get you something?"

"Would a Diet Dr. Pepper be too awful?"

"First thing in the morning?" She winced but checked the refrigerator. "I don't see any but I think we have more in the bar in the garage."

She led as they descended to the main garage and then over to the stairs to the lower level. He checked the fit of her designer jeans as any good detective would. Perfect as far as he could tell. He dropped his camera and notebook while she retrieved his soft drink from a refrigerator behind a bar in the corner.

"I have a question for you, if you don't feel it is too personal."

His inquiry produced the evil smile. "Ask away. I'll let you know if you get off-limits."

"You seem like Peter's daughter rather than his niece."

"Why don't we sit down a minute before we get started with the cars?" Several sofas and chairs had been arranged in a corner for local car clubs to use from time to time. Tanya took a seat in a chair across from Michael and immediately crossed her legs slowly and adroitly before she continued. He thought his heart might have stopped temporarily.

"A lot of people mistake Peter for my father. My father died when I was twenty-five. He was nothing like Peter. He was fun-loving, easy-going. Peter was always a workaholic. Don't get me wrong. My dad was a gifted software writer, but he was happy when they got bought out. He enjoyed life to the fullest when he retired. I don't think he missed work a bit."

"May I ask what happened to him if it's not too painful?"

"Skin cancer. I guess our family has a history of it. He went quickly. It's been more than fifteen years now. Anyway, I think Peter tried to step in a little when I lost my dad. We kind of needed each other."

"What do you mean?"

"Like I said, Peter had some challenges with addictions. He had plenty of women after him in his younger days but he had a mean streak that was poison to relationships. I seemed to be immune. I was able to keep him centered a little bit, keep him out of trouble."

She had a habit of tucking her hair behind her right ear when she talked. He found it most distracting.

"What about your mother?"

"I have my own town house not too far from here. She's in the same area. It works out well for us. I drop by for coffee with her almost every day, except recently. I like to make sure she's okay. Sometimes we shop for groceries together. She's fantastic."

"What was it like growing up in San Francisco?"

She crossed her legs the other way and flipped her hair behind her ear again. She took a drink of her coffee and stared directly into his eyes.

"Hmmm. How do I answer that? I'd say it was great until I became a teenager. I attended private school. Lots of drugs and bad behavior. I try to apologize to my mother at least once every time I talk to her. Some of my friends went over the edge. I was probably headed in the same direction. I was saved by a trick my father and Peter played on me."

"A trick? I can't imagine them pulling something over on you."

"Like I said, Peter had his own challenges with drugs. I guess he recognized my bad behavior. He came up with a brilliant plan. He decided he'd interest me in kart racing. Do you know what I mean by karts?"

"Of course. That's how many of the Formula One drivers got started."

"Exactly. Well, he came up with an interesting idea. He hired a professional to build this gorgeous kart in the garage at his old town house. When I saw it, I thought it was the most beautiful machine I'd ever seen. He asked if I'd be interested in racing. Of course I said yes. He warned me we would have to get my dad's permission. When we went to my house, Peter and my dad had a terrible fight, or so I thought. My dad finally said I'd have to prove to him I could handle the kart. I'd have to show him I could drive safely. He added I'd have to train for driving, just like any athlete. That was the deal. I had to put everything into it."

"How'd you do?"

"The first year was a learning experience for both of us; me learning to drive and Peter figuring out how to run our team. We finally found a really good mechanic. He knew all the tricks to make the car fast. The second year we started to win. The third and fourth years, we won almost every race. The last year, I think I was eighteen by then, I had a bad wreck. I got beat the week before by one of the boys and the next week I tried a bad pass on him. My front wheel got hooked on his rear tire and it flipped me. I broke my arm. That was the end of racing."

"So what was the trick?"

"I found out years later the whole thing was cooked up by Peter and my dad. I was rebelling against everything at that age so my dad had to appear to be against racing to get me to really put myself into it. I even ran cross-country for my school team to improve my conditioning. I lost interest in my drugged-up friends and learned to work hard toward achieving my goals. It was a lesson I've used in every challenge since then."

"A clever plan and well executed."

"Oh yeah. I think they had more than one good laugh about it. There's no doubt it saved me from drugs."

A voice echoed down the stairs. "Tanya, are you down here?"

"Over by the bar."

Peter came down the stairs and took another chair with his own coffee in hand. Michael seized the opportunity. "Peter, I have a few questions, if you don't mind."

"Not at all. What would you like to know?"

"I don't quite understand how you gained possession of the cars. From the brief conversations I had with your guests at the party, it seemed to me many enthusiasts were pursuing the Waldorf Jaguars. How'd you find them?"

"Completely by luck. Come over here and look at this trophy in the case."

He led them to a fine wooden case filled with trophies against the back wall; mementos from Jack Waldorf's racing career. In the center a graceful silver cup posed regally, polished to a mirror-like sheen, engraved, "Jack Waldorf, Monterey Champion, 1957."

"This trophy led me to the cars. Let's go back and sit because this is going to take a few minutes." As soon as they were situated he continued. "I attended Stanford University at the same time as Jack Waldorf, although I was just starting when he was finishing. I didn't really know him or anything but I certainly saw him driving the one-twenty around campus. He was a true legend with the women. I'm sure that's what started my craving to own a Jaguar. There was a gentleman at the party, Buck Snider. Do you remember him?"

"Yes. You made a toast to him and his wife because it was their anniversary."

"Good memory. Yes, it was Buck and Rosalina's fifty-sixth wedding anniversary. Buck was Jack's spitfire mechanic during the war. I think he was actually the reason Jack decided to attend Stanford after the war. Buck's dad was the owner of the first Jaguar dealership in San Francisco. I think Jack's father somehow helped him get the dealership. Anyway, I used to go down to the shop and drool over the cars. Of course, I couldn't afford one back then. I got to know Buck a little bit because he worked for his dad at the dealership. When Jack got the C-type, he started racing. I used to attend the races because Buck was always talking about it. I was actually at the race in fifty-seven when he won this trophy.

"One morning, a few months after I managed to buy this house, I was reading the paper and noticed a small ad about the trophy coming up for auction. I found it very strange."

"Why would it be strange to auction the trophy? I'd think this kind of object would have quite a value to collectors."

"It didn't make sense because Jack was from a very wealthy family. His father was an industrialist. From what I understood he made a fortune after the war. There was some kind of accident at one of the factories, I think a wall might have fallen during an inspection of one of the buildings causing his death. Jack's mother sold the businesses and moved to California to be close to Jack. He persuaded her to build the house in Los Gatos and lived there with her. It just didn't make sense she'd sell something like the trophy. She adored Jack. Why would she sell a memento with such a link to her son?

"I tracked her down, which, incidentally, wasn't easy. I was flush with money from selling the company so I said I wanted to buy the cup immediately. She asked for a personal meeting, I guess to size me up. The next day I drove the E-type down to her estate. I'd just finished with the restoration and thought it would be a nice drive.

"I was shocked when I arrived. The estate was in ruins. The big saloon you see here was rusting. It looked like it might not even be running. She only had one staff member taking care of her at the home. I had a tea with her in her library and we talked for a while. Emma, that was her name, was a lovely woman. She had the bluest eyes. I finally got up the nerve to ask her what was wrong. She confided in me. I guess it might have been because I drove the Jaguar that day. It turned out she'd been swindled in a stock deal and lost everything. I felt so sorry for her. On a whim, I offered to buy her estate. I can't explain exactly why. My mother spent her final days in a lovely home in Monterey. It was situated on a hill with a view of the ocean, surrounded on the sides by a pristine pine forest. I promised her I'd buy her estate and make sure she had a nice apartment at the home. I'll never forget what she said next."

The story had completely absorbed Michael by this point. Peter paused. He looked over at Tanya and she just smiled at him.

"So, what did she say?"

"She said, 'What about the cars in Jack's garage?' I'd completely forgotten about the C-type and the one twenty. When Jack was killed in the accident, she'd apparently put a padlock on his garage and the cars were kept in a time capsule. I never dreamed I might own the same cars I'd idolized during my college days. I offered her a million dollars for her entire estate, cars and all. I promised I'd restore the cars and keep them. I wasn't interested in selling them off for profit. She seemed relieved. I guess she was at her wits end trying to figure out how she was going to survive.

"It took a couple of months to get the paperwork done. I made good on my word. She took a place in the home in Monterey. I had a quick restoration done to her car to make sure it was safe to drive. I also found her a driver so she could go into town any time she wished. She had a couple of good years. I even met her a few times at the Stillwater Café at Pebble Beach for lunch. Her health wasn't good, though. Eventually she passed away.

"When she moved, I took a crew down to inspect the garage. I'll never forget one of the men knocking the lock off the double doors and swinging them open. The electricity was off and the garage was like the tomb of King Tut. The cars were lined up with a half-inch of dust covering each one. All of the trophies you see here were in the cabinets with the checkered flags mounted above. I left them until Tanya finished the house and then moved everything here. By the way, the D-type was a complete surprise. By the mid-fifties the other cars were catching up to the C-type. Jaguar developed the next generation racing car, the D-type. It was one of the most successful racing cars in history. Jack must have realized that if he wanted to continue his winning streak, he'd have to get one. However, they were tough to come by. I found out he looked a long time before he heard about one that had been wrecked in Europe. It was a local hill climb. The driver crested the hill at full speed and lost control. He crashed into a ditch and was killed. The family parked the wreck in a garage. I guess Jack used his charm to persuade them to sell it to him. He kept it a secret because he wanted to surprise the other drivers the next season. Colin Hunter had been brought over with Emma as head mechanic of the estate. He'd been with the family for many years in England. Colin was about to begin the restoration of the D-type when Jack was killed."

"So you had them restored as they are now."

"That's another story. I think I'll let Tanya tell you that one."

"Why was Lucille sold when the others were locked away?"

"Another good question. You need to ask to Buck Snider about that."

"We should drive down and visit Buck and Rosalina," Tanya offered. "He could tell you the story about your car. They live in Santa Cruz. It'd be wonderful if we could drive Lucille down for a visit. We could make a day of it. We could even visit the old Waldorf mansion on the way back, if you like."

"After the stories you've been telling me, I can't wait."

"I'll call Buck and set it up." Tanya disappeared up the stairs.

At the end of the day, Michael assessed his productivity. He felt he had accomplished very little with regards to the car story, but that he had made great progress spending quality time with Tanya. Overall, he considered the day a complete success.

————————⋇✷✷⋇————————

Peter sat at his desk that evening as he prepared for bed. The design and decorating of the entire house had been completely up to Tanya, but not his bedroom. A long but rather narrow room ran the entire east side of the house, divided into three parts. At the back he had a sitting area with a view of the bay. At the other end a bathroom was situated with a large dressing closet, stocked with the finest clothes arranged with military precision, a testament to the care he took in his appearance.

What most people didn't know was that he used the same attention to detail with his businesses. In the middle room, the bed was on one side, but a bespoke desk and cabinet took up most of the remaining space. The cabinet structure was built into the wall. On the desk, a portable keyboard commanded a large CPU hidden from view. On top of the nearly six foot wide desktop were stationed three over-sized screens arranged in a semi-circle. Visitors weren't allowed into this inner-sanctum. He liked it that way. Even his beloved Tanya wasn't aware of the investments he'd made with new start-up companies on the cutting edge of computer and software design. It was his habit to study for any meetings he might have the following day before he retired. A maze of storage cabinets were built into the desk on each side; drawers that were wide but not tall. The folders on his investments were strategically placed in the drawers in an intricate but eccentric system only he could understand.

Tonight was different, though. Instead of preparing for an important meeting the next day, he was scouring his brain in an effort to figure out who had used his party as a method to attack Tanya. The invitation list from the party was the only paper on the desk. A nagging throb at the back of his head told him he must be missing something. Maybe he was somehow to blame for the attack. It was even possible that he had been the true target, and the culprit had settled for Tanya when they couldn't get to him. The harder he thought about it, the less progress he made. For a man with a strong mind used to puzzling out complicated issues, the lack of understanding was frustrating. He ran his fingers through his hair in despair.

A light tap on the door interrupted his thought process. He shoved the paper into the desk drawer and turned just in time to see Tanya open the door. When she stayed over, she had the habit of coming in for a late night chat before bed. She flopped in her favorite chair next to the desk wearing an old full length flannel nightgown.

"What do you think of Michael?"

Peter folded his hands together and sat back in his chair. "You mean as far as boyfriend material?"

A slight red glowed on her cheeks. "I wasn't going to be quite that blunt."

"To tell you the truth, I think the guy has possibilities."

"Wow. How did you reach that conclusion so quickly? Usually you're quite skeptical of my gentlemen companions."

"In my opinion, you've done nothing but run around with the most beautiful men this town has to offer, but every time I took a closer look I found each one to be either a con-artist intent on separating you from your money or some dumbass from a rich family."

"That's a little rough."

"Maybe so, but you asked me, so I'm going to tell you what I think. That's what you count on me for, right?"

She nodded.

"I was intrigued when I met him, but still skeptical. He's a good-looking guy, I'll give you that, and certainly polite to a fault, but what's under the covers? That's where my interest lies."

"So how did you go about answering that question?"

"Detective Clark did a lot more checking on him than you might think. He had to be sure he wasn't involved in the attempt on your life. Clark knew he was a police officer before Michael told us."

"You knew, too?"

"I'm afraid so."

"Why didn't you tell me?"

"Mostly because Clark made me promise not to, but I also saw the way you two were looking at each other from the first minute you met. He had the name of a local detective who knew Michael very well so it became convenient to do a little more checking on him on my own."

"You had a background check done on him?"

"You might be surprised to know he's not the first one of your boyfriends I've had checked out. I wanted to find out everything I could about him."

"You make it seem like I don't have any judgment when it comes to men."

"I'll give you one thing. You're doing a lot better lately."

"I don't even have a boyfriend. I just work all the time like you and dad used to."

"That's a lot better than being with a chiseler."

"We've been over this a thousand times before. Get back to Michael."

"I have to admit I was a bit skeptical at first. After all, he was a civil servant for twenty years, not the most ambitious way to make a living in my opinion. However, the more information I got, the better he looked. For instance, he scored the highest score on the detective exam ever in Tulsa. They made a point of noting it in his report. He was a natural. Very high IQ. He was their golden boy until the killing."

"The killing?"

"Michael hasn't talked to you about it?"

"No, he hasn't. He was involved in a killing?"

"He didn't just catch the serial killer. Word was he assassinated him. He was lucky he wasn't prosecuted. There wasn't enough evidence to prove anything but the consensus was he killed him when he tracked him down. He didn't quit the force. He was pushed into an early retirement. Probably a compromise to protect him from a prosecution. I'm sure a lot of the officers considered him a hero but others thought he was a murderer, no better than the man he had caught. I'd like to ask him about it if I get the chance."

"I couldn't quite put my finger on what I was feeling all this time but now I know what it was. He seems a little bit damaged. He's been hurt."

"Anyway, he's off the force, nice little pension and healthcare, and nothing to do so he got involved with the Jaguars. That's when it got interesting."

"Go on." She leaned forward placing her elbows on her knees.

"His father died, like he said, right after they finished the restoration of Lucille. It seemed the ranch was located right in the path of Tulsa's growth south. Michael sold the property to a developer for three million dollars. That scared me. I thought I'd see him go through the money pretty fast. Instead, he started driving the old Jag and invested the money with his financial counselor. He stayed in the same house, which was already mortgage free. He's basically been doing his stories. That's about it."

"You said Clark had access to a detective. You didn't find out all the money stuff from him."

"No. I guess I used some other sources for that. If the guy's sleeping under my roof, I want to know everything I can about him."

"So you think he has some possibilities. I'll keep that in mind."

She gave him a kiss on the forehead and quietly left the room for bed. Peter was intrigued by Tanya's behavior. She always kept the upper hand where men were concerned. She seemed pretty interested in this Michael McAllister fellow. God help the poor man. It wouldn't be a fair fight.

Chapter 12

He awoke at eleven in the morning, although regained consciousness might have been a better description, the result of a four-day cocaine binge. The bed fought back when he tried to roll over to get up. The taste in his mouth was unfamiliar and not pleasant. The best idea to stop the pounding in his head seemed to be more cocaine. A neat pile beckoned from the nightstand with razor blade and a hundred dollar bill at the ready.

Just before he took his first snort of the day, a little reminder about a meeting clicked far back in his mind. Five minutes later, he had managed to dig a calendar out from under several old newspapers in disarray on the kitchen table. Tomorrow was a big day. Some fool had offered him six million dollars for his company. All he had to do was make it down to the lawyer's office in the morning, but that meant he had to cool it on the drugs. A shave and shower were a first for this week. As he admired his naked body while drying he noticed his ribs were showing for the first time in years. The scales confirmed he'd lost weight. When he finished dressing, he clambered back downstairs to make an attempt at breakfast.

On the outside, the house appeared normal to his neighbors, thanks to the crew of Latinos that cared for the yard. Inside was a different matter. Several rooms on the first floor were empty thanks to the fact that the ex-wife had removed her fine furniture.

Keeping the days straight was becoming quite a challenge, so he didn't feel he could risk a cleaning lady. He certainly didn't want anybody snooping around the garage. Occasionally, if there were no way to avoid a meeting at the house, he would hire a service to clean it thoroughly. A vain attempt at a little vacuuming would have still left any visitor aghast. A trail of food crumbs and coffee stains could be easily tracked from the kitchen to the dining table overlooking the backyard and up the stairs to the bedroom. The few meals he ate at home were usually in bed while he watched television. Plates were stacked precariously in the sink and piled along the countertop, all of which he ignored. An inspection of the refrigerator yielded nothing edible. He double-checked the date on the calendar. Yes, tomorrow morning.

One of his biggest competitors had visited unexpectedly two months previously and made a low-ball offer for the business on the spot. Sure he'd missed some business that would have been his for the taking had he not forgotten to submit his bid on time, but that didn't mean he was going to give his life's work away. He'd somehow managed to appear indignant and negotiated a fair price for his holdings. All he had to do was appear at the signing tomorrow morning and an additional six million dollars would be transferred to his account. An idea occurred to him to hide a knife inside his boot for the meeting in case there was trouble with the deal. When he tested his idea the point jabbed him along the side of his foot. He decided against it, feeling that he could handle himself in hand-to-hand combat, if necessary.

It took every ounce of his self-control to avoid using cocaine during the twenty-four hours before the meeting. His lawyer handled the proceedings while he looked on silently. The eager gentlemen across the table disgusted him. What had they ever accomplished with their lives? If they only knew what he'd been up to during the last few years they would've shown him more respect. The strongest urge he had during the meeting was to kill them all. Finally, his lawyer pushed the papers over to him with a pen.

He was rich and totally free of commitments now. Nothing would ever interfere with his true passion again. Back in his bedroom, wearing only a pair of shorts, he assembled his research, which consisted of various newspaper reports about his crimes along with crumpled pieces of papers covered with incoherent scrawls that had seemed important when he had written them. The media had been good to him, reporting almost every step of the police investigations in great detail. He couldn't quite understand why they were allowed to tell him all the secrets but he was certainly grateful for the treasure trove of information.

After a half hour of flipping through television shows he landed on one done by an expert profiler. The local police had consulted the FBI and had drawn a detailed analysis of his methods. The most surprising fact was how much data had been gained based on his victims and the locations of the crimes. Somehow they had figured out how he took the two victims in bars. Authorities even had a rough sketch done by a bartender. In his opinion it resembled half the male population in California. All they really knew was that he was white. DNA and fingerprints still eluded them. After careful consideration, he decided he needed to change his tactics as much as possible with each victim. It was the only way he could hope to avoid detection and keep doing what he loved. It suddenly dawned on him how incredibly lucky he'd been not to get caught before now.

As the first part of his new plan, he rode the bus and train to the San Francisco airport, then took the BART out west and got off at Pleasanton. The darkness when he arrived made him feel safe. A different type of vehicle was called for this time, but he wasn't sure exactly what he was looking for. A Ford Taurus caught his attention. The locking and ignition systems would be the same as an Explorer so that would be easy. A car instead of a truck seemed like a good idea.

The car put up little resistance and in minutes he was heading home. This time he decided not to stop at the side of the road to change the plates.

The next challenge was to throw off the investigation as much as possible by changing up his hunting location. He'd seen the map the police were building of the crimes on television with San Jose was at the center, a little too close for comfort A completely new location might throw the computers for a loop. After a long consultation with his own maps, he chose Bakersfield as the next site where he'd hunt for a victim. Bakersfield was a large enough town with plenty of nightspots to look for victims. He used the computer to build a list of bars he could check.

A quickie paint job changed the color of the Taurus from red to grey, one of his favorite Jaguar shades from his shop. Again, it wasn't a great job, but at night, it would look good. New plates completed the transformation. The drive south on Tuesday took over three hours and landed him in front of a country and western bar that seemed promising. The enormous parking lot was ideal and he took a spot at the back. The size of the crowd on a weeknight surprised him. From his spot at the bar, several women seemed available. One took a shine to him right away, but was not particularly attractive. He snorted most of her coke in the bathroom before finally giving her a stern brush-off. She moved to the far end of the bar and glared at him from time to time.

Around ten o'clock, he zeroed in on his prey. Initiating a conversation with the attractive young woman sitting alone at a table was surprisingly easy. She started pouring out her heart about her husband having an affair. A few drinks were all the encouragement she needed to keep telling her sad story. The first time she looked away, he poured a bit of the vile into her glass. At 10:30, he steered her out the door. She was barely able to balance herself against the side of the Taurus while he checked for witnesses. When he didn't see any he quickly clicked the opener and shoved her into the trunk.

A pit stop for gas on the edge of town allowed him to snort a few rows of cocaine in the bathroom, enough to make it through the boring drive back to his house. At least he would have plenty of time for his fantasies. Something new was in order. None of his victims regained consciousness for hours after they were drugged, so he didn't bother to find a place to pull over so he could tape his victim. The terrain was unfamiliar anyway and pulling over was a risk not worth taking.

About two hours into the drive north, he heard the first moans coming from the trunk. In minutes, they became louder and more frequent. She started screaming and kicking at the trunk lid. The exits on the freeway were miles apart. He feared she'd somehow release the trunk lid and other drivers would see her, or that she would get away. After what seemed like an eternity, which was actually less than five minutes, an exit came into sight. He carefully pulled off and drove past the same gas station and fast food restaurant combo that seemed to repeat itself along the highway every so many miles. A small dirt road offered a dark and lonely setting so he could attend to his problem. The screaming and kicking in the trunk were now constant. An even smaller road turned into a field and he followed it to the edge of a stand of trees far from the main highway. The road was very bumpy, and he could hear his victim hitting the sides and top of the trunk as the car bounced along. Just as he stopped the car, the trunk lid popped open either by being sprung violently by the rough road or possibly by the victim. The cause didn't matter.

He lunged for her but missed as she ran for the open field. The barbed wire protecting the field had large gaps and she was through one in a heartbeat. The only weapon in the trunk was the crow bar for the jack. Apparently his victim had found it in the trunk and used it to jimmy the latch. The moon was full so he could see her running across the field, screaming at the top of her lungs. Both pursuer and victim tripped repeatedly over the ruts in their drugged states. The first time he caught up with her, he tripped just as he grabbed for her arm. The second time he hit her across the head with the crow bar and she went down hard.

She looked up at him in terror as he hit her again, with his fist this time. She didn't pass out, but the fight in her seemed finished. He grabbed her by her hair and pulled her to her feet. The walk back to the car seemed to take forever. She didn't resist but they still continually tripped over the furrows. He taped her wrists and ankles tightly by the back of the car. He added two rounds of tape around her head, covering her mouth but trying to leave enough room for her to breathe through her nose. If she couldn't, that was her problem. When he was finished, he threw her back in the trunk roughly, slammed the lid, and found his way back to the highway.

Mud covered his torn clothes and several ugly scratches adorned his neck and face. He was very careful to keep his speed within the limit, so he didn't attract the attention of the police. Lady luck got him home without further incident.

When he arrived in his garage, he changed his routine slightly. The stripping and taping of his victim were the same, as was his ritual of stripping himself but this time he snorted an enormous amount of coke before he started working on her. Sex wasn't part of the plan this time although she was a beautiful woman with a killer body. Instead, he tortured her for the next three hours. When she died, it was probably the best part of her evening. Another massive coke session followed the last glimmer of life leaving her eyes. In the end, he passed out on the floor covered in her blood.

When he awoke late the next morning he was cold and the dried blood actually caused his back to stick to the floor. It took over an hour to accomplish the clean-up. Wrap the victim in plastic, clean the floor, hose down over the drain, pour chemicals down the drain to kill any human remains; all part of the ritual of the killing zone. By the time he headed upstairs, he was completely exhausted. The trip back to Pleasanton to dump the car was uneventful. The BART station was only a block away and the train delivered him safely home. On the way back, he wondered if his new tactics would confuse the police. He hoped so because it had been a lot more trouble than he'd bargained for.

Chapter 13

The sharp ring of the phone on his desk caused Detective Clark to jump.

"This is Officer Simmons from Pleasanton. I'm the chief investigator on a homicide. Someone reported a car with blood on the trunk lid. When we opened it, we found a victim. It looks like the work of your boy."

"Ford Explorer?"

"No. It's a Taurus, but the way the body is wrapped in plastic, it looks just like the info we've received from the task force. It's a young woman from what we can tell. We haven't touched anything since we popped the trunk."

"Keep it that way. I'll be there in forty-five minutes."

Clark made record time getting out of downtown, traversing the Oakland Bay Bridge and then heading south and west to Pleasanton. When he arrived, he saw a crowd beginning to form on the far side of the parking lot of a grocery store. The crime scene suddenly appeared through the mass of onlookers as he arrived at a yellow barrier. The local team had done a good job of protecting the area. They'd positioned three patrol cars, used a light pole for the fourth corner, and then run the tape around the perimeter. His badge gained him entry to the crime scene as he ducked under the tape and went directly to the trunk. He identified himself to Officer Simmons.

"Looks like you've done a good job of protecting the crime scene. I want to take a look."

He leaned over the trunk, being careful not to touch the back of the car. The scene was almost identical to the others, a young woman tightly wrapped in several layers of heavy clear plastic and held together with box tape. The woman curled into a fetal-like position, but he could see her long hair and the side of her face. She might have been pretty once but he could see the deep angry slash marks across her face even through the plastic.

Blood splatter was clearly visible in several places inside and outside the trunk area of the car, hopefully some from the killer. He turned back to Simmons.

"Thanks for waiting to let me have a look. I want your team to go over this car with a fine tooth comb, inside and out, and get lots of pictures." He stopped and tried to control his emotions. The frustration over his continued inability to solve the crime spree had resulted in another victim. "Sorry. I know you'll do an excellent job. Please copy me on your report and the pictures as soon as you're done."

He removed a card from his upper shirt pocket with his direct number and handed it to Simmons. The grocery store caught his eye so he decided to get a coffee for the trip back to the office. As he walked, he thought about what he'd seen. Why had the killer used a new type of car? Clark worried about him changing his tactics. As he exited the store, coffee in hand, a loud horn sounded close by. The BART Station came into view around the corner, and the idea hit him at that moment.

"That's it. He's using the train to get home after he abandons the cars!" He spoke aloud to himself.

This information needed to be added to the database as soon as possible. Maybe there'd be other new evidence from the car.

Clark worked in a frenzy over the next two days. The first report he received was from the license tag. An older couple had been shocked when two police cruisers appeared at the curb in front of their house. After a few minutes, the police pieced together that their license plate had been switched with that of the stolen car. They hadn't even noticed it had been replaced. They lived just south of San Jose. The location fit the profile. Clark was sure the killer lived in the area. Since the car was stolen from Pleasanton, Clark surmised the killer had probably ridden the BART both to steal the car and to get home after he abandoned it.

Clark checked the entire state for a female of about the right age missing for the last few days. A day later, he found her in Bakersfield. Tammy Sheridan had been reported missing two days before the car was recovered. The location confounded Clark. Another big change. The Bakersfield police were cooperative and managed to get her picture on the evening news, asking for help from anyone that had seen her.

The next day Clark's phone rang again. "This is Officer Stanley from Bakersfield. We think we have a witness to Tammy Sheridan's abduction."

"A witness?"

"Yes. A woman in a local bar saw a man dump her in his trunk."

"Why didn't she try to stop him?"

"She did. It's a long story. We've got a bartender and the woman as witnesses. You want to come down here and talk to them?"

"Yes. Set it up for first thing in the morning, about nine. I'll probably drive down."

The long, boring drive down State Highway 5 would be dreadful, traveling through the San Joaquin Valley, but the department budget frowned on a plane trip. He left about two hours after the call, grabbing a small bag with a change of clothes from his apartment on the way out of town. Night made the drive even more boring than he anticipated. He couldn't see much more than vague shadows and tumbleweeds, but he knew from experience that there really was not anything to see. He arrived stiff and tired, and dragged himself through checking into a cheap motel the local cop had recommended. Even his anticipation of the interview the next day couldn't stir up any energy in him. He was even too tired to eat. Instead, he hit the sack after scheduling an early morning wake-up call.

The next morning, at nine sharp, Officer Stanley escorted Charlene Dupre into a small, drab room at the Bakersfield station with Clark the last to enter the room. Stanley had begged to sit in. Clark allowed it because he needed all the help from Bakersfield he could get.

He smiled as he sized her up across the table. She was forty-five years old but looked closer to sixty, thin as a rail with bleached hair. Her coif was brushed from the front but from behind it was mashed down like she'd just gotten out of bed. His bet was she was either a drug addict or an alcoholic.

Clark didn't waste any time. "Mrs. Dupre."

"It's Miss Dupre." She offered Clark a yellow-toothed smile.

"Miss Dupre. Why don't you start by recreating the night of the abduction? Try to think of every detail you can. I might ask some questions as you go along."

"Okay. Well, it was Tuesday night at The Corral. I usually go down on Tuesday nights because they have a good deal on drinks. Ladies night, you know. I like to sit at the bar and look people over as they come and go. This guy comes in, a pretty good looker, about my age. I gave him a smile every time he looked my way. Finally he came over to chat."

"You sat with him and had a drink?"

"Yes."

"What did he look like?"

"He was about my age, mid-forties I'd say. Strong build. Not too tall. Dark hair. He was dressed well. Not fancy, but nice slacks, tassel loafers. He looked rich."

"If you saw a picture of him, would you recognize him?"

"I think so."

"Okay. Go on. Sorry to interrupt."

"Well, we talked for almost an hour and I thought things were going pretty well, if you know what I mean." Both officers nodded with poker straight faces. "Then we got in a fight, so I went back down to the other end of the bar."

"What did you fight about?"

"I'd rather not say."

"Miss Dupre, this is a murder investigation. You need to tell me exactly what happened. It might help us find the guy."

"Can I get in any trouble if, you know, I was doing something bad?"

The question confused Clark until he thought about it. "Were you using coke?"

Her face turned white. "How could you know that?"

"I've been tracking this guy for quite a while. This is something new with him. We found a significant amount of trace evidence of cocaine at the last crime scene. I think he's getting high now right before he commits each murder."

She looked down at the table. "That's what we got in a fight about. I thought I was going home with him. We went in the bathroom and snorted all my coke. When we got back to the bar, he dumped me. He just ignored me after that."

"That made you mad."

"It made me mad as hell."

"What happened next?"

"I kept my eye on him. He spotted this hottie, younger than me, and went over to her table. I guess she bought whatever he was selling. About thirty minutes later, she got up to leave with him. It surprised me. I don't know why, exactly. She didn't look like a one night stand kind of girl. They went out the door together. She seemed kind of drunk. She was having a hard time walking straight. I guess that was it, she was drunk."

Clark knew from toxicology reports of the previous victims the killer had been using a date rape drug but chose not to divulge anything to the witness. Keeping her talking was his main goal.

"Well, anyway, I was surprised she left with him, so I waited a minute and then walked to the window by the door. He was across the parking lot. I saw him look around a minute and then he opened the trunk of the car and pushed her in!"

"Did you try to stop him?"

"I ran back to the bartender, John, but he wouldn't help. I had to explain everything to him and by the time I got him to take a look, the car was gone."

Stanley piped up. "They filed a police report. We couldn't find any evidence in the lot, though."

Clark thought a minute. "Stanley, do you have a good sketch artist?"

"We have a great sketch artist. She's a student at Cal State studying to be a police officer. We use her part-time to do our sketches."

"I need you to have her work with Miss Dupre and see if you can get me a good picture of our guy." He looked back at Dupre. "Thank you for coming forward. We never know when a piece of evidence is going to be the one that solves a case."

Stanley ushered the other witness into the room with Clark and then went to tend to the sketch artist matter with Miss Dupre.

Clark stood and extended his hand. "Detective Clark. San Francisco Police."

"John Graves."

"I just got a statement from Miss Dupre. Why don't you tell me what you saw?"

"The guy sat at the bar for an hour or two."

"Describe him."

"White guy, middle aged. Looked wealthy. Didn't exactly fit in."

"What do you mean by that?"

"The Corral is a country bar. Most of our patrons are cowboys or oil workers. They wear boots and jeans. This guy was dressed nicer. He was with Charlene for a while then he moved on. I didn't notice him much after that. He wasn't at the bar."

"Why didn't you check the parking lot when Charlene alerted you?"

He sighed and waited a few seconds. "Charlene's a coke addict and an alcoholic. She gets in a fight with somebody almost every night she comes in. I saw her get in a fight with the guy that night, too. She ran up babbling about someone throwing someone in the trunk of a car. I couldn't make sense of what she was saying. When I went outside, the parking lot was empty. I thought she was just drunk or high."

"Was the girl at the table a regular?"

"No."

"You seem pretty sure about that."

"She was hot. I would have remembered her."

"Could you identify the guy if you saw him again?"

"Maybe. I didn't pay that much attention. We were kind of busy."

Clark checked back with Stanley before he left. Dupre would work with the sketch artist that afternoon.

"Officer Stanley, can you tell me why Tammy was in the bar that night? She wasn't a regular."

"We talked to her husband. She'd just found out he was cheating on her. She ran out of the house that night. I guess she just wanted to have a stiff drink."

"She picked the wrong shoulder to cry on."

The drive back to San Francisco seemed even longer than the trip down. The road offered Clark a lot of time to think. He felt so close to solving the case, he could taste it. If he just kept feeding information into the computer, he had to get a break. Clues were starting to pile up.

A day later, the sketch artist's picture of the killer was enlarged and put on the wall in the strategy room. Every day Rick Clark took a few minutes to gaze at it. Something was familiar about the face, but he couldn't quite put his finger on it. He wracked his brain trying to remember the piece of information from their investigation that would jog his memory about the picture. Still, this picture seemed to be a much more accurate representation of the killer. Top brass were discussing the possibility of putting it on the news to see if anyone could possibly identify him. The challenge was that he was a middle-aged white guy. The picture would match a huge number of males in the bay area and therefore would cause a rush of new leads they would have to track down.

Chapter 14

The next morning, Michael went with Tanya for a run down by the marina. It seemed she'd made him her fitness project. The effort proved both painful and embarrassing. How could she manage to glide along in an effortless jog like a damn gazelle? The steep hill at the end of the run brought him to heel a couple of times. Tanya smiled and walked along with him. He was going to have to work very hard to get in good enough shape to keep up with her.

He descended the stairs about the same time as Tanya after their showers (taken separately, unfortunately) for a snack and coffee. After a quick check of the fluids, he fired Lucille's engine and let her rumble for a few minutes. She could be grumpy after a few days off, so it was best to give her five minutes to get her bearings. At nine they eased out of the garage and began the winding journey south for a visit she'd scheduled with the Sniders in Santa Cruz. The streets in San Francisco seemed to travel in circles so Michael was glad Tanya knew the way.

She was dressed stylishly in a pair of olive colored silk Capri pants with a textured white top. A black Jaguar baseball cap with her strawberry blonde hair pulled out the back in a small ponytail topped off her sporty look. A pair of Ray-Ban aviator-style sunglasses hid a pair of mesmerizing slate blue eyes. The highest paid fashion model on the way to a big shoot paled in comparison to her natural beauty. Her skin was flawless but sprinkled with the freckles. The night before, while they we had been looking at some pictures on the computer, her hair had brushed against his cheek, wafting over him an intoxicating fragrance, a mix of the perfume she wore and the shampoo she used. The same fragrance filled the small cabin of the old Jag even though the top was down for the trip.

"Those freckles translate to tender skin so you better protect yourself for the drive today."

"Don't worry. After what happened to my dad, I never go out without sunscreen." She turned and looked directly into his eyes. "I've got freckles all over. Maybe you should try to count them some time?" She had her wicked grin going full blast.

"Could it be arranged?"

The dimples in her cheeks told him she was grinning even though she turned away slightly. Another development offered him further encouragement. She wasn't texting as much as she had the first day he had met her. She seemed to be getting a little more interested in him and a little less interested in her business. Maybe she just did it so fast he didn't notice as much anymore. Anyway, he felt like he was with the hottest girl in town as he enjoyed her company on the way south.

After a few minutes, she turned back to him, serious this time. "You asked me several questions yesterday. May I ask you a few today?"

"I'll tell you what. I'll answer a question for you and then you answer one for me. Sound fair?"

"Sure."

"You first."

"I haven't noticed you calling home. Isn't there a girl waiting for you?"

"I'm afraid the girls back home don't think I'm much in the way of boyfriend material."

"I find that hard to believe."

"Like I said before, I got too involved in the serial killer case. I guess it took over my life. Every waking moment, I was trying to go over the facts. I thought I must have missed something that could solve the case." He gave her a quick look and smiled. "There were some nice girls, but I guess they all decided I was a lost cause. I'm sure some of them think I lost my mind. They might be right."

"If you really were crazy, you wouldn't worry if other people thought you were crazy."

"I never thought of that. Maybe I'm not crazy after all. Now it's my turn. Why aren't you involved with someone?"

"Peter says I'm the poster girl for bad relationship choices. I seem to pick cute ones who are no good. The last few years I've kind of given up."

"I don't think you've ever met anyone who could keep up with you."

She didn't answer that one, but wrinkled her brow a little while she seemed to think about it. He couldn't stop thinking about the freckles she had said were all over her body. The road got a little more interesting south of San Jose. It was a two-lane job and the local version of oak trees bowed inward from each side. In some areas, the trees formed a complete canopy like a tunnel through the forest. Just after San Jose, they passed through Los Gatos. He still hadn't looked at a map, but with Tanya as his navigator, he didn't have to worry about how to get to the Sniders' house.

"Los Gatos. There's a city named after cats?"

"Yes. When this area was settled, mountain lions were common in the area."

"Mountain lions. I hadn't thought of that. Are they still around?"

97

"Yes, but in much smaller numbers now. You'd have to be quite lucky to see one."

They passed an exit for Highway 9. "The Waldorf estate is just over that way. We'll stop in for a visit on the way back if you like."

"You were going to tell me the story about the restoration of the cars."

"Okay. As Peter told you, Colin Hunter was the mechanic at the Waldorf estate in England. When Emma moved to California, Colin was offered the same job over here. With five Jaguars, there was plenty of work to do besides repairing just about anything else that needed fixing around the estate. When Jack died, his cars were locked away and the one fifty sold, so there wasn't much for him to do. He decided to open his own shop. Emma gave him a generous check to help him get started. He could still repair her saloon when needed.

"Colin was pretty good with money, from what I've heard, and he did very well with his shop. He got married and had a son, Derek. As Derek grew older, he slowly learned everything about the Jaguars. They were so busy, they kind of lost touch with Emma in her later years. When Peter bought the place and she moved, we later learned Colin couldn't find her.

"When Peter got the cars, he and I started looking for the right person to restore them. There aren't many shops around that know what a C-type or a D-type is supposed to be like or how to work on them. We finally attended a show a year later and stumbled onto a C-type restored to perfection. The owner of the car gave us a card. It turned out Colin's shop had done the work. Peter knew all along that Colin was the right guy for the job. He just hadn't known what had happened to him. Even Emma had lost track of him during her last days. Colin was also looking for the cars, but didn't know where they'd gone. We finally arranged to meet with Colin and Derek at their shop. Colin was pretty old by then and Derek was doing most of the work. It took Colin a while to remember Peter from the races in the fifties, but he finally made the connection. They struck a deal to restore the four cars. The work took several years. Another D-type showed up about halfway through the project, and Peter decided to let Colin do that one first. Colin kept the whole thing a secret. We planned to do a grand showing of the cars in some special way. Unfortunately, Colin died shortly after the last car was finished, just over a year ago. When Pebble Beach made us an offer to display the cars, we had the ultimate venue to announce the cars had been found and restored. I know a lot of car people had been searching for the Jags for many years."

The road to Santa Cruz was even better than the others, winding its way down to the coast in a never ending gentle set of curves. They exited the small highway and made their way through a dense forest. When they emerged, they were in the city. It took a few minutes to reach the coast from there. Finally they found themselves driving along the bay. When he turned in to the Sniders' residence, Tanya reached over and beeped the horn. The sound brought Buck out to greet them in the driveway.

"Tanya and Michael, so nice to see you. Please come in."

A cozy front room with an overstuffed leather love seat awaited them inside. Buck sat across from them in a matching chair. Rosalina brought them lemonade and then disappeared. The sun shone through a large picture window and warmed the room. It was the kind of place that came at a dear price or one had to have bought it a long time ago. Buck and Rosalina had bought it a long time ago.

Buck was over eighty now and wasn't getting around very well. He started with the story about how he'd inherited the San Francisco Jaguar dealership from his father then sold it many years later. From what Tanya had told Michael, Rosalina came from an even wealthier family.

"I have a lot of stories, so maybe you should tell me what you want to know first."

"I was wondering how my car was sold when the others stayed at the estate. That doesn't make sense to me."

"Good question. I'll have to give you some background first, though. Jack was a pilot during the war. Not just any old pilot, an ace. It was life and death every day during the Battle of Britain. We found it difficult at the end of the war to come back and return to the

99

university. My dad got the Jaguar dealership in nineteen forty-eight. Jack had been helping his father put their businesses back into production for a couple of years but was given an ultimatum to get an engineering degree. I think his father was a second-generation mechanical engineer. Jack never wanted any part of the business. He couldn't see himself sitting behind a desk all day. Well, he threw his dad a curve. He agreed to get his degree but wanted to come to Stanford. I think the stories I had told him about California made this place sound like heaven. His dad grudgingly agreed.

"I was almost finished with my degree when Jack got here. We rented a house off campus, and my god, did we throw some parties. This was before I was married, of course. Jack was one hell of a womanizer. I worked at the Jag dealership part time while I finished my degree. One day, I went down to the shop and they had the XK one twenty sitting in the showroom. I called Jack immediately and told him to get his ass down there. That silver body with the bright red leather interior was like nothing we'd ever seen. Basically, it was the closest thing to a fighter plane you could drive on the road. He bought it on the spot.

"He used to drive that thing around town like a madman. The girls begged for rides and then he'd just about make them pee their pants. Some would be crying when he dropped them off. He drove that old car very fast.

"Then his dad got killed in an accident. I think one of the plants had some bomb damage from the war. A wall fell in when they were doing an inspection. His mother wanted him to come and take over, but he wouldn't have any part of it. She gave up and sold everything, for a pretty penny, mind you. He finally convinced his mother he was staying in California so she decided to move over here."

Tanya interrupted, "Buck, why did they build the house in Los Gatos? I always wondered about that."

"Jack was invited to some party at the old Montalvo estate. It's up there in the same area. He really liked the place. Kind of close to the beach but not too close. Rosalina's family was from Santa Cruz, so we were kind of neighbors, too. Emma and Jack worked together on the design, and after a year or two, Jack finished school and they lived there."

"What was Jack planning to do for a career? He had a degree in engineering, right?"

"Jack got his degree but I don't think he ever had a clue what he was going to do. Like I said, after the war we were just happy to be alive. I sat in the bar with him many a night and listened to how some kid went up with him the first time and got blasted to pieces. He never could relax after that, day after day not knowing if he was going to survive. He couldn't settle down. Then he saw the C-type.

"Went to a little club race and he saw the car and that was it. He walked over to the owner right after the race and paid him double what it was worth. He built that big racing garage down the hill from the main house and lived there from then on. I think somehow he thought he might be able to make a living from racing. Of course, in those days, you couldn't. He was good all right, but not as good as a Phil Hill or Carroll Shelby."

Buck was getting a little worked up and tired. Rosalina came back in and refreshed their drinks. Michael decided Buck had completely forgotten his question so he tried to steer him back.

"So, the one fifty."

"Oh yes. I'm afraid I'm taking the long way around to that. Emma was actually the first one to have a Jaguar. She owned that Mark four saloon back in England. When she moved to California, she brought it with her. She hired a driver and that was how she traveled. It was funny because it was right-hand drive but she wouldn't change it over. Jack used to take his mother to dinner every Sunday afternoon. It was a ritual with them. However, she refused to ride in the one twenty. She considered it rough and he drove way too fast. So Jack had to ride with her in the saloon and that drove him crazy. She wouldn't let the driver go over thirty miles an hour. They used to feud over it all the time. When your one fifty came in the dealership, I called Jack. It was a good compromise. It was much roomier than the one twenty and more civilized. It had the lined top so when it was up, it was warm and dry but still could be put down on a nice day. Emma agreed to the compromise and Jack could drive to dinner. She was a beautiful woman. Jack was a good son to her. They finally made their truce and had some very nice Sundays in your car. That was just before the crash."

"What exactly happened?"

"Jack found a spitfire after the war and had it restored. I'd maintained his plane during the war so I helped him with it. He kept it at a little field close to here and would fly it from time to time. The day of the crash, witnesses said the wing broke off when he was doing a loop."

"The plane was just too old?"

"Too old, hell! There was something fishy about the crash. That plane was in perfect condition. I looked it over plenty of times. The thing was he had almost a full tank of gas and the wreckage burned 'til there was nothing left. There wasn't anything to investigate for the cause of the crash.

"It hit Emma hard. Jack was all she had. She'd hoped he was going to settle down and have a family. In fact, he had met a local girl. He was forty when he died. I got the impression he was going to get married. Anyway, Emma went into this big depression and put a lock on the door of the racing garage. She called me up and told me to come get the one fifty. She told me to sell it to someone far away so she'd never see it again. That's why we sent it down to Brentwood Motors in LA. That's how your father found it."

Michael looked at Tanya and then back at Buck. "That's quite a story. Thank you for telling me the history of my car. I guess I never thought about it before. The car was in our barn covered by a sheet for as long as I can remember. I used to play in it like it was a fort when I was a little kid. My dad wouldn't talk about it much until we got it restored. Lucille has had two full lives already."

Tanya added, "And now beginning a third."

Buck entertained them with war stories for another hour. It was thrilling to hear firsthand about his adventures. Finally, they sensed it was time to leave. Buck had a shock for them as he was getting up.

"Sometimes I see Jack in town. I know it's just my age playing tricks on me. He might be driving along the road or walking down the sidewalk. I'm not ashamed of it and it gives me peace inside."

Michael gave Tanya a startled look that she returned with an arching of her eyebrows. Buck went to a bookcase and returned with an old worn manila envelope.

"Take these pictures from the old days and have a look. I'll get them back from Tanya later. Keep any of the one-fifty you want."

"Thank you very much, Buck. I'll enjoy going through these."

As he walked outside, Buck asked Tanya, "Are you going to take him to the point?"

"Yes, of course."

Buck walked them to the car. "It's been a long time since the old girl was down here. If you can imagine, she was parked right on this spot when Jack visited me almost fifty years ago. She sure looks fine. A little walk will do you good before your drive home."

Tanya took Michael's hand as naturally as only she could do. "Come, walk with me. I want to show you something."

On the land side of West Cliff Drive some grand, older homes stood in a stately manner enjoying a spectacular view of the ocean. On the sea side of the street a large park bordered the cliffs. To the south, they could see the Ferris wheel and rides for an amusement park towering over the entrance to the pier. The structure led far out into the ocean and gave the appearance of a centipede with a thousand legs standing in the water. Michael could see couples walking to the far end and back and fishermen casting their hopes for dinner over the side. A strange building dominated the very end, round in shape with light blue walls and a conical red roof, offering burgers and fries to tourists that could handle the trek. A few sea lions were making a racket, clearly audible across the several hundred yards of water. Tanya led Michael along an ancient pea gravel path and watched the surfers below. The ocean formed a unique area because the water got deeper slowly but surely. The longer they walked, the deeper the water was below, the bigger the waves, and the better the surfers. It was a natural surfing school. The beginners were in close to the beach, and the more experienced ventured farther out. The experts were beyond the point, where the waves were much bigger and rougher. Tanya said the area was known as Lighthouse Point.

When they reached the end of the point, they turned a corner and headed north for a short distance. They came upon a monument of a larger-than-life surfer with his board standing behind stretching high up in the air, a memorial to all surfers, which was a nice touch for the area. A garden surrounded the surfer, and inside, almost hidden from view, was a much smaller monument. The garden contained some large blue agave that almost covered the marker. Most people passing by probably missed it. Tanya made sure Michael didn't miss it. It was a memorial to Flight Lieutenant Jack Waldorf!

"I don't believe it!"

"This is where he crashed and died."

Just as she spoke, a church bell rang. He spun around to see a bronze statue of a pastor reading from a Bible on the grounds just across the street, pronouncing an eternal prayer for Jack. As they walked back to the car, Tanya continued to hold his hand. They drove quietly to Los Gatos still lost in thought about the memory of Jack Waldorf.

On their return, they exited the highway just past Los Gatos and headed what seemed to be north, but Michael was so turned around he wasn't sure. A smaller, two-lane highway curved gracefully through estate homes protected by huge lots. Soon enough they turned off again and encountered a large oak tree in the center of the road. He wasn't sure what kind of city government allowed a tree right smack in the center of the road, but he decided it had been there long before any of the city managers. It must have been fifty feet in circumference at the base with five or six main trunks supporting branches extending a distance of what must have been well over a hundred feet. The oak formed a kind of roundabout for the few residents who used the road. The entrance to the Waldorf place was just to the left of the tree but they actually had to drive around the tree and come back. An ornately designed copper gate guarded the residence with spikes on the top, now green from oxidation. A wall started at the top of the turrets on each side of the gate, dropped gracefully down to just over Michael's head and ran out of sight in each direction. An elegant hedge had lined the wall a long time ago, but now it was badly in need of a trim. He inspected a large plaque embedded on one side of the gate while Tanya fumbled with a set of keys until she found the right one. The inscription on the plate announced the residence as La Casa de Bougainvillea. She swung the gate wide and they returned to the car. A gravel drive curved gracefully a short distance under more large oak trees. The house was a shambles. Vines grew from the ground and the surrounding trees to almost cover it. Michael noticed a three-car garage at the side so he parked there.

"I haven't visited in a while. I guess I need to get someone down here to clean the place up. Come around back with me."

He snatched the package of photographs from behind the seat and obeyed. Possibly, there would be a chance to compare some of the old pictures with the garage. The rear of the house had fared only slightly better than the front. A large porch commanded a view of the grounds as they gently sloped away. Another small road curved down the hill and out of sight. Tanya used the keys to open the main door. She pulled back some heavy curtains to allow a little light inside. The electricity wasn't working. She sighed as she looked around.

"I always thought this would be my masterpiece. It has good bones."

"The house has bones?"

"Oh yes. There's only so much you can do with a property if it has a terrible design. This one was top notch in its day. I'll have to take out some walls, redo all the wiring, put in new bathrooms and a kitchen, but it has good bones."

"I wish I had your eye. It seems dark and lonely here."

"Well, for instance, imagine the whole back of the house with large windows to take advantage of the view down to the stream."

When they walked back outside, Michael asked if he could look at Jack Waldorf's racing garage. She nodded and he followed her down a smaller road. It curved through the trees another hundred yards. The garage was in the same condition as the house. Three double doors faced them with a stairway to the right leading to a second floor. It seemed quite austere for the residence of a wealthy man. The double doors put up quite a fight but they finally managed to raise the middle one that wasn't locked. A musty, sickly sweet smell assaulted their noses as soon as they entered the old building, neglected for fifteen or more years. The garage had been emptied and swept clean, but now was covered in cobwebs. A board was broken out on the back and the birds had made a mess of the place.

A search through the package of photographs Buck had given him produced a view almost identical to the one they had now. The prints were like jewels to him; antiques. In the scene three men worked on the C-type with its bonnet raised. One was obviously Jack Waldorf and another looked like a very young Buck Snider. He didn't recognize the other man. Trophies were displayed on one side in the cabinets that were now in the basement of Peter's house. The same checkered flags were mounted high on one wall. Tanya looked at the picture over his shoulder.

"This place is starting to grow on me. It has such a history. I see what you mean about it being the most important renovation you'll ever attempt."

"I want to show you something else."

She took his hand again and led him around the garage to the back. A path followed the road down to the garage from the main house and ended behind the garage at a small grave. They approached reverently and read the marker.

Emma Waldorf
1900-1991
Wife of Robert, mother of Jack
How our lives led us down a flowery
path, in mysterious ways, only to
end here by the tranquil Blue Sea

"Jack's mother's buried here on the estate?"

"Yes. That was her last request."

"The inscription seems strange to me."

"We'll ask Peter about it later. She was adamant about it. She might have been a little off her rocker at the end."

As they walked back to the main house Michael began to understand how magnificent the estate had once been. Tanya made sure the doors were locked and did the same for the main gate as they left. The skies remained warm and sunny late in the afternoon as they headed back to San Francisco.

Tanya wasn't quite finished with her interrogation. "My turn again." He nodded. "You've spoken very highly of your father but hardly mentioned your mother."

"From the time I was six years old, I was allowed to spend the summers with my mother. She had a small apartment at the back of a grand house in Malibu. It was hard for me as a child to understand, but later I kind of put things together. My mother was just able to get by while my father was quite wealthy. He gave me an envelope for her each time I visited. It must have contained money. It was always sealed so I never saw the inside but I remember it was very fat. I think he must have been quite generous with her.

"The house wasn't on the ocean as most people think of Malibu. It was inland several miles and high on a hill. I absolutely loved it there. My mother was a free spirit. She let me roam with abandon. I captured every lizard and snake within miles."

"What was her name?"

"Jane. Eventually the summers began to cause some trouble."

"How do you mean?"

"I started to like California better than Oklahoma. I loved it at the ranch, don't get me wrong, but I identified with California. As I got older, I spent more time at the beach. I got totally hooked on skateboarding and surfing. Over the years, I made up my mind I was going to move to California and take care of my mother when I was old enough."

"What changed your plan?"

"When I was sixteen, she disappeared."

"Oh my God."

"She vanished from the face of the earth. My father told me he contacted the police but they never found a trace of her. I've never made another trip to California until now. You might as well know I was going to accept Peter's trip from the moment he offered. I was hoping to head down to Malibu after the party and look around some before the Pebble Beach event."

They finished the journey in silence. His mind was back in Malibu as a young boy, surfing all day and laughing with his mother. He wasn't sure where Tanya's was.

At dinner, Michael broached the subject of Emma's grave with Peter.

"The situation was quite strange. One day she called me out of the blue. She had to see me immediately. I drove down the next day for lunch. She had the complete instructions on where she was to be buried and the inscription on the headstone. I warned her I might not be allowed to have a grave on the property. She gave me a look like I've never seen before or since. Her blue eyes were blazing. She made me promise I'd do as she requested. When she died, I managed to get it done. I didn't exactly ask the city for permission. After her death, all of her business papers showed up on my doorstep. I still have them upstairs."

As they walked upstairs to end the evening, Tanya started to turn down the hall toward her room, which was in the opposite direction from his. Michael gently caught her arm and turned her around.

"I'd just like to say this was the most wonderful day I've had in a long time. Thank you for spending so much time with me."

"It was the best for me as well. I have another question for you but I'm not ready to ask you just yet."

She leaned over and kissed him gently on the cheek then turned and went to her room. He stared at the ceiling as he prepared to go to sleep and thought about her. He'd had his share of women during his life but Tanya was the one. Unconditional surrender seemed to be in his near future.

Just as he was about to doze off he heard a light tap on the door. Tanya entered and closed it behind her. He sat up on the side of the bed. She was wearing a robe and her hair was wet and combed straight back, like she had just taken a shower.

"So you're kind of like a detective with the San Francisco PD now."

"I guess you could say that."

"Then I want you to investigate me."

With that, she dropped her robe to the floor. She was only wearing the smallest G-string. Freckles did cover her body and the faintest six-pack showed across her stomach.

"I guess you should turn around so I can get the rear view as well. I need all the facts."

She smiled and turned to reveal a very fine ass, gazing at him over her shoulder with her wicked smile at full force.

"Are you discovering any clues as to my motives?"

The next morning he woke up before Tanya and tip-toed downstairs. Peter was already in the kitchen. Michael retrieved two cups from the shelf and prepared coffee.

"Tanya takes hers with one low calorie creamer and two artificial sweeteners."

"You know we were together last night?"

Peter looked Michael directly in the eye. "There isn't much that goes on in this house I don't know about."

Michael realized he should tread carefully. "I wasn't going to try to keep anything from you. I just wasn't quite sure until now how she felt. I hope I haven't offended you in some way."

"You've charmed her in a way I've never seen any other man manage."

"I'd have to say I'm the one that's been charmed."

"She does have a way of casting a spell. Anyway, I'm very worried about her. We've got to figure out who tried to kill her. Detective Clark called first thing this morning. He's coming over for lunch. I think he's ready to institute your plan."

Paul McNabb

Michael carried a small tray back upstairs and placed it on the
nightstand then opened the door to the bay. A gentle breeze mixed
the sunlight with the aroma of the coffee. As he sat on the side of the
bed, Tanya began to rouse. With one gentle brush of her hand
through her hair, she was as beautiful as most women after an hour of
fluffing.

"I'm sorry but I didn't catch your name last night."

"Detective Michael McAllister."

"Oh, yes. Now I remember. That was quite an investigation you
conducted. You didn't seem to miss anything."

"I was intent on finding an ugly spot. I'm afraid I failed.
However, it was dark. Perhaps I should conduct another quick search
in the light of day."

"I think I'd prefer something slow and methodical to make sure
you don't miss anything. However, I want to ask you that question
first." She paused and turned her blue eyes and smile on high beam.
"I'm thinking about sleeping with you every night for the rest of our
lives. How does my idea strike you?"

Michael's heart stopped. It was like a dream come true and he
was afraid "Some might question your judgment."

"I don't care what other people think. I'm interested in your
opinion. I want to know if a drop dead handsome cowboy who could
charm the pants off just about any woman he met could settle down
in a monogamous relationship."

"When we met, it was like being struck by a thunderbolt. I've
thought of nothing else since."

The wattage of her smile went up another notch.

"That's a damn good answer. I'm going to put a small
checkmark in the plus column for you."

He made love to her again, a little slower this time. Afterward
they took a long shower together, holding each other close with the
warm water running between their bodies. He gently scrubbed her
back and shampooed her hair. When they finally descended the stairs
it was practically time for lunch.

Chapter 15

The television blared. A beer warmed on the nightstand. His office was now the bed, and on it, everything served to help him do his new job, which was to watch the news reports and look for ways to improve his skills. The news review of his new career was quite satisfying. From an accidental killing, he had progressed to a succession of murders, most committed according to plan. Women would now show him some respect if they knew what was good for them. A celebration seemed in order, but he couldn't come up with something appropriate. Fate made the decision for him.

When the news outlets caught wind of his sixth victim, the coverage his work had previously received paled in comparison to the firestorm they created now. He watched it all, absorbed it with pride and satisfaction. He wondered how the public would react to the extreme violence of her murder. The way the journalists were selling it, he could just imagine their fear. One of the main newscasters was Kelli Emerson. During her local evening show in San Francisco, she ranted in a long diatribe against the police department for not making enough progress bringing the killer to justice. At the end of her telecast, she had quite a finish with the following statement: "If you're watching tonight, I want you to listen to me. You're sick. What you've done to these victims is the work of a madman. You need help. You need to turn yourself in to the police or call me at the number on the screen. I can help you." She finished her broadcast with a long look into the camera.

It was an obvious ploy to increase ratings for her station. A grin began to cross his face because he had an idea to really help them with their ratings. Instead of picking women at random maybe it was time to select a more famous victim, one who could really generate some interest in his work. He knew from the information on television and in the papers that it would be a good idea to change his mode of operation as much as possible, to keep them guessing, and make it hard to predict his next move. The Bakersfield idea had been a disaster. Time to try something different.

The television station was located on the outskirts of San Francisco. Observations could be made of Miss Emerson's comings and goings from a few blocks away, using a good set of binoculars. He drove his Jaguar sedan, showing care not to spend too much time at any one vantage point or keep the same schedule. One evening he caught her leaving work and managed to follow her home, which turned out to be a condo in town.

On a Friday night a few weeks later, he drove to San Francisco using another stolen Explorer. A parking spot available six blocks from her condo was perfect. This time he wore a black hooded sweatshirt because he'd read about hidden cameras placed around the city and how close they'd come to taping him on several occasions. With the hood pulled up to cover his face, he got out of the truck. Her condo was located on the second floor near a trellis he felt he could easily climb. The balcony had an expansive view of the bay. He'd chosen Friday night because he thought she'd probably have a date or some event to attend after work. He had guessed correctly.

Pedestrian traffic posed a great risk so he waited for a lull and then quickly scaled the trellis to the balcony of her condo. He slid back into the shadows and waited to make sure no one had noticed him. A few minutes later, he easily broke the catch on the door and entered. The rooms were dark, but a tiny light over the stove cast a pale glow like moonlight throughout the condo. Her kitchen provided a nice set of knives so he selected the largest one as his weapon for the evening. He removed his goodie bag of cocaine from his pocket and formed several lines on the granite countertop. When he was loaded, he waited in the dark of her bedroom closet for her return.

A noise jarred him awake. Apparently, he'd passed out for a while. The door shut firmly, keys landed on a table, and he heard her listening to her messages. The illuminated numbers on a clock near the bed told him it was a little past 1 AM. When she finally came into view, he watched with anticipation as she removed her dress and jewelry and moved to the bathroom.

He moved silently across the bedroom and watched her from the shadows for a full minute as he reveled in the thrill of what he was about to do. When he made his move, he came from behind quickly and gripped his hand firmly over her mouth before she could cry out. With a knife held under her throat she was completely defenseless, and he warned her not to scream. He enjoyed her for a moment, shaking in her bra and panties. He was particularly brutal with her because he knew she was going to get him a lot of media attention. He kept her alive as long as possible while he tortured her. When she died an hour into the ordeal it filled him with rage. Her lifeless body was ravaged for much longer, acting out a fantasy he'd been planning for days. When he was finished he moved to the door of her bedroom and turned to observe what the Police would see when they entered.

The scene needed to be something they would never forget. After using her shower, he dressed, wiped down the tiles and then put back on his gloves. As he prepared to leave, he peeked out the door. Seeing no one he left the door slightly ajar, not wanting to have to wait for her to be discovered. With his sweatshirt hood pulled up over his head so any surveillance cameras couldn't record his face he walked calmly out of the building, raising a hand in a wave of defiance.

Chapter 16

The jangle of a ringing phone sent a sharp pain directly into Detective Clark's brain. No sleeping in this Saturday morning. "This better be important."

It took him a moment to process the information before bolting upright in bed. The Slasher had struck again, but they'd discovered the body quickly this time. There might be an opportunity to catch him.

"I'll be there in ten minutes. Send all available cops on the beat to the BART stations. Pull over any Ford Explorers in the area or on the highway. Take down the license number of anyone driving an Explorer in the area, even if they don't seem to be a match. Check the condo for surveillance video. Get on that immediately."

Police cars, news crews and bystanders were already congregating around the entrance to the condo complex when he arrived. He double-parked and was shown to the second floor condo. The beat cop quickly filled him in as they scaled the stairs.

"An elderly woman across the hall was apparently a big fan of her famous newscaster neighbor. She was up early and heard someone leave the condo. She came out to get her paper and noticed the door ajar. She called out, but got no reply and finally went inside to see what was wrong. She's down at the hospital now. I think she had a heart attack."

"A heart attack?"

"You won't believe what is inside. I took a look and then sealed the place off."

"I can't take a chance on disturbing any evidence until after the CSI Unit finishes but I also can't waste any time. You've got to tell me in detail what you saw inside."

"Okay. Like I said, I got the call because the lady across the hall called the police. She was scared to death. I had to show my badge at the peephole of her door before she would open up. Just when she was getting to the part about investigating the condo across the hall she clutched at her heart and fainted. When I couldn't revive her I called an ambulance. I called for back-up while I waited. Once she was attended to I entered the condo across the hall because the door was still ajar. The entry way was small. A set of keys and a purse sat on the table undisturbed as far as I could tell. I could go right or left so I chose left, which led me into the kitchen and living area, open with a big island in the middle. I noticed a white powder spread all over the counter top. I tasted it to confirm it was cocaine. Nothing else seemed out of place so I back-tracked and went right which led me to the bedroom and bath." He paused a minute as he remembered what he saw. "The corpse, or what was left of it, looked like it had exploded. Body parts were spread haphazardly across the bed and floor. Blood spatter covered the walls and ceiling. The head was staged on the pillow looking right at me. I never entered the bedroom, just looked in from the door. I knew better than to go any further."

"You did very well in preserving the crime scene. I'm heading back downstairs. I think we might be able to catch him this time."

"Two more things real quick." Clark nodded. "Part of a leg was near the door. I felt it to see if it was still warm. It was. The other thing was the hall was clean, no bloody foot prints. How could that be? I think he might have undressed in the hall before he started on her then showered and dressed out in the hall before he left. I don't think the perp will be covered in blood if you catch him."

Chapter 17

The sun surprised the Slasher as he exited the condo building. He'd taken a long time with his victim after he had killed her and then showered. Now he realized it was a mistake to leave her door ajar, but he was afraid to go back to close it. If she were discovered quickly, the police might put out an all-points bulletin on Ford Explorers. He quickly pulled off the sweatshirt to change his appearance. The BART station was only a few blocks away but he got lost in the complexity of the streets in the downtown area. The track was in plain view, tantalizingly close, but he couldn't find the right road to the station. When he finally approached, he noticed a police car parked near the track and two officers talking near the entrance. Was it possible the police had figured out how he was getting home? He couldn't take the chance.

The next two hours were spent driving down endless side streets, only to be blocked by the freeway or train tracks, and having to double back to another route. The original plan was totally shot. A few times he pulled to the side of the road and banged on the wheel in rage, and then hit more cocaine. When he saw commercial airplanes low in the sky, he knew he was quite a bit south, near the airport. He risked the freeway to the San Jose Airport and dumped the truck in the parking lot. The bus ride home gave him some time to consider his latest murder. Leaving the door open to her condo had been a huge mistake. Apparently the police had figured out he was riding the BART too, because they were waiting for him at the station. By the time he arrived home, it had been almost six hours since he left Miss Emerson's condo. Only blind luck had allowed him to elude the manhunt in San Francisco.

He stripped in the garage and performed his cleaning ritual. Upstairs he put on his pajamas and crashed into bed so he could watch television. The body of Kelli Emerson had been discovered only minutes after he left. Someone had investigated the open door in the swank complex. The scene he had staged in Kelli's bedroom yielded results even better than he had hoped for. Reports on the police band radio set off a media frenzy. One of their own had been murdered in a sensational manner providing an orgy of emotional and police drama the media could gorge on for weeks. It might not have gone according to plan, but he was proud of his work. The fear in the city went up another notch. The pressure on the police force had to be unbearable, and he felt more powerful than he ever had in his life.

Chapter 18

When Detective Clark arrived, the meeting took on a different tone than the previous ones. Clearly, it was time to get down to business. Michael's black eye was fading. The cut wasn't as angry as it had looked a week earlier. His hair covered most of it, anyway. Tanya's neck still bore faint blue traces of fingers making Michael's blood boil every time he saw them. The marks were a daily warning for him to stay alert. Another attempt on her life could come at any time.

They gathered around the large kitchen island with sandwiches and drinks. Detective Clark looked haggard. It wasn't hard to imagine what his last week had been like with the latest of the Slasher's victims being a prominent television reporter.

"You look tired, Clark." McAllister commented.

"If you think my face looks bad, you should see my ass, or what's left of it. Excuse me for being blunt, Ms. Stafford.

"You both look like you've healed up enough for us to get started with our investigation. I have three guests I want Michael to investigate. The names are Roger Simms, Mark Barrow and Steve Williams."

Clark looked at Peter and Tanya for an opinion of his three suspects.

Peter looked at Tanya. "None of them seems likely to me but, of course, I can't imagine anyone we know being behind this so…"

Michael didn't remember much about any of the three suspects. He'd met too many people at the party in a short period of time.

"Do you see any problems setting up the meetings?"

Peter answered again. "I don't think so."

Clark looked at Michael. "Do you want a gun?"

"No. It would just raise suspicions if it were noticed."

"Then proceed with your first appointment." Clark turned to Tanya. "I'm going to have officers trail you. We'll work out a scheme where you preset your cell phone so you can punch a button for help if you need it."

Peter objected strongly. "Now just a second, you are not going to put my niece in harm's way like this. I don't like this one bit."

Michael offered him a promise. "I won't let anything happen to Tanya."

Peter seemed to grudgingly accept the plan. Setting up a meeting with Roger Simms took only a few minutes on the phone.

Tanya asked an interesting question. "What exactly are we looking for when we visit each suspect?"

Detective Clark looked at Michael. "Why don't you answer that question?"

"We're looking for lies. The guilty party will lie about the smallest things. He'll lie for no reason. Lies always lead to the right person."

Clark offered one more instruction before he left: "Tanya, remember you said you bit your attacker on the hand during the fight in the basement. Don't forget to look at the hands of each suspect, as well as anyone else in each house. It's a long shot, but you might get lucky."

The next evening Michael rode with Tanya north in her new Jaguar. Roger Simms lived on the far side of the Golden Gate Bridge, on the road to the coast that passed through the Muir Woods. She drove with a natural motion, quick but not jerky. Little wonder she'd been successful at kart racing. The road wound through a eucalyptus forest. An intoxicating aroma filled the cabin with the windows down. If it weren't for the directions they'd been given, it would have been almost impossible to recognize the house from the road. Roger had given them a warning about a red mailbox at a certain mile marker. A couple of off duty police officers, hired by Peter to watch his house twenty-four hours a day, trailed close behind. Clark agreed to have them follow for backup. A cell number was programmed into Tanya's phone in case of emergency. The officers waited a block away in case of trouble. If the phone rang with a call from her and there was no one on the line, they would be through the front door in two minutes.

As they drove up the long entry, Michael commented, "This looks like a haunted house out of a horror movie. Maybe we should have set this up for daylight."

"Oh come on, you big scaredy cat. We can handle this."

Gravel crackled under the tires as they approached a darkened house. The wind was picking up as the sun went down. The grounds weren't very well kept. A big Bentley sedan parked at the front of the house looked lonely with wet leaves stuck to the windows. Roger answered the bell at the front door and showed them in. Michael vaguely remembered him from the party. Simms was well dressed, but pudgy and soft. Tanya told Michael on the drive over Roger had inherited quite a sum of money from his grandmother. Simms had the look and manner of someone who hadn't worked a day in his life. Although he seemed surprised to see Tanya along for the ride he asked little about the murder attempt. Michael judged his behavior as somewhat insincere.

At least Roger had the good manners to offer them a glass of wine. At Michael's urging they were shown to a large garage in back, almost empty save for a gleaming gun metal blue E-type. The Jag wasn't the normal kind, though. It was what was called a lightweight, a club racer. The body was all aluminum with flared fenders and various racing upgrades, truly a rolling work of art. Michael set about taking photographs. In thirty minutes he'd taken a hundred.

Tanya's job was to engage Simms while Michael appeared to be busy with the photographs. The suspect didn't have much to say, didn't seem interested in photographs of his car or if a story ever appeared. Simms owned a scrapbook containing many newspaper and magazine articles that filled in the history of the car. Michael asked if he could borrow it for the story. Simms reluctantly agreed but made Tanya promise to get it back to him.

A wave to the bodyguards a block down the road signaled the all clear. They followed them back to Peter's house for good measure.

"Well, princess, how do you think we did with our first interview?"

"I didn't get any kind of a vibe from him at all. He certainly didn't seem to be upset I was along."

"I agree. I don't know if we can remove him as a suspect based on what we saw, but he seemed pretty disinterested. He wasn't nervous. I got a good look at both of his hands a couple of times and didn't see any cuts or bandages. He certainly didn't lie about anything as far as I could tell. He either has absolutely nothing to do with this or he's one great actor. I wouldn't bet on the actor proposition. Still, he's a loner. He's got plenty of money and nobody's checking up on him."

"I still don't see how you're going to know when we run across the right guy."

"I'll know, all right. Don't worry about that."

Mark Barrow proved to be quite a different story. His home was in Saratoga, not far from the old Waldorf house, requiring another trip south. Mark was in his forties and still working, a little younger than most of the Jaguar crowd. Tanya remarked that he wasn't very active in the club anymore. This tended to happen to some members; they'd get all charged up for a few years and then lose interest later and eventually sell their vintage cars.

Paul McNabb

"Mark? This is Michael McAllister. Do you remember me from the party at Peter Stafford's house?"

"Yes. We talked a few minutes. You're a writer or something, right?"

"Yes. That's what I'm calling about. I was wondering if you might allow me to come down and take a few pictures of your cars for an article. I can get some notes down quickly so it shouldn't take long. I've heard you have some nice cars. What about this weekend?"

A long pause followed. It seemed like he was trying to figure out a way to avoiding a meeting. McAllister knew the trick was to stay quiet and force him to respond.

"This weekend's not good for me. Tell me again how long you think this would take?"

"I'd say an hour or so is all. I can be quick."

"The only time I'd have this coming week would be Tuesday evening. Could you make it then?"

"Tuesday it is. Give me your address and I'll look up the directions. What if I showed around six?"

Barrow gave him the information he needed, so the team began preparing for the meeting. Detective Clark seemed well connected with the police in nearby Los Gatos. A cell phone number was provided for the visit. An officer would be positioned close by around six. Again, if they had trouble, a call from Tanya would have someone coming through the door within minutes.

Tanya's Jaguar would make the trip easily so they headed south after lunch. The old Waldorf mansion was on Tanya's mind more than ever so she wanted to make a visit to consider some new ideas on a complete renovation. The mid-day drive allowed them to miss rush hour traffic, spend some time at the house, and then make the short trip over to Barrow's residence.

The house seemed less intimidating on the second visit. The main house received a lot more attention this time. Tanya shared some ideas about a final design. A few walls would come down to open up the kitchen and living room requiring beams for support. The kitchen would have to be enlarged, as would the master bedroom.

Eventually, they walked down to the garage. This time they investigated the suite above the garage where Jack had lived. It was like opening a time capsule. The room apparently hadn't been disturbed since his death. The bed was still made and personal items still lay on the dresser. On a shelf, Michael found the pilot's logbook from World War II, listing every mission. He suggested Tanya should donate it to some air museum, since it was a priceless piece of history. Waldorf's mother undoubtedly came down from time to time, walking through the room and looking at all that was left of her son. Tanya never took her eyes away from Michael as she pulled back the covers on the bed, unbuttoned her blouse and then unfastened her jeans.

"Get your clothes off, cowboy. We need to break this place in."

A wonderful passionate love-making session was interrupted after a few minutes when her phone buzzed on the dresser.

When he looked deep into her eyes she whispered, "To hell with that thing and don't you dare slow down." Progress.

The water wasn't turned on in the garage, so they had to get dressed in their dirty, sweaty state and walk back to the house. Luckily Tanya had a large bottle of water in the car so they cleaned up as best they could. Soon enough it was 5:30. The GPS in Tanya's Jag made the trip to Barrow's house easy. While it wasn't too far from the Waldorf residence, they had to drive back to Highway 9, then around to Saratoga and then back via some very windy roads to get there.

As they walked up, Mark opened the door. "Tanya. I didn't know you'd be along. Good to see you. You've sure been in the news since the party. I hope everything's okay."

The hair stood up on the back of Michael's neck. He always trusted his instincts and Barrow set off alarms from the first instant. Suddenly he wished he'd taken Clark up on the offer of a gun. Maybe they'd gotten lucky the second time out. Barrow gave Tanya the once over, twice, and didn't seem shy about it. It was obvious Mark had some nasty intentions if the opportunity ever presented itself. Barrow shook his hand with a vice grip that spoke of a life of hard work. A quick glance at Barrow's hands didn't show any obvious injuries. Too much time had probably passed anyway. The house was even more elegant inside than out. A lovely view of the backyard rolling down to a creek provided the backdrop for their meeting in the kitchen. It seemed to be the same one that meandered its way past the Waldorf house further downstream. Barrow apologized because the living room furniture was being reupholstered.

"May I offer you both a glass of wine?"

It was clear he was only really addressing Tanya when he said "both".

"Just a couple of soft drinks would be fine. Diet if you have it."

"You certainly don't need to be on any diet, Tanya, but I'll see what I have."

For someone who didn't want to be bothered on the phone, Barrow seemed quite willing to spend as much time with Tanya as she'd allow. After several more minutes of tiresome comments about Tanya, Michael decided to push their agenda.

"May we have a look at the Jags?"

Barrow showed them down a flight of stairs. The house was a walkout with the front at ground level, but the back followed the slope of the hill providing a large garage at ground level with the door opening to the rear of the house. True to his word, Barrow had several very nice Jags, all of them show winners. Michael immediately began snapping pictures of the cars and the shop. He also noted serial numbers and quizzed Barrow about how each car had been found, as well as information about the restorations.

Tanya's job was to keep him distracted, an easy task. "How's your wife, Alice, these days?"

"She's fine. She's visiting her sister for a couple of weeks back east so I've been playing bachelor. That was a shocker about the murder attempt at the party. I had to leave early and missed the whole thing. I couldn't believe it when I read about it in the paper."

Michael needed a little more information. "You had to leave early?"

"Yes. Rosalina Snider called when she saw me on the party list. She asked if she and Buck could pick me up on the way. They're getting pretty old now and she wanted me to drive up and back. They had a new long wheelbase sedan I wanted to try out. I don't think Buck can really drive anymore. They were pretty tired after dinner so we were one of the first to leave."

"What exactly do you do for a living?"

"I own a machine shop. We can custom build just about anything. It's a great money-maker but the challenge is keeping an eye on the staff."

"Why is that?"

"Most of the full-time guys are welders. We build custom parts, some big stuff. You'd be amazed at some of the things they've done after I gave them full instructions. If I'm out half the day, there's no telling what I might find when I come back. If I want to make sure we build something only once, I have to supervise everyone closely. Building things twice isn't a good way to make money."

Michael finished with the pictures and notes so they made their way back upstairs. A nod to Tanya motioned toward the door. Disengaging proved difficult because Barrow really didn't want Tanya to leave. They finally managed an exit and began the drive home.

When they were safely away from the house, he asked, "What did you think about him?"

"I definitely felt something a little strange going on in there. I can't put my finger on it, but there's something. I know his wife pretty well. She's the nicest person in the world. I may have to make a couple of phone calls to check up on him. They're very wealthy but it's all her money. Frankly, I don't see it. I guess I have a hard time believing anyone we know could have done this, though."

"He fits the killer's profile in several ways. He has the right build and he's very strong. However, he seems to have an alibi so we'll have to confirm that. He certainly had some nasty intentions when it came to you."

"I'm not available."

Her response placated him a little but alarm bells were still going off in Michael's head. Something wasn't right about Mark

Paul McNabb

Barrow. Years on the police force had made him pretty good at checking people out. He didn't like anything about the guy. Maybe he was just jealous because Barrow obviously wanted a chance at Tanya. If his alibi checked out, though, Barrow would be crossed off the suspect list.

Steve Williams was the last suspect, known to be having some money problems. Other information pointed to a possible driving contract with Phil Roberts for the coming season. The lead seemed legitimate so McAllister made a call the next day.

"Steve, this is Michael McAllister."

"Are you okay? I read about the murder attempt at the party. I couldn't believe it. I wanted to call Peter, but I thought I should stay out of it at least for a while."

"Yes, I'm okay. As a matter of fact, I'm still staying at Peter's place."

"How's Tanya doing? I was so worried about her."

"She's doing much better, thank you. I wanted to ask if you'd consider letting me take some pictures of your Jag? You could give me a little history of the car and I could include a few lines in my story about my trip out here. Peter said you had a nice early E-type."

"I do but it's not been restored yet. It doesn't look too great right now."

"Actually that's good. I need some before pictures to go with all these cars that are done better than new. A little patina can go a long way toward making an outstanding story.

"Well, I don't know if you can make something out of it, but you're welcome to come over."

"We're going to be busy with Pebble Beach pretty soon. Do you mind if we set something up right away?"

"You can come over any time. My daughters are here from school so the place might be a little busy. We can certainly sneak out to the garage for a while."

"Then I'd like to come over this evening if that would work."

"Sure. Do you have a pencil and paper? I'll give you directions."

Since they knew Williams' family would be present for the meeting Clark didn't bother with back up for the third meeting. As they pulled up to the house, Tanya pointed out Steve's wife talking with the neighbors.

"Tanya, it's so good to see you. I wasn't expecting this. Please come inside."

Michael was introduced to Steve and his two beautiful daughters. The Williams family seemed to know Tanya very well and swarmed around her with tons of questions. He eased Steve into the garage after they each found a soft drink.

"Well, I have to tell you, I never dreamed this old Jag would ever be in a magazine article."

"It's a very interesting car. It'll make a great restoration."

The usual picture session ensued but as he talked, Michael began to dig for more information.

"I heard something about you having a driving contract with Phil Roberts for next season. Is that right?"

"To be honest, it's kind of embarrassing. I had an angle on a D-type replica that was qualified for a special series of racing. It was much less expensive than the real thing but still not cheap. I probably could have gotten it for under a hundred fifty thousand dollars. I've been a commercial pilot for a long time and I do pretty well. The problem is my girls are attending Pepperdine University on softball scholarships. One is a talented pitcher and the other is a catcher, who probably got a full ride only because of her sister.

"Pepperdine is a private school. It's very expensive. I could afford to send my girls to a public university without much trouble but Pepperdine is another matter. If they pull the scholarship from the catcher, the pitcher wants to quit. Suddenly, I might be on the hook for some serious tuition and books so I decided to back out of the purchase of the D-type. I love cars but until the girls are off the payroll, I guess everything's on hold. I told Phil at the party. He seemed cool about it. He said he had a lot of offers for next year and not to worry about it. That was such a tragedy about him. At first it was pegged as a suicide, but then I read in the paper it's looking like a murder."

"The police seem to have accepted the murder theory from what I've heard."

"Who would do a thing like that? It doesn't make any sense."

"No solid leads and no motive. It's going to be a tough one to solve."

Tanya joined them in the garage as the interrogation was ending. She looked over the old E-type.

"You need to get going on this project, Steve."

"One of these days."

When they were safely in the car, Tanya gave a sigh. "He isn't involved."

"I totally agree with you. He wasn't the slightest bit nervous. He was genuinely pleased to see you, as was the rest of his family. He was completely open about his money problems. He just doesn't fit. I got a good look at his hands. They were lily white. Not a mark on them."

The next morning Tanya took her mother grocery shopping, allowing Michael some time to himself. The manila envelope he'd borrowed from Buck Snider beckoned from the desktop. Slowly and carefully, he browsed through the pictures, which included various news clippings and other pieces of information. The vintage pictures were tiny works of art, precious time capsules. The racing pictures from Monterey and other local tracks were the most interesting. The fifties in California seemed to have been heaven on earth for cars and motorbikes.

One shot drew his attention just as he was about to put the photographs away. A trophy presentation after a race depicted three men on a winner's stand. As usual, Jack had won and was holding up the trophy with a big smile. What caught his attention in the writing below the picture was that third place went to a driver named Dave Terrell. Positioned on the third rung of the podium was a very young version of a man he'd spoken to at the party. No one had mentioned anything about Terrell and yet he definitely had a history that seemed worth a little further investigation.

A quick data search on his laptop computer revealed a surprising amount of information. Terrell had his own website, seemed to be extremely wealthy, and owned a number of companies integrated into a maze of businesses from computers to finance to insurance. The brief conversation he'd had with Terrell at the party didn't bring anything important to mind. He vaguely recollected some vain and insecure bragging about an extensive car collection. Terrell had given him a business card, though, with his cell number and an invitation to come do a story about his cars. The card was still in his wallet with an address listed in Palos Verdes. He wasn't sure of the location. At the time of their brief discussion, it hadn't seemed important. He made a mental note to discuss Terrell at the meeting in the morning with Detective Clark.

The next day they gathered around the table with drinks; coffee, or in his case, a Diet Dr. Pepper.

Michael began, "Clark, Tanya and I did exactly what you asked, and we couldn't see a fit with the three names on the list. I'd say Roger was the most difficult to read. He was uncommunicative during our visit but he didn't seem nervous. He didn't appear to try to hide anything. My instincts would say he's not involved but I can't give you any facts to back that up.

"Mark Barrow was quite different. He seemed to be a possibility. There was a kind of tension the whole time we visited. Something didn't feel right. Very high class family, though. Hard to believe he'd be involved. No motive of any kind. He said he had an alibi, too."

Clark interrupted. "An alibi?"

"Yes. He said he rode up and back to the party with Buck and Rosalina. She asked him to drive because they don't get out much anymore. They were with him the whole time."

"I'll check that out with Buck to make sure Mark's telling the truth. This is exactly why I need your help. There's no telling how much time we might have wasted checking on him. If what he said is true, he's off the suspect list. What about Steve?"

131

"He was quite straight forward about his money problems, and we don't think he's involved, either. He has two girls in college, and they are the source of his financial challenges."

There was a silence within the group for a moment.

"I see another problem with these three suspects from our brief look into their backgrounds. We know it was a team involved in the murder attempt. One man attacked Tanya but she saw two more take Phil away. Steve certainly doesn't have a team at his disposal. Roger's interaction with the world as we know it is limited, at best. That leaves Mark Barrow. At least he owns a business, but it's a machine shop. I don't think welders make the best gangsters. He's the one with an alibi, too." More silence. "I do have something to bring up. It's probably nothing, but I'd like to hear what the rest of you have to say. Yesterday I was looking through the pictures Buck Snider lent me. I noticed a man in one of them who attended the party. His name is Dave Terrell. I was wondering why we haven't looked into his background?"

Tanya and Peter looked at each other when he mentioned the name.

Peter said, "I knew I was missing something. I feel pretty stupid about this. There does seem to be some bad blood between us."

Detective Clark asked, "Bad blood?"

"Yes. You see, he was actually the first owner of the C-type Jaguar, one of the cars in the basement. I don't remember how he managed to get it because in the early fifties they were hard to come by. Jack attended a race and saw it there. He offered Dave a price he couldn't refuse. Buying the C-type was really how Jack got into racing. He fell in love with the car the first moment he saw it."

Michael asked, "What do you mean by bad blood?"

"It was the way Jack bought the car that started it. When the transaction was done and Jack was loading it up on a trailer, Dave asked why he wanted the car so much. Jack made some offhand comment about he couldn't bear to watch someone as untalented as Dave drive the car one more second. Dave had the best car and still only finished third. They developed a rivalry right away."

"Dave used the profit from the deal with Jack to buy another car, but he could never beat Jack. The C-type won everything with Jack at the wheel. He was on the verge of becoming a professional racing driver. I guess when I acquired the C-type, I inherited the rivalry, so to speak."

Detective Clark seemed confused. "Dave Terrell wasn't on the guest list. I haven't heard anything about him until now."

"That's true. I guess that's why I said I didn't take him seriously. It was kind of an accident that he attended. He wasn't invited, or rather, I should say he invited himself. He heard about the party and called me the day before asking if he could attend. He said he wanted to see the C-type again. I don't know exactly how he knew I owned it but the word has gotten around among some of the car guys. I couldn't think of a way to refuse. He owns a Porsche racing team and there was an event the same weekend at Sears Point. He kind of bullied his way in since he was going to be in the area. I remember he came by himself and left right after we viewed the cars."

Michael looked at Detective Clark. "There's a lot of information on his website. I think you need to take a look at him."

Clark was already packing up his leather case and papers. "So, here's where we are at this point. I'm not taking Simms off the list, at least not yet. I'll check out Barrow's alibi. If it's legit, he's off the list. I'm taking your word about Williams, so he's off the list. That means Dave Terrell might end up being front and center. I'm going to get our researchers on him today and see what we come up with. I'll be in touch."

Chapter 19

The murder of Kelli Emerson was the Slasher's most satisfying to date, providing appropriate media coverage for a killer of his stature. As far as he could tell, all of northern California was trembling in fear. He was thrilled with his notoriety. Life was exciting now. Targeting specific victims seemed to be a good idea, especially famous ones. Random victims were proving to be a bad idea. The cops were gathering too many clues. Searching bars with the hope of finding just the right victim and then pulling off the abduction without being caught seemed way too risky. Research and planning were the keys to success if he expected to continue avoiding capture. He'd been smart enough to pull off the murders so far without being caught. A change in tactics might throw the cops for a loop.

He compiled a list of five women he'd met or seen in the media who lived in the San Francisco area. One of the five names was Tanya Stafford. Since she was a Jaguar enthusiast, he'd seen her many times at shows and other events. She'd make a wonderful trophy. Since she was from a wealthy family, she'd certainly generate a lot of coverage in the media. He made a note by her name because he knew she'd attend the Pebble Beach shows. Maybe the event would provide an opportunity. Big crowds. An opportunity to take her? Probably worth a trip down to take a look.

Chapter 20

A few days later, the crew met with Clark again. Maria served iced tea as they sat under the Japanese maple in the courtyard. The fantastic sculpture of the jaguar resting beside the water drew Michael's attention again. Clark seemed excited as he looked at each of them. Michael could sense he had found something.

"I checked out Mark Barrow with the Sniders and he's off the list. Since then I've focused our attention on Dave Terrell. The more my team looked, the more we found. He's a person of interest for some of the detectives who work in the drug crime division. They like him for some things but haven't been able to pin anything on him. He has a complex business organization. We had to bring in some extra help from a special unit to start unraveling the maze of corporations. It's pretty intricate. We still haven't quite got it figured out, but we're beginning to see some patterns."

Peter asked, "Like what?"

"First of all, the companies don't make money. While he has vast holdings, including a lot of cash and real estate, his various companies haven't generated income. They're all losers and kind of borrow from each other and funnel money around. The bottom line is we can't figure out how he's making money."

Peter frowned thoughtfully. "Clark, it's been a long time since I've dug into a business to take it apart and figure out how it works, but I used to be pretty good at it. I also used to be pretty good at using a computer. What if I came down and had a go at your system, with you looking over my shoulder?"

"We'd have to do it on the sly. You can't legally look at our files as a civilian. I could probably slip you in at night and let you have a shot."

"Let's do it tonight. If Dave is involved in this, I want to know."

That night Clark picked up Peter at eight. Peter knew Clark still considered him somewhat of a suspect. They were uncomfortable being alone together, but they had a common purpose and had to make the best of it. When they got to the station, Clark took him up the back stairs and led him to a room with a couple of other detectives. Peter tore into the computer system with a vengeance. It was pathetic and woefully out-of-date by modern standards, but with some help from one of their experts, he successfully queried the databases. The myriad of companies proved little challenge to his business genius and he quickly put together how they related to each other. One company called Investment Index rang a bell. He couldn't quite place it, but was sure he'd seen it before. He thought it was strange that he'd know about it since it was a small private company wholly owned by Dave Terrell. He asked for a pen and paper and jotted the name down for consideration later. More digging turned up a property in Costa Rica. It appeared to be a condo written off for business; probably used for partying. A lot of money had been expensed for trips south in a Learjet.

"I think someone needs to look into this one. It's immune from your system because it's in a foreign country, but several paper trails lead there. I'd suggest you put a tail on whoever goes there and see where it takes you."

"I don't know exactly how we're going to swing that one but we'll find a way."

"I agree that these companies aren't making money. Mr. Terrell doesn't seem to be much of a businessman. However, there's plenty of money. There's some money laundering or something fishy going on here."

"Okay, thanks for your help. We better get you out of here before you're noticed."

As they were leaving, Peter stood at the open doorway of the massive operations room of the Slasher task force headquarters. A large staff buzzed around the room. Pictures on the walls denoted each of the crime scenes.

"Are you making any progress?"

"I think we're getting a little closer every day. The problem is we're getting all these prank calls we have to treat as real. If we could concentrate on the facts, I'm sure we could figure this out. He's leaving a lot of clues. We just have to find a way to link the right ones together."

"You know, I could be a big help to you here, too."

"It's too hot for an outsider. If you have some ideas, you can always call me and I'll check them out."

Chapter 21

"Where exactly is Palos Verdes?" It seemed a fair question since Michael already knew he was going to investigate Dave Terrell.

"Los Angeles. It's just south of LAX, right on the coast," Tanya responded.

A break had finally surfaced in the case. Michael was sure he would be able to tell if Terrell was lying during a face-to-face meeting.

"I'm going, too."

Peter quickly objected to Tanya's comment, and this time so did Detective Clark.

However, Michael agreed with her. "It's the same situation as before. He won't be expecting it. We'll have help nearby, but I think if he's our man, Tanya will really bring it out when we visit. We might have to talk about a gun, though."

Detective Clark slid a picture across the island in the kitchen where they were having a coffee.

"Ever see this guy before?" All eyes focused on the photo but no one had an answer so Clark continued. "His name is Klaus Kremer. We got the picture off Terrell's website. He's listed as the head mechanic of the Porsche racing team. He won a gold medal in the Olympics for Germany in the nineties in weightlifting. We think he's most likely the person that tried to murder Tanya. The Palos Verdes police have been watching Terrell's place for several days now and haven't seen him once. Be on the lookout for him. If you don't see him, try to push Terrell on it. See what he says. I have a feeling he's been eliminated. Keep in mind if Terrell's our guy, he's managed to get away with this for a very long time. He didn't manage that by being stupid or taking chances. I think whenever it's been necessary, he's eliminated witnesses or anyone he didn't trust, for that matter."

The meeting with Dave Terrell was surprisingly easy to set, probably too easy. Possibly his ego was so big he couldn't resist showing off his cars, even if it might jeopardize his criminal activities. On the other hand, he might want to use the opportunity to find out what was going on with the investigation without appearing too interested. Michael's bet was the latter.

Saturday evening, all the details of the trip were set. The meeting with Terrell was scheduled for Wednesday morning at 11 AM. Tanya requested they drive Lucille, which was fine with Michael. She also insisted they drive down the Pacific Coast Highway. He'd heard about the drive from many classic car owners. It was the chance of a lifetime to drive the old car down the scenic road. The trip held a few more surprises as well.

"I'd like to leave on Monday."

"I thought it was only about a day's drive?"

"We could make it in a day if we had to, but the PCH is a difficult drive. We won't make good time along the coast. I was hoping we could camp one night in Big Sur."

"Camp? Like in a tent?"

"Yes. My friends used to camp there all the time. I always wished I had. You do know how to camp, right?"

"Of course, but I don't have any camping equipment with me."

"I've already taken care of that. I know a spot that will be perfect. We'll stay Tuesday night in the Ventura Keys. My old college roommate lives there. I haven't seen her in years. It'll be great fun. Then we can drive down to Palos Verdes on Wednesday morning for the meeting with Dave Terrell. We can stay another night with Barb and then hustle back on Thursday. How does that sound?"

"I have a request. I was going to head down to Malibu at some point to nose around some. I'm not sure I can find the house where my mother used to live after all this time, but I'd like to try."

"Do you remember the street name? I could look it up. It'd be a lot easier."

"I looked through the few papers I could find before I left but came up empty. It's been thirty years. I remember a canyon road leading down to the coast. I think, if I go there and look around, I'll stand a better chance of finding it."

"Okay. We'll stop by after the visit at Dave's house. We should have all afternoon. If you want to go back the next day, we can. I'm sure we can stay with Barb as long as we want."

Packing Lucille was an all-day event on Sunday. The tent and sleeping bags were the modern type and quite compact. Two tiny seats in the back, only adequate for small children, provided some much needed storage space. Soft bags were a must for everything else because the trunk was flat and irregular inside. Tanya managed almost a week's wardrobe in a small hand bag, a miraculous achievement.

Monday morning they started the day with a jog through the marina, then showered together. After a light breakfast, and a lot of advice and warnings from Peter, they hit the road around ten. The first leg was the identical route through Los Gatos and Santa Cruz they'd used to visit Buck Snider, then on through Monterey and finally a pit stop for gas at a retro station in Carmel. The old building looked like it had been built in the fifties and never changed. Gasoline would be at a premium on the trip through Big Sur because few stations were allowed in the pristine area. They snacked on Tanya's special oatmeal cookies, a recipe she had learned during her college days. Michael managed to snap a few quick photos of his glamour girl beside Lucille before they left. Tanya insisted that Carmel was simply too beautiful to miss so they took a short detour down Ocean Avenue. The main thoroughfare through the fairy tale village was lined with gingerbread houses converted into bed and breakfast establishments. Tanya mentioned they were lucky to visit during the week when the locals had the run of the town. Modern shops designed to separate tourists from their money as quickly as possible were fronted in the same gingerbread style.

Just south of town, Bixby Bridge afforded a spectacular view of the ocean far below, a mere prelude to the scenery that followed. Steering proved a constant challenge. The old Jag didn't have power steering and the large wheel required a lot of effort and concentration. The road continually changed elevations and switched back and forth as it followed the rugged coast. Tanya had been spot on about not making good time, but the sublime scenery of thick forests of Monterey Pine more than made up for their slow progress.

Nepenthe was the first stop about an hour down the road. Michael knew that the name of the town must be a nod to someone or something from Greek Mythology, but the name didn't make a connection in his head. An elegant phoenix carved out of wood stood proudly over a restaurant perched on a peak with a spectacular view. Café Kevah, a coffee shop one level down, turned out to be their final destination, quite adequate for a snack to tide them over 'til dinner. Tanya found a small ornate table where they could relax for a few minutes. Birds of every imaginable color begged and attacked at any opportunity for a crumb. After a twenty-minute break, they were back on the road.

As they continued south, Tanya asked, "What do you think happened to your mother? What was her full name, by the way?"

"Jane Francis. I think she changed it back when she divorced my father. As to what happened to her, I have no clue. I was too young at the time to be able to tell if my father lied to me about her. I don't think so. He told me he called the police. They supposedly looked into all the cases of unidentified deaths of females about her age. My

142

father never brought her up with me until the end of his life. He talked about her while we were restoring the Jag. I think he would have told me the truth if he really knew what happened to her. I'm sure he blamed himself in some way. As I look back now, I don't blame my father. I think maybe she was a little off. Maybe what we know now as manic-depressive."

"So what do you expect to turn up in Malibu?"

He shrugged his shoulders as he drove.

"I don't know. Like I said, I'm just going to nose around. I'm pretty sure nothing is going to come of it, but maybe I'll feel a little better if I at least make an effort."

"One more question and I promise I'll leave you alone for at least a couple of minutes."

Michael smiled, knowing there was no way she could possibly leave him alone for any amount of time, no matter how small. He found it charming. "Maybe you should think about a career as a detective. You seem to enjoy asking questions."

"I know. I'm sure I'd be good at it. Anyway, you've got to explain to me how you went from being a detective to being a writer for a classic Jaguar magazine. I've tried to make a connection somehow but I can't figure that one."

"It was completely by luck. When I left the police force, I didn't have much to do. I had a pension and healthcare. My house was already paid off. I'd been in that life for about twenty years. I was pretty lost. As I look back, it's probably why my dad came up with the car project, trying to get me involved in something. The local Jag club invited me to bring the car to their show that summer. Several of them helped us with the car, so they wanted to see the finished product. You know, dad and I were incapable of a restoration like the other Waldorf cars but Lucille's still a nice car. I started going to a few shows here and there; taking pictures of the cars. I'd e-mail them to my friends. Well, one day, out of nowhere, I got an e-mail from the Jag magazine asking if they could use one of my pictures. I agreed, but asked for a credit on the photo. The editor e-mailed back and asked for a caption. I loved the picture they selected. A silver-haired guy was sitting beside his red on red XK one forty coupe, fully restored, but the work had been done a long time ago. I thought the Jag and the owner made an elegant pair so I asked him how long he had owned the car. He couldn't quite remember. Then I asked him how he found it. His face lit up as he told me the story. In about nineteen eighty he was driving his nineteen seventy-six XJS sports car on a business trip to Dallas. He stopped for lunch in some restaurant I didn't recognize the name of. When he came out, the one forty was parked beside his Jag and the owner was inspecting his car. The stranger said he'd been looking for an XJS. The first guy said he liked one forties. They retrieved their pink sheets, signed them and drove off in a new car."

"That's an unbelievable story."

"Apparently the magazine thought so, too. They offered me a job writing about owners and cars in North America the next day. Of course, if you consider the pay, I don't think I beat out a lot of other writers for the job. Still, it got me through a bad time. It kind of forced me to be sociable; got me out of the house."

After a couple of hours of driving through the Los Padres National Forest, they turned into the Klespett Creek campsite per Tanya's order.

The site was fairly crowded. After all, it was summer, which was a prime time for camping, according to Tanya. A campsite on a corner with a bit of privacy beckoned. A small level area offered a spot for the car, room for the tent and a circular cement pit for cooking barbeque style.

"Follow me."

After filling out a small white envelope with their campsite number and stuffing it with a ten dollar bill Michael was instructed to drop it in a box provided with a slit on top and a strong lock on the side. Admission entitled them to a bundle of wood as well. With the wood deposited by the fire pit, Tanya set about pitching the tent in deadly earnest. All didn't go exactly as planned but Michael knew enough to stay out of her way. Eventually she managed a picture perfect tent, with the door pinned back and two sleeping bags on each side like a vacation post card.

Now that she was done, he felt it was safe for him to make one small adjustment. "I think the sleeping bags work better this way." He unzipped each one and then zipped them together to make one large sleeping bag.

She frowned at him. "How did you know how to do that?"

"Cowboys know things."

She took his hand and led him back down to the highway. They had to use care to cross due to the heavy traffic. On the other side they found themselves high on a cliff looking down at the waves crashing on the beach. Immense elephant seals loafed in the surf. The steep path leading down to the beach below required constant concentration. Their descent took almost thirty minutes. At the bottom, they sat together on a large rock and watched the seals while the waves crashed against the rocks. Eventually, they made their way back up the path, which seemed much steeper now. When they reached the summit, they were rewarded with a sunset richly bathed in pink and blue pastels.

Michael found that starting a fire in the pit was a bit of a challenge to his masculinity, but eventually Tanya was able to cook some hot dogs for dinner. A half bottle of wine stashed in the cooler turned up as a secret surprise. No king or queen in Europe ate as well as they did that night. As they lay side by side on a blanket, looking at a million stars, she asked the one question he'd been dreading: "Please tell me about the serial killer case in Tulsa. It seems to bother you so much. I want to know what happened."

"You know the basics of how it started. A young girl was murdered and dumped on our ranch. I was the one who found her. I became obsessed with the case to the point that I joined the force. I should have known then that nothing good was going to come of me getting involved. After years, I was finally put in charge of the case with my partner, Vic. We made a pact that we were going to solve it. Two more girls had been murdered in the time between me joining the force and getting to work the case. With each victim we collected more evidence but we didn't seem to be getting any closer to solving the case.

"The last few years, I had started touring the small towns outside of Tulsa, giving talks to the locals. One thing we learned from the evidence was that the killer had to be an outsider. I stressed preventative measures with the kids. Another thing I stressed was that when locals noticed a car that didn't fit in the neighborhood to write down the license plate number.

"After the ninth disappearance, an old woman came forward with a description and license number of a car seen nearby at the time of the abduction. I got an APB out and got a hit back in town. I raced over while my partner organized a search warrant. I interviewed the hotel owner as soon as I arrived. The information he gave me looked promising. I thought he might have the girl upstairs at that very moment. I was torn between storming his room and waiting for the others. I decided to go to the room and confront the suspect; try to keep him busy until back-up came with a warrant. I heard noises inside but no one answered. I knocked harder. The suspect finally answered the door. I talked to him for a minute, but he was uncooperative. The longer I insisted on talking to him, the harder he sweated. He tried to lock me out so I made the decision to force my way in. We struggled briefly and I was able to get the better of him. I forced him to the floor, facedown, and handcuffed him.

"I left him and did a quick search of the hotel room. I found a young girl in the bathtub. She'd been drowned but her body was still warm. I realized that while I had been downstairs trying to decide what to do, he had killed her. I tried, but couldn't resuscitate her."

"It wasn't your fault, you know."

"I appreciate you saying that, but I can't help feeling I was too slow—too late.

"I don't know how long I tried to resuscitate the girl but when I finally gave up, I checked on the suspect. He'd just managed to get to his feet. We looked into each other's eyes, and I think he knew in that instant that I knew everything. He turned and jumped through a picture window. He hit the pavement just in front of the first patrol car to arrive at the scene. The two officers looked up and saw me staring down from the broken window. They didn't say anything but when I came downstairs they wouldn't look me in the eye. I realized they thought I threw him out the window. He might have slit his throat on the glass from the window or just hit headfirst on the pavement, but either way, he was dead.

"By the time it happened, it had been almost twenty years since I had found that first girl, of the two friends who had helped get me onto the police force, one had become the district attorney and the other was the chief of police. The papers decided to go with the story that I'd thrown the killer through the window. It put my associates in a bad spot. If they went easy on me, they could be accused of a cover-up. I'm sure some people in the department thought I was nothing more than a cold-blooded murderer, no better than the man I'd caught. I was immediately put on paid leave pending an investigation. One night, the two of them paid me a visit at my townhouse. They said a trial might ruin their careers. I guess they weren't worried about mine. They promised that if I'd take early retirement, the whole thing would blow over. I bought their sob story and retired. I didn't realize it made me look even guiltier, and insured that I would never get a chance to clear my name. The investigation into the killer's death was inconclusive. I was never charged, but I guess I was pretty bitter about the way it all worked out.

"There's one thing I want you to know. I started having nightmares right after I found the first little girl. They worsened over time, and they've never left me, but they vanished the first night we spent together. I've been sleeping like a baby since then. I feel the most rested I have in years."

She hugged him and whispered, "I'm pretty sure a good dose of me is all you need."

It must have been midnight when they finally retired to the tent. A full moon caused the gray plastic of the tent to glow as a background for Tanya as she undressed. It revealed her form in a most erotic way, almost as if she was performing on a stage with only him as her audience.

She noticed he was staring and smiled her wicked smile. "When camping one must sleep naked. It's one of the laws of nature."

Her body was flawless from head to toe, just like every other day of her life. He decided she enjoyed stripping in front of him and he enjoyed anything she enjoyed. She backed against him spoon style in the sleeping bag. The night was cool even though it was summer, because they were so close to the water. Their bodies heated up quickly when they touched. They made love until they were exhausted and fell asleep.

The next morning, Michael got the fire going again while Tanya took a shower. When it was his turn, he dutifully carried a towel and a bar of soap to a cinder block building that proved anything but opulent. Even though the water was cold, it felt good to get clean. When he returned, Tanya had toasted a couple of bagels and added peanut butter. The tent decided to put up a fight when it was time to take it down. It seemed impossible to get everything rolled back to the size it was originally but they finally succeeded and continued south.

Hearst Castle loomed high up in the foothills an hour later. The cliffs eventually disappeared as the coast flattened against the sea. The ocean disappeared just south of San Luis Obispo but returned near a jewel called Santa Barbara. UC Santa Barbara was where Tanya had attended college.

"I came down here to get away from home and surf. A degree in design had just been added to the curriculum the year I began. I found out what I wanted to do with my life completely by accident."

Michael thought maybe his mother had visited the area with him on a day trip one time but he couldn't remember for sure. Late in the afternoon, their journey ended at the home of Jon and Barbara Steele.

A dark-haired woman Michael assumed was Barbara ran out of the front door and screamed, "HB!"

The girls embraced and were soon deeply enthralled in stories. Jon was friendly and offered a glass of wine. The two men wandered out to the back patio, which turned out to be a deck. The Steele's home was in the Ventura Keys so a channel ran behind their house complete with a smart-looking sailboat tied up along their private dock. The sky was clear and the warm sun and gentle breeze provided an idyllic end to the day.

The home had a particular appeal to Michael. Even though it wasn't ostentatiously large, nothing had been overlooked in the design. The living area had an immense fireplace with a most interesting sculptured conical head that eventually blended into the wall. An intricately wood-lined cupola capped the ceiling. The room was two steps down from the kitchen, which made it cozy, especially with a fire. The flooring was composed of one-foot square terracotta style tiles, both downstairs and up. Subdued Mexican tiles finished the countertops in the kitchen and baths. An intimate suite upstairs near the street, formerly the room of the Steele's only daughter, who had grown up and moved off to college, was Michael and Tanya's home during their visit.

They finished the evening and a couple of bottles of wine while lounging on a leather sofa that curved gracefully around the fireplace.

"Barb, you called Tanya 'HB'. May I ask what that stands for?"

Both girls erupted in laughter. "I'm afraid you're busted, Tanya. It stands for heartbreaker. She had so many boyfriends in college; it was like a sporting event. She'd hook one and then set him free, like a catch and release program."

Michael gave Tanya a stern look and she blushed.

"That's an exaggeration. Maybe I should tell some stories on you, Barb?"

Now it was Barb's turn to blush. They looked through a few college pictures. It appeared Barb had been living the good life for some time. She must have put on twenty-five pounds since college. Tanya was still trim. Michael decided it was the same reason he was still the same size he'd been since college. They'd never been married, never enjoyed the tranquility of a lasting relationship and never had someone to care for them. He hoped that would to change now. Maybe they'd get fat in their old age. After a night of fond memories, engaging stories and good wine, they finally crashed in bed. The attempted murder seemed a long way away, but tomorrow they had

149

to deal with another suspect. They kept that information to themselves, simply explaining they had some business the next day in Palos Verdes.

At eight sharp they hit the road the next morning, driving south on the Pacific Coast Highway to avoid the rush hour traffic of the major highways. Beyond the topmost reason for the trip, Michael was anxious to see Malibu again after so many years. The further south he traveled, the less he recognized the place. So many houses had been built along the road it almost seemed like a different city. The one thing that hadn't changed was the sculpture of the land meeting the ocean. Tanya pointed out Cher's house on an outcrop jutting into the sea. She'd been interviewed about doing some work there a few years back, but it hadn't panned out. Around the next corner, he saw what he thought was the road leading up to the house where he'd spent so many summers. The last time he'd visited, Pepperdine University had been a small establishment. Now a large manicured campus nestled in the foothills, looking out to the ocean. He remembered the area fairly well because his mom had worked for the university in the library. On the south side of the campus he found what he was looking for, a street called Malibu Canyon Road. It would have to wait though.

Tanya called the local police on her cell at ten sharp as they'd been instructed. Another cell number was programmed into her phone in case of emergency. She was to call it immediately if they had any problems. Furthermore, the police in Palos Verdes had Terrell's house under surveillance. If they were out of sight longer than an hour, the PV police would call Tanya. If she didn't answer, the police were to figure out a reason to visit the house.

The fantasy of the last two days with his dream girl quickly evaporated into reality. There was a good chance they were preparing to meet the person responsible for her attempted murder. A series of questions intended to evoke a response, had been rehearsed on the drive down. Practice was over now. It was show time.

When they reached Santa Monica, they traveled on Lincoln Boulevard, still technically the PCH, but now a crowded four-lane street with traffic lights every few blocks. Just past LAX airport, they veered right and entered what appeared to be an Italian village. The main road wound around a steep hill with the ocean on their right. A strict housing code seemed to be in effect because each residence was colored in a uniform manner, all with stucco walls and tiled roofs. Tanya guided him through the last few turns using the GPS on her cell phone until they were finally confronted by a large gate. The guard was expecting Michael, but not Tanya. After some discussion they were allowed in. Dave Terrell was waiting for them on a large circular drive near the front of the house.

"Tanya, what a surprise! I wasn't expecting to see you as well."

"Michael and I have become sort of inseparable."

Terrell quickly turned an eye on Michael, a look of both respect and jealousy apparent. Even this octogenarian had ideas about Tanya. They were invited into the house and led to the back patio, which provided a spectacular view of the ocean a mile away.

"I was shocked to hear about the trouble after the party, Tanya. From what I read, you're lucky to be alive."

"I think Michael had a little to do with it, rather than just luck."

"Ah, yes. Michael. You bravely saved the day. Has there been any progress on the case?"

Tanya answered, "No. The police can't seem to find a motive. I have a feeling we're never going to find out who was behind it."

Terrell seemed to enjoy her response. He quickly began to brag about himself in a most spirited and self-indulgent manner. McAllister decided they should let him continue, giving him the possibility to slip up and entrap himself with his words.

"You know, Tanya, I'm a lot like your father and Peter. I'm truly a self-made man."

Michael thought Tanya might convulse at the comparison of this waste of human tissue to her father, but she displayed a remarkable control of her facial expressions.

"I decided to reward myself with this magnificent mansion. I thought about San Francisco, but I couldn't stand the climate. Much too cold there. I scoured the southern coast until I found this perfect piece of land with an unparalleled view of the ocean. I worked out the design myself. You know, Tanya, I think I even contacted you about handling some of the work, if I remember correctly."

"Yes. I was in the middle of a big project and couldn't fit it in. It was a little too far for me as well. I don't know the suppliers in LA like I do in the bay area. It's too bad. This would have been a nice project."

Her interrogation techniques were impressive. Dave was smiling with rich satisfaction from the compliment of a designer with her reputation. Too bad he had no idea she was setting a trap.

"Thank you for those kind words. Let me show you more of the house."

They were dragged through the entire upstairs and endured more of the same self-indulgent rhetoric. When Terrell took them to his massive master bedroom, Michael couldn't stand it anymore.

"Dave, Tanya and I would love to spend more time viewing the house, but we have another appointment later today in Malibu. I want to do justice to your cars. May we have a look?"

Terrell grudgingly turned and took them down a flight of stairs at the back of the house. The lower level was one enormous room, as large as the footprint of the entire house above, and packed with cars. In one corner of the garage, a group of men were working on a racing Porsche. Michael casually nodded to Tanya in that direction. He took his camera out of the case and began snapping a few photos, distracting Terrell by asking him to pose with the cars from time to time, which he was most willing to do.

Tanya wandered near the racing preparation area. Michael took a few side-glances, noting that the staff acted like she was the plague descending on them. There was no doubt they all knew who she was, and their collective nervousness was palpable.

The layout of the room filled in a piece of the puzzle for McAllister. Nothing was haphazard about the design. A large hand-painted mural commanded attention on the main wall, maybe twenty feet square. A young Dave Terrell racing the C-type was celebrated in vivid color. The other cars from the collection were arranged in a semi-circle facing the mural in mock adoration. He snapped a number of pictures of the layout for future study. From time to time he was able to maneuver himself around one of the cars so he could get a shot of each one of the men by the Porsche, turning up the magnification so he'd have clear facial shots. When he was finished he nodded back to Tanya and looked up at the mural, a sign she correctly took as her cue. The giant picture of the C-type was a surprise, but they'd already decided the car was going to be the tool they'd use to unnerve him, so it was perfect.

"That's you driving the old C-type if I'm not mistaken."

"Yes. Those were the good old days."

"You sold the car to Jack Waldorf for a few thousand dollars. The car must be worth two million now. Why would you do something so foolish?"

Dave's face turned a little red but he controlled his reaction. "You have to remember, all the cars were just a few thousand dollars back then. I sold it for about double what I paid for it. It was a good deal at the time."

Tanya didn't let up. "Did you ever actually beat Jack in a race?"

"A few times, here and there."

"That's odd because Peter and I have done a lot of research on the cars for the tribute at Pebble Beach and we couldn't find a single time you beat him."

Redness flared on the skin around Dave's neck and moved slowly up toward his ears. Their game seemed to be wearing on his temper. "I'm sure if you continue to do your research, you'll find some instances where I clearly got the better of him. One time for sure but that's a long story. It's in the past now."

It was time to play the final card. Tanya walked back over by the racing Porsche and asked, "Which one of you is Klaus Kremer?"

Dave almost ran to answer before any of the men could speak.

"Why would you want to speak to Klaus?"

"Peter had a technical question for him about the cars. They'd discussed the C-type at a race a while back. He's written it down for me on this paper."

"Klaus quit the team. I'm afraid it's my fault. We had a tough time qualifying at Sears Point after the party. I guess I chewed him out too much. He quit before the main race and I haven't seen him since. I'm sure he'll be back soon."

Tanya crumpled the paper and put it back in her purse. McAllister knew there was nothing written on it. Dave stared at her a few moments.

"Why don't you give it to me so I can get the answer for you?"

"That's okay. I'll tell Peter. When he returns, please let Peter know so he can call."

"I'm hoping he'll be back for the racing during Pebble Beach week."

"You're going to have the team at Laguna Seca?"

"Yes. As a matter of fact, Porsche is the featured marque for racing this year. It should be a lot of fun."

"Be sure and come over to see the exhibit at Pebble Beach on Sunday. I think you'll enjoy seeing your old car as part of the exhibit." A final subtle dig by Tanya that Peter now owned the C-type.

"I'll make a point of it." Dave was clearly becoming exasperated.

"Dave, I really appreciate the opportunity to include your collection in my story about my trip to California. However, I'm afraid we've got to leave now."

Michael tried to maneuver Tanya toward the stairs. He held his breath for a few seconds, half expecting Terrell to call out after them. It seemed possible they'd played their hand a little too strongly. Would Terrell try to detain them? Michael was relieved to see Tanya with her hand on her phone. Would the reception be adequate in the underground room? The unique ring tone of her phone allowed them both a small sigh of relief. She made a big production of answering and pretended to be talking to a business associate they were supposed to meet soon. Michael kept her moving toward the door while she talked.

"Sorry about that, Dave. You know with these new cell phones people can track you every minute of the day. I'm afraid we've got to rush along."

The ringing of the phone was a strong reminder to all in the room that people knew where they were. Terrell didn't seem to like it, but he had to let them go. Outside on the circular drive, they made false promises to get together at Pebble Beach. Michael couldn't wait to fire up Lucille and get them out of there.

"Cool, you drove the one fifty down. How's she doing?"

"Very nicely, thank you."

He gunned the engine and didn't breathe again until they were through the front gate. They rode in silence a few minutes.

Finally, Tanya asked, "How do you think we did?"

"I think we learned a lot today. Maybe too much."

"Why do you say that?"

"I think you did a great job provoking him, especially about the C-type. Did you notice anything about the setup of the room?"

"It just looked like a whole bunch of cars to me. Do you mean the Porsche racing stuff in the corner?"

"What about the mural?"

"Well, yes. That was impossible not to notice. What about it?"

"I thought it was the focal point of the room, placed at the front, larger than life. The other collector cars were arranged in a semi-circle, all of them facing toward the mural. What was in the center?"

"There wasn't anything in the center. Did I miss something, Sherlock?"

"The point is there was nothing in the center. It was reserved for a special car."

"The C-type?"

"Exactly. In some sick way, I think this has all been about the C-type. He wants to get it back. I think we pushed too hard when we brought up Klaus Kremer. He's onto us now. You better call Detective Clark and fill him in."

He listened while Tanya gave Clark the information about their meeting. Clark seemed to be doing a lot of talking on the other end of the line. She finally ended the call.

"Detective Clark said there have been some big developments on his end. We need to get back as soon as we can."

"I'm not sure it was a good idea to bring you along on this trip. I think he considered getting rid of us. That cell phone call came just in time." Michael glanced at Tanya, putting everything he felt into the minute meeting of their eyes. She seemed to notice because her expression was just as earnest.

"Michael, I wish I'd met you a long time ago, but unfortunately I didn't. We have to make up for lost time. We have to make memories. I'm going to be with you on everything you do from now on, no matter what it entails."

He reached over with his right arm and pulled her close to him. She was his girl now, for better or worse.

"I still want to drive up Malibu Canyon and see if I can find the old house."

Malibu Canyon Road proved a lot easier to find on the drive back. Hope faded a little as they drove inland, though. When he had visited his mom, the land was undeveloped. Now there were houses, even small villages and shopping centers along the road. A large tunnel through part of a mountain provided a short cut he didn't remember existing earlier. The road continued a gentle climb in an unending set of graceful curves. Just when Michael was about to give up, the old stone house on top of the hill appeared on their right.

"There it is."

As they turned off on a road called Mulholland Highway Michael pointed out the house to their left on a hill. A long curving drive delivered them around to the back of the house. A smaller detached stone house was positioned across the drive. The main house and the guest quarters were much smaller than he remembered as a boy. The stone castle of his boyhood became a smallish home constructed entirely of river rock, quite antiquated by the standards of the other houses.

"My mom lived in these quarters in the back."

The place seemed deserted. Now that he'd found it, he wondered what he was looking for. The gently rolling hills brought back a thousand memories of playing there as a boy. A couple of motorcycles cruised by on Mulholland below.

He motioned to the bikes below. "There's a big biker hangout a little way north from here. It was the only place off limits to me when I was visiting, but I used to sneak down there sometimes and look at the bikes. On the weekends, there seemed to be millions of them.

A voice made them both spin around. "I haven't seen that car in fifty years. I can't believe it."

A tiny, shriveled woman who looked more like a walking mummy was looking back at him.

"Aunt Heidi?"

She gave a gasp when he called her by name.

"It can't be... Michael?"

"It's me, Aunt Heidi."

He wanted to hug her but worried he might break her into pieces. He couldn't believe how hard she hugged him back.

"I've wondered so many times what had happened to you."

After a brief introduction, she led them both to the main room of the house with promises of a cool drink. Michael explained to Tanya that Aunt Heidi wasn't a blood-relation, but rather the kind a person adopts along the paths of life by close and affectionate association. Too soon they ran out of words. He had not been prepared to actually find anything on this trip. They both seemed a little overwhelmed, wondering if maybe too much time had passed them by. Heidi excused herself and returned with a cardboard box.

"This box contains all I have left of your mother's possessions. I'm not exactly sure why I saved them, but I guess I hoped you'd come back some day."

He eagerly inspected the meager contents of the box. It didn't matter that it was all worthless trinkets left behind and deemed unimportant. For him, it was filled with treasures he knew had touched his mother's hands.

"Heidi, do you think my mother was—well, you know, a little off in the head?"

"That's a tough question. I think possibly she had some issues that could have been controlled nowadays, with the right medication."

"Do you think she might have killed herself?"

"I don't think so, but again I don't have anything to back that up. Just a feeling. I think we would have found her if she'd killed herself. She didn't seem depressed or anything. On the contrary, actually. I talked to her the night before she disappeared, left for work the next morning, and never saw her again. Your father and I checked with the police and every other agency we could think of but never found a clue. She just disappeared off the face of the earth."

They came to another uncomfortable silence. Michael sensed it was time to go. He entered Heidi's phone number in his cell so he could contact her if he thought of something else. He also entered the address so he wouldn't have to hunt the place down again. Soon enough, they were back in Lucille and heading north on the coast to Ventura for the night, nursing a vague sense of stunned dissatisfaction and wondering why.

"Do you think she might have been murdered?"

"That's always been in the back of my mind. It would explain her not contacting Heidi again, but who knows? I've been driving myself crazy for thirty-five years. It's been too long. I don't think I'll ever figure it out. I guess I just had to try. At least I know where the house is now. I can contact Heidi if I think of something."

Tanya nodded.

The next morning, all duties as detectives were abandoned in favor of a sail with Jon and Barb. Tanya hopped to the bow of the boat as they left the harbor, as nimble as if she'd been doing it all her life. A gleaming smile made it clear she was having fun. They sailed a short course halfway out to the islands and then returned to the harbor. A large plant of some kind on the coast, sporting a huge orange and white striped smokestack, caught Michael's attention. Barb identified it as an old nuclear power plant. Shut down years ago, it had recently been scheduled for demolition. A modern replacement with much greater capacity was scheduled for construction in the desert. The wind blew just strong enough to make the boat glide effortlessly through the waves. A group of dolphins played alongside for a few minutes then lost interest.

Jon and Barb were treated to a late lunch on Main Street in downtown Ventura, Tanya's last chance to spend some girl time with Barb. The next morning they left early. The 101 would have returned them home faster but they chose the PCH again. The campgrounds provided a pit stop to enjoy a snack Barb had packed for them, and they made another for a drink at Nepenthe.

The last few days together had given them time to learn a lot about each other. Michael hadn't found a thing about Tanya he didn't like. A week of memories had been deposited in their bank, a good start in that department.

Chapter 22

Detective Clark rang the bell at the Stafford house at nine sharp the next morning. Many new pieces of the puzzle surrounding the attempted murder of Tanya Stafford had emerged and he was eager to get down to business.

"Right after you left, we tracked Terrell's plane on a trip to Costa Rica. The FBI had a man waiting at the airport. The plane was locked in a private hanger for a day but another plane was allowed to enter later in the afternoon, from Colombia no less. A drug connection seemed obvious and appeared to be the source of Terrell's money all these years. The FBI wants him bad now. The problem is Dave didn't go along on this trip, just his flunkies. The Feds want to wait until he makes the trip. If they can catch him with the drugs, they could take him down for good."

Peter added another useful piece of information. "I found a reference to a company named Investment Index while I was searching through Dave's companies. It rang a bell but I just couldn't remember where I'd come across it. A couple of days later, I was

160

downstairs looking at Emma's saloon and it came to me. I searched through her papers stored in my office and confirmed my suspicions. Investment Index was the company that ruined her."

Clark said, "That means this whole plot, from what you two told me from your trip, has possibly been to get back the C-type. It's been going on for a long time, maybe almost fifty years. The murder attempt was just the latest part of his plan. We were also able to determine Dave's Porsche team didn't have any trouble qualifying at Sears Point. They qualified first right out of the box. I think there's a very good chance Klaus Kremer was the one who tried to murder Tanya. I doubt we'll ever see him again. Terrell doesn't seem like the type to accept failure."

Something had been nagging at Michael since they'd visited Dave's house. "Dave made an interesting comment while we were interviewing him. We'd asked him whether he ever beat Jack in a race. He said he had definitely got the better of him one time. I think Terrell might have murdered Jack Waldorf. He couldn't help bragging about it. I think he did something to the plane."

His statement brought a stunned silence.

"I'll add that to our list but I'm not sure we'll ever be able to prove it. Again, I think we're just scratching the surface with Terrell."

"So what's our next move?"

"What we really need to do is figure out Terrell's next move."

Tanya said, "I think I know." They all turned to her. "I think he's going to try something at Pebble Beach."

"Why there?" Detective Clark asked.

"First, he's racing at Laguna Seca, just like he was at Sears Point last time. He'll have his whole crew with him. Secondly, this exhibition we're giving honoring Jack Waldorf is like rubbing salt in an open wound. Terrell wants his C-type back. Peter's going to show the automobile world that he owns it. I think that's what pushed him over the edge.

That gave Michael an idea. "We could use that to our favor. Why not dangle the C-type as bait? I don't think he'll be able to resist a shot at stealing it."

"It's time we started taking the initiative. We've been reacting. I like the idea of a trap," Peter said.

Detective Clark asked, "How big a deal is this Pebble Beach show?"

"It's a week-long event if you attend everything. There are five or six auctions, vintage racing at Laguna Seca most of the week and a few other special events. The attendance for the concours alone is over fifteen thousand."

Clark frowned. "I hope we haven't bitten off more than we can chew. At least we're beginning to form a plan. We don't have much time. I think I'll go down and look the place over tomorrow. I want to get a feel for the layout. McAllister, would you be interested in tagging along?"

Michael was stunned. Until that moment, Clark had been using his first name, treating him like a civilian, even as he used him to inconspicuously interview possible suspects. Hearing Clark use his last name, it was a concession, one cop to another, recognizing skills and accepting him as an equal. Michael had thought he would never have that again. It felt momentous. But he wasn't just 'him' anymore. He was part of a 'we' now. He looked over at Tanya. She seemed to understand that this was important to him, and she smiled slightly and nodded, giving him permission.

"I could use the day to go check on my project." He gave Detective Clark a nod.

Clark nodded back. "Good. Do you mind if we take Lucille?" Michael agreed. "Peter, can you give me the highlights of the events and help me with a map? I need to handle this in one day."

Peter spent thirty minutes on a laptop computer with Clark and Michael, advising them of the best routes to avoid traffic and the exact location of each event. They quickly focused on Laguna Seca Race Track and Pebble Beach Golf Course. Detective Clark promised to be back at eight sharp the next morning. Michael showed him out and then turned in early. Tomorrow looked to be a long day.

Chapter 23

Michael heard the banging on the front door. The clock was straight up eight. The two men didn't chat much while Lucille warmed up. Clark inspected the gauges on the dash as they burst into the sunlight.

"I hope you don't mind driving today. I've never been in an old car like this. I spend most of my days in a different world."

"How long have you been a detective?"

"Just over twenty-five years now. Man, just saying it, I can't believe it's been that long."

"What about before you were a cop?"

"Military. Special Forces. Vietnam. Most of the cops in California are ex-military. The force is organized the same way--rank, chain of command, all that."

"Do you ever get tired of it?"

"Interesting question coming from another detective."

"Ex-detective."

"You're still a detective as far as I'm concerned. It can be sort of hopeless dealing with slime balls most of the time. Still, every day is new. It's still exciting. I guess the answer is no, I'm not tired of it yet." There was an awkward pause. "I know what happened to you back in Tulsa."

"What do you mean by that?"

"I got a look at your records with the Tulsa Police Department. I know they think you threw that guy out the window."

"What do you think about it?"

"As far as I'm concerned you're a hero for catching the killer but we have the same politics here as you did there."

"I was forced into early retirement. My good buddies decided I was a liability to their otherwise exemplary careers. Having the benefit of looking back into the past, I think maybe I should have stayed and demanded a trial."

Michael gave Clark a quick look directly in the eyes, trying to gauge his reaction. Clark didn't flinch.

"I doubt if things would have turned out much different. You'd still have some believing you were a murderer." Michael chewed on the comment a minute and then changed the subject.

"Tell me about the Slasher. What have you got?"

Clark gazed into the distance a few seconds before he answered, seemingly mulling over his response.

"This is just between you and me. You can't share what I say with anyone, not even Tanya. Agreed?"

McAllister turned and gave him a quick nod.

"We're getting closer every day. He makes so many mistakes with each murder I can't believe we haven't be able to catch him yet. The only thing he's done right is not leaving prints. He must use gloves. However, blood and DNA has been found on every victim. We have a perfect profile but it doesn't match to any database we can find. That makes me think he's a rank amateur. We know he's a middle aged white male. That's worked against us because too many men would fit his description. We've kept the DNA stuff out of the news because we want him to think he's covering his tracks. Lately, we think he's become a cocaine freak. I think his habit is getting out of control."

"How'd you figure that out?"

"The Kelli Emerson crime scene. Cocaine was splashed all over the island in her kitchen as well as her bedroom. He had himself one hell of a party."

"What else do you have?"

"We think he's in the car business. He painted a couple of the vehicles he stole. He did a quick job, but it was done well. I think he's an expert painter. He used a specific color, a Jaguar red color, as a matter of fact. The plastic covering the victims tested positive for a chemical used in painting, too."

"Do you remember the name of the chemical?"

"It was a virgin solvent, used to clean a car right before it's painted to remove any traces of oil. All of this makes us think he owns a paint or body shop. I think he's taken some of the victims back to the shop for the killing. We're assuming he did it at night when no one else was around. A deserted industrial shop would be the perfect place for something like that. The pattern of the crimes leads us to believe the shop is somewhere in the San Jose area. There's an industrial area a little south of town in Campbell. It's filled with shops that meet the criteria. We're checking them out one by one. Eventually, we'll find the right one. We found a couple of witnesses from the Bakersfield abduction. The bartender and one of the patrons remembered him pretty well. That led to a pretty good sketch. We'd tracked two of the other abductions to bars but by the time we figured it out we couldn't track down any reliable witnesses. We got a couple of sketches but I think we were too late for a really good picture. We'll probably put the new one on the news soon. We just need a lucky break."

Michael couldn't help imagining being part of the Slasher task force. As they neared Monterey, Detective Clark directed him to Laguna Seca. The racetrack was locked up, but a badge changed the security guards' minds pretty quickly. A long curving road challenged Lucille, but at the top they were rewarded by a panoramic view of the track with the grandstands all around and the pits in the middle. Michael tried to imagine it with thirty thousand people in attendance. The security guards said they got up to one hundred thousand people attending the superbike races, but the vintage racing drew a smaller crowd.

The trip over to the Pebble Beach Golf Course was shorter than Michael imagined. Seventeen Mile Road was the only route in. Tourists actually had to pay a fee to drive in this area but Detective Clark's badge took care of that as well. The main clubhouse didn't offer much parking except for police officers. The city of San Francisco bought them lunch at a marvelous restaurant called the Stillwater Café, sporting large windows looking out over the golf course. The ocean waves crashed against a wall just beyond the eighteenth hole. After lunch they found a security guard who provided some needed information. He counseled them with a map showing all the events with locations posted. Michael was surprised by the magnitude of the event. There were auctions, art displays, automobile dealers; the list went on and on. The main event, the Concours d' Elegance, was actually staged on the eighteenth hole. Reality began to hit home that he was going to be a part of a show he could only dream of attending just a year earlier. He knew a little about the event, but only from a television show he'd seen and stories he'd read in various car magazines. The setting was spectacular. The Staffords had made arrangements to stay with a friend who lived just a block from the clubhouse. Clark suggested a brief visit to check the place out. The house seemed a little small for a castle.

On the way home, Detective Clark had another good idea. "We should stop for a visit with Buck Snider." A cell phone call to Peter produced the number, then he called the Sniders. A detour through Santa Cruz added an hour to their day. Detective Clark apprised Buck of the situation with Terrell. Buck didn't seem very surprised that Terrell might be behind the whole thing. Buck was planning to attend the Pebble Beach event on Sunday to see the Jaguars, so Clark noted he needed someone to watch him. Michael was impressed by Clark's thoroughness. He personally had to admit that he might have missed the close connection between the Waldorfs and Buck Snider. Lucille ran flawlessly and delivered them back to the Stafford house late in the afternoon.

Chapter 24

Private parties extended the Pebble Beach celebrations to over two weeks for some of the attendees. If Michael had accompanied the Staffords on their original plan, he would have attended five auctions, the Concorso Italiano, the Rolex Monterey Historic Automobile Races at Laguna Seca and, of course, the Concours d' Elegance at Pebble Beach. Since he'd never attended any of the events previously, the Staffords were prepared to make sure his first experience at Pebble Beach would be unforgettable, as a further reward for bringing the car over for the show. Peter turned out to be a very generous man. The tickets to enter those events weren't cheap, some as high as four hundred dollars each. Now the original plan was out. They had to cut down the events they would attend to give the police the chance to gain the upper hand by only having to cover a few locations. Catching a master criminal would be difficult, but the exhibition of the Waldorf cars was an ideal set-up for a trap. Transmitters were mounted secretly in each of the five cars.

Others were hidden in the trucks and trailers transporting the cars along with various other equipment needed to keep them running.

McAllister vowed to stay at Tanya's side every second during the events. Spending most of their time at Pebble Beach would make protection a little easier on the police. When the group departed for the event on Tuesday, he drove with her in Lucille and Peter followed in the saloon, arriving around lunch. Derek Hunter followed with a crew in a big sleepover cab rig and trailer with the C- and D-types and the XK120. Parking for big rigs and trailers was reserved in a special lot near the equestrian center. Derek and the crew were stashed at Casa Palmero, which was as convenient as it was expensive. The Staffords' host, the one with the smallish castle, was well prepared for them when they arrived. The classic cars were arranged artfully in the courtyard even as they enjoyed their first cup of coffee. The house was only a block away from The Lodge at Pebble Beach, headquarters for the show, but blocks in this neighborhood were a bit longer than they were in others. Special parking passes, obtained for a hefty bounty, allowed access to coveted spots near the epicenter of activity. Passes arriving via e-mail stating "Entrant" with a big gold background, were printed and placed on the windshield of each Jag. The badges on the windshields allowed them to skip the $8.50 fee charged to normal visitors for the privilege of driving on Seventeen Mile Road and the long lines at the security booths. Residents carried a permanent sticker on their windshields for the same purpose.

On Wednesday evening, all of them, including their host, drove up to a party in the hills high above Carmel, held at Clint Eastwood's home. He'd driven a Jag in *Play Misty for Me,* so Michael asked Eastwood if he still owned it.

"Follow me." The movie star responded.

For a few minutes he was alone with an Academy Award winner. A paved walk along the back of an impressive house led to an equally impressive six-car garage. The facility was as spotless as any surgeon's operating room and framed with ivy growing obediently on the sides. The floor was constructed using an intricate matrix tile design. In the corner Eastwood's 1959 Jaguar XK150S roadster crouched menacingly. The classic was white on the exterior, but aged in a pleasant patina, and red on the interior with ancient leather sporting wrinkles that mimicked its owner's face. Eastwood was kind enough to let him snap a few pictures of the car, some including the star himself. He'd apparently noticed Michael's arrival in Lucille and that had scored him some points. Michael thought it was pretty cool that the movie star still owned the car.

"I didn't own the one used in the movie, but I bought this one shortly after. I still drive it sometimes if it's a sunny day. Mostly I just drive a Mercedes because I turn the key and it goes. I don't have time for all the maintenance issues anymore. Too busy."

The private party schedule seemed to be non-stop. Massive booths were being erected at Pebble Beach, and on Thursday, Michael and Tanya took their first tour through the displays. A shop had recently been built in Irvine, by Mercedes, for doing restoration of vintage cars. A large display with ten cars restored to perfection featured a 1956 300SL Gullwing painted in a show-stopping gray-green with plaid interior. The shop had been open less than a year and already had a year's waiting list.

Special badges allowed them to enter a VIP lounge across the street from the main lodge. Michael wasn't sure how Peter had managed to arrange it, but the tent provided a good place to pick up a snack or a drink and sit for a few minutes. Copies of the book prepared for the concours event on Sunday had just become available, thick as a phone book and smelling of expensive paper and ink. As promised, six pages were devoted to the Waldorf display. Apparently quite a bit of interest had been generated by the Waldorf Jaguars. His favorite picture was one of Tanya and Peter taken by the C-type. No other woman, even considering the plush ads that filled much of the book, was as strikingly beautiful as Tanya. Many of the car people attending instantly recognized her. Most commented on the article and the display set for Sunday. The discovery and restoration of the long-lost Jaguars caught even serious collectors by surprise. Others overheard the conversations and recognized Tanya as the beauty pictured in the book. If they stayed in one place very long, she ended up signing books. The organizers were also kind enough to make a small thumbnail article about Michael and Lucille. A few people even recognized him. He began to realize the Pebble Beach book would reach far more people than his stories in the classic car magazine. It seemed he had a lot to learn about marketing himself as a writer.

Saturday was the first day at Laguna Seca racetrack in which the Jags were competing. Clark decided to relent and allow them to attend when media badges materialized for the event. Michael and Tanya enjoyed walking through the pits and talking to some of the drivers. A couple of plain clothed police officers stayed close to them at all times because Dave Terrell's team was present in full force. Michael's best estimate was that Terrell had at least ten men in his crew. A visit to Terrell's pit found him basking in the limelight of team ownership.

Dave gave Michael a cool stare. "I want you to get some good pictures of the racing today, especially when we cross the finish line first."

The races consisted of ten laps for each class. Michael and Tanya toured the rest of the cars and then about an hour later moved to the start/finish line to observe Terrell's car in action. Racing cars passed within inches of them as they formed up on the inside, facing the wrong way. When all the cars were out of the way from the previous race, the next class was waived onto the track in a U-turn maneuver to start the race. The noise was deafening as the old racers with straight exhaust pipes and no mufflers gunned their engines and took off. They set-up in order of qualifying on the assembly lap and began racing from a flying start as they passed the start/finish line.

Porsche racing cars were broken down into several classes. Dave's team was entered in a vintage 911 class. His driver began in third but was right on the tail of the second place car as their race started. Dave was positioned only a few steps away from Tanya and Michael at the side of the start/finish line as they watched the cars fly past. On lap four, his driver managed to move up a spot, setting his sights on the number one car. During the next three laps he closed the gap, and finally on lap eight, he passed to go into first place. Michael dreaded the bragging he was going to have to endure if Dave's team won. He dutifully snapped pictures from the wall as the cars came by. On lap nine, Terrell's driver turned the corner onto the straightaway and gunned the engine for the long uphill run. Just as he was approaching their vantage point, the left front wheel spun free! Something must have broken in the suspension. The wheel shot down the track as if it wanted to win the race by itself. The driver lost control of the car and cut straight across the track and ran into the pit wall with a big thud only about twenty yards from them. As he looked up, McAllister snapped a picture with the driver looking right at the camera. Dave turned towards him just as he took the picture.

Michael whispered to Tanya, "That ought to piss him off."

"I should say." Tanya smiled as she waved to Dave.

Eventually a tow truck retrieved the injured hulk. A cheerful goodbye to Terrell seemed the perfect finale to set him off.

"Quite an effort, Dave. However, I don't get the wheel thing. What was your strategy there?"

"Go to hell."

"See you at Pebble Beach." Michael and Tanya were giggling as they left the pits and made sure he noticed, feeling safe being surrounded thousands of witnesses. The plan was to provoke him in every way possible. Pebble Beach might be their last chance. Detective Clark intimated at an earlier meeting that he thought Terrell would make a run for it if he failed at the venue.

The rest of the afternoon was consumed by a tour for all the cars entered in the concours. Tanya drove the C-type, Michael drove Lucille, Peter drove the XK120, their host was allowed to drive the saloon and Derek Hunter drove the D-type. They took it easy and managed to do a drive to a party and back down late in the day without incident. Tanya was lucky enough to be right behind the XJ13, a legendary Jaguar built for Le Mans with a V12 engine. A last minute rule change on engine size made it ineligible. Legendary test driver Norman Dewis crashed it when Jaguar introduced the V12 motor to the public a few years later. Norman, now eighty-five years old, drove the XJ13 all weekend and relished his status as a true legend.

Sunday morning finally arrived. Entrants were instructed to bring the cars to the field at seven o'clock in the morning for setup on the eighteenth fairway of the historic golf course. The marine fog layer was thick on the ground as Michael, Tanya and Peter drove cars onto the grass in formation. Derek wasn't far behind with the C- and D-types. Expensive cars emerged from the fog with only their running lights outlining the hulks, much like battleships entering a port at night. The Jaguar factory was present in full force because they'd sponsored the exhibit in partnership with Peter. As the group of five cars arrived, staffers motioned them to the correct area for the Jack Waldorf display. The cars were positioned at precisely the same angle, their backs near a monstrous sand trap that ran almost the entire length of the hole with the ocean beyond. As soon as the Jaguars were aligned perfectly, oversized posters were placed around the cars allowing everyone attending to learn about the life of Jack Waldorf. The scene created was truly a masterpiece with manicured grass in front, a stone retaining wall at the back of the sand trap, and finally, the ocean with an occasional sailboat silently floating by. At ten o'clock when the event officially opened, the marine layer burned off and the sun began to win the day over the fog. By noon it was perfect. Michael took over five hundred pictures of Peter and Tanya to fully appreciate and record this once-in-a-lifetime event. If he hadn't been there to see it himself, he would never have been able to appreciate the setting. This was an event best experienced in person. When the crowds descended, it became impossible to get any clear pictures of anything. Thousands of people surrounded the cars in a matter of minutes.

As the Pebble Beach event drew closer on the calendar, the Slasher realized it would be a long shot to make an attempt at Tanya. First, there were too many car people attending who could possibly recognize him. Secondly, for the same reason, he couldn't try to mask his identity. A disguise would certainly appear odd to anyone who knew him. Using a stolen car was out of the question for the same reasons. He finally decided to drive one of his classic Jags down and just have a look around.

It took him a while to find Tanya with her companion, but once he did, he followed them for most of the afternoon. He was correct in assuming there would be little chance for abduction because her new boyfriend never let her out of his sight. He continued to watch them, just in case. It was frustrating to fail, and he vowed to be successful on his next attempt, which he hoped he could plan soon.

Michael and Tanya stayed together to make it easier for the police to keep an eye on them, and Peter was almost always nearby. Still, there were so many people by noon, it was impossible for the police to keep tabs on them at all times. They took some time and looked at the other cars on display. Duesenbergs, Cords and Rolls-Royces representing the grand touring cars from the thirties and a special exhibit of French art deco cars like Delahaye, Delage and Bugatti were displayed in various classes. Each car was a work of art, perfect in every way. The level achieved by the owners during the restoration process was simply stunning. Michael was glad to have experienced the fifty-mile drive and was amazed how well the old cars ran, too. Michael tried to imagine how luxurious it must have been to ride in these cars when they were new.

He found out a poster nothing short of a fine work of art was prepared each year for the event. With Jaguar being the featured marque, another star of the show was the XJ13, sitting regally on the grass with the ocean in the background. The poster depicted a similar setting. He bought a couple as souvenirs. When he was back down by the cars, he placed them in Lucille's trunk. Later when he saw Norman Dewis near the XJ13 he shamelessly asked Norman to sign one like a little schoolboy, not caring what anyone else thought. Dewis was a legend as far as he was concerned.

One of the local Jaguar dealers rented one of the suites that backed onto the fairway for a private party. They were allowed in because everyone seemed to know Tanya. A cool drink and a place to sit were a welcome respite from the ever-enlarging crowd. A quick investigation of the luxurious suite offered some insight as to how rich people expected to be treated. The sale of his father's ranch had deposited three million dollars in Michael's bank account but he could never seem to bring himself to spend it. Tanya continued to have constant requests to sign her picture in the Pebble Beach book. Ten of them were squirreled away in Lucille's trunk for posterity. A few spectators asked Michael to stand by Lucille for a picture. At the first opportunity he would disappear back into the crowd, uncomfortable in the limelight.

At four o'clock, the attention turned to a large podium near the lodge. A crowd amassed just below the microphone so the master of ceremonies could announce the winner in each class. Each winning car drove up past the podium, and a ribbon was ceremoniously placed on the windshield. After the class winners were announced, a few talks were given to build tension for the "Best of Show" award. A very professional gentleman from the Jaguar factory gave a humorous talk about their adventures, offering a few words about each car they had on display. Peter was also asked to come up and say something about the Waldorf cars.

Peter gave Michael an odd look as he was walking to the podium. He wasn't sure what it meant. Maybe Peter was worried something was going to happen. Michael pulled Tanya close and looked around, but they were completely overwhelmed by the mass of people. Peter gave a very fluid overview of the history of Jack and the cars. Then he paused.

"I've made a special arrangement with the owner of the auction company. I must thank him immensely for going to so much trouble for me. I've been blessed with great wealth in my life. I'm sorry to say I've spent way too much of my time and energy thinking of ways to spoil myself. I've battled addictions. The only way I'm going to overcome them is to start trying to help others. Therefore, as many of you know, the auction will begin at six o'clock at the Equestrian Center. I'm going to sell the D-type to the highest bidder with no reserve. All the proceeds are going to go toward a new rehab center I'm personally going to build on a location near San Francisco. The auction house has graciously agreed to forego their normal commission this one time since all the money is going to this cause. I'm also going to match from my own pocket whatever money is raised."

The crowd erupted in a great cheer as he stepped down. Several men immediately hurried to look at the D-type, cell phones held close in frantic conversations. Michael noticed Tanya furiously pounding away on her smart phone. When Peter walked up to them, Tanya threw her arms around him.

Michael even hugged him when she was done. "It's a great thing you're doing."

An elegant Voisin won Best of Show and by five the awards ceremony was over. The crowd quickly began to thin as the cars began leaving the field. Peter was slated to drive the saloon back home because it was nice and warm inside, and Tanya and Michael would drive the XK150, but the C-type and the XK120 were loaded on the special trailer for their return trip.

The auction house was actually a large tent with blue AstroTurf covering the dirt below. In the middle a stage rose four feet high. Each car emerged from one side of the stage during the bidding and then motored across the stage and out of sight when sold. The auctioneer whipped the crowd, seated below in folding chairs, to a frenzy attempting to get the best possible price for each car. Two wealthy bidders fighting over a car was the ultimate. Seventy-five cars were slated to change owners with the D-type slotted in about half way through the proceedings. The pre-sale estimate, the responsibility of the auction house to give bidders a fair appraisal of each car, was two million dollars. The crowd cheered when the D-type hit the stage and bidding began at a million dollars, increasing in one hundred thousand dollar increments. It slowed as it got near two million dollars. A master of suspense, the auctioneer would pause and then start to hammer the car down, only to draw another bid from the crowd. As the room grew silent, it appeared two million might be good enough.

Suddenly a bid came from the phones stationed on the side. Bidders were allowed to use agents or even bid by phone. "We bid three million dollars."

Everyone gasped and spun to see a woman with a phone to her ear with her hand raised. The crowd cheered, but then a grey-haired man in the audience stood up. "Three-and-a-half."

He looked back at the woman on the phone. She spoke on the phone for a few seconds. "Four." She looked back at him.

He drew his hand across his throat meaning he was done. The car sold for twice the expected price. The phone bidder remained anonymous, but someone else had apparently battled some addictions and was willing to ante up for Peter's cause. He found Michael and Tanya while balancing three flutes of champagne, smiling widely as if the weight of the world had been lifted from his shoulders.

"You sure are happy for a man that just spent eight million dollars!" Michael said.

"Yes, I am. I certainly am."

Michael spied Detective Clark in the corner. Clark lifted a glass to him with a broad smile. He hunched his shoulders up with a question mark on his face as if to say, "I guess nothing is going to happen." They made their way back to the cars and prepared for the drive home at nine o'clock, exhausted from several days of activities and still facing a three-hour journey home. They'd drive together in case one of the vintage cars had a problem, especially using the lights at night. A detective called Michael on his cell and assured him they'd tail them on the journey.

As they rolled by the main lodge, Tanya turned to him. "Stop here just a minute. I've got to run to the ladies' room before the drive home. Just wait at the curb." Peter parked immediately behind him in the saloon with the engine idling.

Clark called Michael on his cell. "Are you okay?"

"Yes. Tanya just ran inside for a minute, but we're getting ready to head back with the two cars."

"Can you see her right now?"

"Well, no, she's inside."

"Go find her immediately. Something's going on with the big rig."

No further encouragement was needed, waving to Peter as he ran inside. The ladies' room was just down the hall and he opened the door to some startled women.

"Tanya, are you in here?"

No answer. He spun around and looked both ways. At the very end of the hall he saw a man escorting Tanya roughly through a door toward the kitchen. He jostled his way through the crowd as quickly as possible. When he burst into the kitchen they were exiting a back door. As he broke into the cool evening air, a dark car was easing away from the loading dock at the back of the kitchen onto the road away from the club. The occupants didn't seem to realize he was in pursuit, as they weren't rushing. Michael's feet almost went out from under him on a big stone as he hit the parking area. He picked it up and threw it helplessly at the car. It struck the right rear taillight and broke it, showing a bright white light where it should have been red. The driver gunned the motor when he heard the rock hit. Michael ran around the corner and back to Lucille. The saloon was empty. No Peter. He had no time to find out what had happened to him. Lucille was still idling. Slamming her into second gear he pulled around in pursuit. The police escort had arrived with lights flashing but was blocked by traffic.

Several roads led out of the club, all twisting with lots of turnoffs. Michael decided they'd try to get to the highway as soon as possible so he stayed on Seventeen Mile Road. He wanted to use his phone to call Clark, but the road was too twisty for him to manage it. Catching them before they got to the highway was essential. He roared through the curves and ran a couple of cars to the side as he pushed Lucille for all she was worth. After a minute, he caught a glimpse of the car ahead. Thank God he'd broken that taillight or he would never have been able to tell it was the right car. It appeared to be a sixties Cadillac or something like that, and Lucille started gaining very quickly. The hulking sedan was easy prey for the agile sports car.

An arm came out the side window and flashed twice causing the windshield on the old Jag to pop. Clearly one of the shots had ricocheted off the steeply slanted glass. At the next corner, he gunned Lucille hard inside of the caddy, pulled up beside and turned into them. Both cars left the road and slid down a steep ravine, flashing through small trees until the caddy hit a larger one head on. Michael slid right into the back of them and smacked his face on the big steering wheel. The door was buried deep in the dirt making the window Michael's only way out. He stumbled up to the car ahead just as a man in the back got out and pointed a gun at him causing him to stop dead in his tracks.

The culprit pulled Tanya out of the sedan roughly by her arm. "Hurry up. You're coming with me."

"No, she's not."

"Just what are you going to do about it?"

Michael started to move closer but he turned the gun on Tanya. For a moment they stood at impasse. Tanya suddenly spun and brought her right elbow up hard under the man's jaw as she dived to the ground. Two shots immediately rang out. The man's head exploded in blood as he collapsed to the ground.

Two police officers slid professionally down the ravine in a second and checked the man one of them had shot. Inside the car they found two more men slumped on the seats. One was unconscious from a blow when the car hit the tree. The other was groggy. They were expertly retrieved from the car, shoved face down, and handcuffed. Michael recognized all of them from the visit to Dave Terrell's place.

"That was some pretty fancy driving. The old Jag still has some gitty-up." One of the officers said.

Michael and Tanya turned to a pitiful looking Lucille heavily damaged on the front end and fenders and sporting a cracked windshield. "Yeah, I think the old girl has still got some fight in her."

He patted her side as they walked by. The trip back up the steep ravine seemed to take a lot longer than the slide down. Back on the road, they collapsed inside a police car just as Tanya's cell phone rang.

It was Detective Clark so she put him on speaker. "They commandeered the truck with the Jags, and they snatched Peter. Stay there. I'm coming to get you."

Clark arrived in minutes and yelled, "Are you okay to travel?"

Tanya said, "You're damn right we are. I want to kick some ass."

"Well, you just may get the chance."

"You don't seem too worried. They may have killed Peter already."

"Something tells me not. Anyway, we'll be able to tell where they're going. We're getting a good signal on the transponders we attached. We know right where they are. They're heading north up the Pacific Coast Highway. We've got Dave's plane covered at the jet center, too. I think the cars and Dave will end up at the same place. We're going to trail them. I'm a little surprised he doesn't seem to be heading to his plane."

Michael offered, "He can't load the cars on the plane."

Clark was still worried. "If he manages to transfer the cars to a different trailer, we're screwed. We better watch closely if they stop."

They continued for an hour up the coast and eventually approached San Francisco. The final destination suddenly dawned on Michael.

"He's heading to the marina. He's going to put the cars on his boat."

A rookie Santa Cruz police officer had volunteered for a job no one else wanted. Most likely he would spend a long evening in the house of Buck Snider waiting for an attack that would never materialize. The older gentleman and his wife had retired early, so now he had the dark, quiet house to himself. The rookie took his job seriously and perched by the window in the guest bedroom upstairs, carefully observing each car as it drove by below. Most wouldn't have noticed, but something caught his attention when a car with two men slowed for a look at Buck's house, then drove by. If these men planned something sinister the stairs would offer a good view of the back door. Moving halfway down he assumed a crouch with his gun ready. Fifteen minutes seemed about right for them to find an out of the way place to stash the car and make their way back to the house. In fact, it took about twenty. Two figures stealthily moved across the porch to the back door and gingerly turned the nob. Finding it open they cautiously entered.

"Drop your guns or you'll die where you stand." The rookie barked in an authoritative voice that even surprised him. The men hesitated for just a second but the policeman descended the stairs with his gun at eye level. "Hit the floor and lose the guns." Kicking the guns out of reach he quickly cuffed both suspects and called his sergeant. The commotion below woke up Buck and the officer noticed him peeking around the corner at the top of the stairs, an ancient shotgun in hand.

"It's okay, Buck. We got 'em. These guys aren't going to be bothering anyone any time soon."

Detective Clark's phone rang, causing Tanya to literally jump in her seat. They were all keyed up and jittery. "Yeah. Yeah. And? Good. Call your boss and tell him to send over the troops. You did well!"

Tanya asked, "Is Peter all right?"

"They hit Buck's house, the bastards. Two of them. That was the Santa Cruz police. A rookie drew the assignment and did an outstanding job. Both of the culprits are under arrest."

"They're going to kill Peter!"

"I won't let that happen. I'm sure he's still alive. We'll catch them before anything happens. Trust me."

Peter had been pulled from the saloon in the melee that ensued during the attack on Tanya. Now he sat in the back seat of a big limo across from Dave Terrell with an assistant training a pistol on him. The 101 carried them on a parallel course to the Pacific Coast Highway toward San Francisco. Peter's arms had been tied tightly to his waist. He wasn't scared about what was going to happen to him, but he'd had enough of the threats against Tanya.

181

"You know you're not going to get away with this."

"I think I already have. We should have taken out Buck and his wife by now, and I think Tanya might even join you for a nice swim later tonight if all goes well."

"The police are on to you."

"I'm resigned to moving south. It's a shame, but I prepared a long time ago in case this day might come."

"If I'm a dead man, why don't you tell me what this is all about?"

"You know what this is about."

"The car?"

"It's about Jack Waldorf and his insults to me. I vowed I was going to get even with him, and I did."

"What do you mean?"

"One night I drove to the airport where he kept the Spitfire. I knew he took it up periodically. I planned for a moonless night. Luckily it was cloudy, too. I remember it like it was yesterday. I parked about a mile away and made it across a field to the hanger where he kept his plane. I brought along a bag with tools, picked the lock and got inside. I set up a small light under the wing and cut a section of the skin open, then used a hacksaw to cut three quarters of the way through each supporting strut in the wing assembly, all three of them. It took me almost all night. I used duct tape to patch the wing back. If he were checking, he could have found it, but I took the chance that he'd just check the engine, oil pressure and that kind of thing. Sure enough, he took it up a few weeks later, and when he did some spins, the wing snapped, making the plane uncontrollable. When I read about the crash in the papers, I laughed my ass off."

"All of this over a stupid car?"

"Then I went to work on his mother. I wasn't going to harm her because I figured she would want to get rid of the Jags after losing Jack. The little bitch wouldn't even take my calls! I had to use my financial guy and slowly win her trust. We started investing her money. The first year we let her make a lot. Then we slowly but surely drained her dry. I knew eventually she'd get low enough to sell the Jags. When she offered up that silver cup from the Monterey Race, I thought I was finally there. Then you came in and spoiled the whole thing. That's when I decided you had to go as well. I'm going to have some fun with Tanya, too, before I send you both to the bottom of the ocean."

"You're a sick bastard."

"You have no idea. I'll tell you one thing--when this is over, I'm going to have my C-type back, and you're all going to be dead. Even Buck. He laughed at me when Jack insulted me, and I made a promise to myself I wasn't going to let that go. I'm going to settle all my scores tonight."

"Why Phil and Tanya? That made no sense."

"If something happened to you, who would own the C-type?"

"Tanya."

"Would she have sold it?"

"Absolutely not."

"Exactly. I had to get rid of her first, and in a way that would not cast suspicion on me. Then if I got rid of you later, who would have owned the C-type?"

"Tanya's mother."

"What would she have done with it?"

"She would have sold it."

"You see, it all made sense. I had to get rid of Tanya first if I were going to get the car eventually."

"So this was always about the car."

"It was always about what the car represents. Some people thought Jack got the better of me. I had to prove in the long run nobody gets the better of me. I've been patient for many years, but I always knew I was going to come out on top."

Peter turned away and looked out the smoked window of the limo. He had no way of reaching out to the passing motorists for help. He hoped the police could somehow save Tanya.

The truck and trailer pulled into the marina just after midnight. A team of men immediately began unloading the two Jags and preparing them for the big yacht at the end of the pier. The police stopped several blocks back and high on the hill. They moved forward and watched with binoculars from above.

Detective Clark was giving orders furiously while monitoring the situation below closely. "I don't see Dave or Peter so I think they're probably already on board. I'm not going to move yet, just in case they're not, but I won't let that boat out of the marina." Over the course of twenty minutes, they watched the XK120 preparing to be taken onto the ship. "I'm not going to wait anymore. Everyone in position? Tanya, you and Michael wait up here." He shouted the order on his phone. "Let's go. Take them down. Shoot first if you have to. I don't want any good guys getting hurt."

Officers descended from three directions. The crew with the cars started to resist, but they were badly outmatched and quickly gave up. Three policemen ran on board the large yacht and rounded up the crew, arresting six men in total. They were quickly put face down in the parking lot and tied with plastic bands around their wrists.

Tanya yelled to Michael, "I can't wait any longer. I'm going down. I've got to see if Peter is alright!"

"I'm right behind you."

The steep embankment made the trip down slippery. Spotlights from several squad cars quickly illuminated the scene while the police rapidly sealed off the area for further investigation.

Tanya ran up to Clark. "Is Peter okay?"

"He's not here. We jumped the gun. But we've cut off his escape route."

Dave's limo crested the hill. The police looked up as two men jumped out and ran into the shadows. Everyone seemed frozen as the limo descended toward the marina, picking up speed as it neared the water.

"Watch out everybody!" Detective Clark yelled.

The heavy car blasted through the marina barrier and plunged into the water. The back door was still open so water poured into the cabin. They ran to the edge, and in horror saw Peter still bound in the back seat and looking up at them. The car sank in just a few seconds.

"Shit," said Detective Clark, as he peeled off his jacket and shoes.

He dove off the dock and disappeared into the black water. For ten seconds, the water remained calm. A second officer stripped down and prepared to dive in and help. Just as he was about to take the plunge, Detective Clark broke the surface with Peter in his arms, both gasping for breath. He cradled Peter's head to keep it above water until help arrived.

Later a police officer asked Michael what should be done with Lucille and even called her by name, which made Michael the tiniest bit happy. Derek Hunter had been driving the truck at gunpoint so he was there and able to give instructions on the type of flatbed they had to use to haul Michael's Jag from the crash site in Monterey to his shop in Campbell, promising to meet the car when it arrived. A visit to the emergency room was mandatory for Peter, but he didn't stay long, determined that Dave Terrell was not going to influence his life for another minute. They all trudged home to the Stafford's house.

The smell of Maria's cooking attracted the clan to the kitchen like a pack of hungry wolves to a kill around noon the next day. The San Francisco paper offered plenty of coverage on the front page but Tanya was finding more information being posted on the Internet. A laptop set up on the granite counter top held her attention while she absent-mindedly wolfed down a plate of huevos rancheros.

"Michael, I'm finding stories, pictures and video of the crash site posted all over the country about your driving expertise and how you saved me."

"I'm a little worried about Lucille. Derek said if the frame was bent, it might be curtains for the old girl. He promised to inspect her in the next few days to see if repairs would be possible."

Detective Clark dropped by in the early evening. "I'm afraid Dave Terrell has a good chance of slipping through our fingers and getting out of the country."

Tanya said, "Well, he can never come here again, so we should finally be safe."

Michael shook his head at Clark. They both knew this would never be over as long as Dave Terrell was alive. He might not be able to come back, but he could easily send someone else.

Chapter 25

A few days later, decision time had arrived for Michael. "I have some business in Tulsa. Would you be interested in making the trip with me?"

"I wouldn't try to get out of town without me if I were you. What's up, Jagboy?"

"I need to attend to my house. I'm thinking of moving."

"Where to?"

"California. The climate seems to agree with me."

"Any place in particular?"

"Something near the ocean."

"Listen, buster, if you think you're going to be living anywhere except with me—"

"Since you brought it up, where are we going to live, if I might ask? I don't think we can impose on Peter much longer."

"My townhouse isn't far from here. We can live there to start with. I have an idea, though."

He raised his eyebrows.

"Peter always said the Waldorf place was mine if I wanted it. I thought we could renovate it and make it our home."

Her quick answer caught Michael off guard. "It seems we have two challenges. The first is that while I have a little money, I don't stack up so well against your family. I might be able to pay the taxes on the place, but to be honest, I'm not even sure of that. I think money might cause some issues between us."

"We have a great relationship. We've been inseparable almost from the moment we met. Therefore, I don't think in terms of whether or not we'll be together. I take that as a given. As far as the money goes, most couples don't bring exactly the same net worth to a relationship. We're no different."

"Most couples are usually within a few zeros of the same net worth."

"The law in California separates wealth before a relationship, so if we split, you wouldn't be due any of my possessions."

California law proved to be a revelation. "Okay. You keep the house and checking account in your name. Maybe that will solve the money issue."

Michael noticed a determined look on her face. He had the feeling she wasn't going to give him any way out, not that he wanted one. "What's the second challenge?"

"From what I've seen of the Waldorf place, it needs a lot of repair. Won't the renovation take a lot of time?"

"I've thought of that, too. We'll start by doing a quick fix on the racing garage. We can live in the suite upstairs quite nicely for a while. I can strip that place and redo it in no time. As soon as the garage is livable, and I'm guessing I can handle that in a month or so, we'll move out of my town house. The space downstairs will be even easier. I want to bring it back up to par as a real functioning garage. When I turn my attention to the main house, the setup will actually work quite well because I usually waste a lot of time commuting to job sites. If I'm living on the site, I can get a lot more done."

"Sounds like you've got it all figured out."

"Are you trying to back out on me?"

"No, princess. I just worry that a broken down cowboy who writes stories about old cars and earns nothing compared to you is going to get on your nerves after a while."

A few days later, they boarded a plane for the flight to Tulsa. An hour after landing, a taxi delivered them to the front of his house. After all he'd seen the last few weeks, it appeared quite humble.

A sign in the front yard that he'd forgotten about caused him immediate embarrassment. Neighbors walking their dogs had been making too many pits stops in his yard, causing him to put up a sign that read "No Dogs!" One of the kids had painted in an additional line below that read, "Just Babes." Subtlety apparently hadn't been high on his priorities when he brought a girl back to his place. Tanya calmly scooped up the sign and dropped it in the garbage can at the side of the house.

The home had been purchased brand new, leaving the design a bit bland for Tanya's tastes, but she seemed to make the best of it. Over the course of the next week, Michael called a real estate agent he knew and got it listed.

During their spare time, he took her to his favorite Western store and completely outfitted her with jeans, shirts, boots, and a summer straw hat. An old neighbor offered to lend a couple of horses for riding. Steaks grilled over an outdoor grill completed their idealistic visit home.

The trip couldn't have been complete without a visit to his favorite bar, The Melrose. Vic, his partner for most of the twenty years on the force, joined them. Vic had advised against moving to California each time they talked on the phone during his absence. Any resistance to the idea vanished at the first sight of Tanya. Her beauty and personality won him over quickly. In fact, he soon proposed a visit to the golden state when the new house was renovated.

The waitress eyed the table nervously as she approached to take their order. Detectives had a well-deserved reputation for terrorizing young servers.

Michael ordered first. "I'll have a bare naked Diet Dr. Pepper."

Tanya looked horrified. "What in the heck is a bare naked Diet Dr. Pepper?"

The waitress knew Michael so he let her give the answer. "No ice, no lime, no lemon, no straw. Straight up."

Vic was next. "I'll have a bare naked traditional."

As the waitress was leaving, Vic called out, "Hey, does a bare naked traditional cost more than a regular one?"

Without a blink, she replied, "At your age, anything that's bare naked is going to cost more."

The next day he started packing. A Fender guitar amplifier, a few pieces of furniture and extra clothes hardly filled one packing crate. A new wardrobe would be needed for California and he was sure Tanya was going to get involved with that project. The crate was shipped to Tanya's town house in North Beach and the rest of the furniture, what there was of it, was donated to a local women's shelter.

As they flew out of Tulsa, he pointed out the location of the ranch to Tanya, although now it was a huge housing addition. Tulsa had been a great place to grow up, but he was headed west for the next phase of the adventure called life.

Chapter 26

The half-hearted attempt at Tanya Stafford was his first failure. A new boyfriend constantly at her side would make any further actions extremely difficult. Grudgingly, the Slasher went back to his list of the five women he thought could offer him the most notoriety. At the top of the list stood the best trophy of all, the mayor of San Francisco. Computer searches offered valuable information detailing her schedule but when he attended a couple of appearances he realized her security was far too sophisticated. The computer did offer a tantalizing replacement, her daughter.

Pamela Stephenson was the mayor's only child. She'd recently finished her doctorate degree at UC Berkeley, and then partnered with another woman in a family therapy center. Tracking down her office was easy, and he invested some time watching her, learning her habits and routines, even following her home. Slightly reclusive in the evenings, a boyfriend or unexpected guest didn't seem to be much of a problem. A trophy of her stature would require patience and planning, but he ached to kill again.

After three full weeks of practice runs, laced and impeded by cocaine binges, he pronounced himself ready. Surveillance of a neighborhood near the bus stop in Campbell revealed a truck that looked to be an easy mark. With the new information that the police were watching the train and bus stations, leaving his personal car in the Campbell area would give him two alternatives. If he encountered no problems at all he could drive the truck back and ditch it anywhere a mile or so away from his car. If he did run into trouble he could ditch the truck anywhere south of the crime scene and board the bus or train at a location the police would not be watching. The first part of the plan went without a hitch. He stole the truck without incident and parked it a few blocks away from his target. In the early darkness of evening he snorted a few rows of coke in the safety of the cabin, gearing himself up for the main event. When he felt relaxed, he left the truck and made his way to the victim's house. He carried a ski mask, a last minute idea to throw off the police with something a little different.

She lived modestly, seemingly an attempt to show her mother she could make it on her own. As per the rehearsal, he made a complete trip around the house to check it out. Pamela appeared to be reading in the front room when he passed on the sidewalk. An alley gave easy access to a screened-in porch on the back of the house. The latch was easy to spring with his pocketknife. The back door was unlocked, as he'd found it on two earlier tests. The knob had to be turned ever so carefully to avoid a telltale squeak. He pulled on the ski mask then swung the door open and entered. Jazz played in the background, which would help cover any sounds that might occur in the struggle. No weapons were in sight as he passed through the kitchen. His bare hands would do the dirty work this time.

Under the plush carpeting, the ancient wooden floor required him to be as light-footed as a cat. The top of his victim's hairdo was just visible over the back of a large leather chair when he glanced around the corner.

Like a lion closing in on his prey, he inched forward a step at a time while controlling his breathing. When he was one step away, he prepared to make his final move. A split-second before he lunged, she glanced up and saw his reflection in the window. Screaming, she slid over the arm with surprising agility, causing him to miss. His hand just touched her dress as he hurtled by and into the wall. A side table with a lamp on it broke his fall. The table disintegrated under his weight and the lamp collapsed onto the floor, shining light and shadows from a crazy angle beside the chair. The volume of her screaming sounded an alarm through the house as strong as any police siren as she ran to the kitchen. When he caught up with her she pushed him across the room with a strength that surprised him, causing him to lose his balance again and crack his head on the side of a counter. When he came up, she was the one with a butcher knife in her hands. For an instant, they just stared at each other. Terrified, but with adrenaline flowing at super human levels, she turned out to be a lot more of a match than he had bargained for. When he lunged for her a final time she let out a blood-curdling scream, slashed him across the arm with the knife and then shot out the front door. With blood gushing from his wound, a retreat out the back porch was his only choice. Running into the doorjamb because the ski mask was twisted so he couldn't see very well was a final insult. By the time he reached the truck a few blocks away, he was gasping for breath and the ski mask was lost somewhere in the alley.

Thinking clearly at this point was impossible. The first order of business was to get out of the neighborhood, so he jammed the gas pedal down hard. A mile later, he slowed down on a large street. He made his way to the highway and headed south. When he could finally check his arm, he saw a clean cut about five inches long. At the side of the highway he tore the sleeve off his shirt and made an impromptu tourniquet that seemed to slow the bleeding. He screamed in rage and pounded the steering wheel as he drove south. The driver's side window cracked when he accidently hit it with his elbow. Parking a mile or so away from his car, he looked through the contents in the backseat. A leather jacket proved to be his best break of the night. His arm ached as he pulled on the jacket to hide the injury.

He abandoned the truck in a small industrial area near the neighborhood without incident, but he got lost a couple of times trying to find his way back to his car. The jacket seemed to keep blood off the seats. The sun was just beginning to show as he drove into his garage. He rinsed the cut in the garage with a hose over the drain. In his bathroom, he did a better job of disinfecting the cut. Thankfully it wasn't as deep as he'd feared initially. Awkwardly he covered it with gauze then applied bandaging over the top.

When he finally sat down on the edge of his bed, he screamed again several times. His victim had gotten the better of him. Everything had gone so well up to that point. Why had everything gone wrong this time? Aching to kill again, he immediately started formulating a new plan.

Chapter 27

As soon as they returned to San Francisco, Michael and Tanya began the task of moving to Tanya's town house in North Beach.

A few bags of clothes stuffed into the back of her car weren't a very ambitious start. Tanya dropped Michael at the front and drove around to the garage to unlock the townhouse so he could experience it ideally for the first time. The downstairs was open concept. The kitchen drew his attention first because it sparkled. Stainless steel appliances gleamed over a limestone floor, which he was informed, was heated. The highlight was a bronze metallic-colored glass tile backsplash that reflected golden tinged lights around the room. A half-moon kitchen bar with a granite countertop framed with maple panels leaned into the dining area. A small table was set for two people. He ran his fingers over the plates to feel the texture, colored in rich earth tones, but grooved toward the center with a ridge around the rim. The napkins were silk with a pattern woven in. The flatware had interesting shapes, curved but not symmetrical. The walls were covered in fabric that seemed to be silk. Two steps dropped down to the living area furnished with leather chairs, a sofa and a big screen television over the fireplace. She motioned him back to the front door and she pushed lightly on a maple panel in the wall causing it to spring open revealing a small powder room. The walls were covered in the same small bronze metallic glass tiles. The sink was raised off the granite counter but very shallow.

The upstairs bath was as interesting as the kitchen. The shower had a steam unit, and the glass was a full two inches thick. The tiles were like the metallic ones downstairs but in a turquoise color, truly a town house worthy of a top designer. Every color, every fabric, every light, nothing was left to chance. The rooms exuded a rich texture that aroused the senses.

"Well, what do you think?"

"It's exactly what I would expect of you. It's very sensual, just like a Jaguar. I like the textures most of all. I want to touch everything. It stimulates the senses."

"I'm going to take that as a compliment. Now, let's see if this new bed I bought is the high performance model they promised."

In a few days the move was complete. Michael was worried Peter would be upset about losing Tanya, but he seemed to be quite busy with construction of his drug treatment facility. Tanya's big project was coming to an end so she got very busy designing and selling the next one. She offered a copy of the book *The Maltese Falcon* for Michael to read. The author lived in the area when he wrote the book, making it a primer for investigating North Beach. Michael made a valiant effort to feel at home, but he found downtown too busy. The peaceful and wooded landscape of Los Gatos called to him.

Detective Clark dropped in on short notice one evening. Although it had only been a few weeks, seeing him was like reliving ancient history.

"I've got some good news for you two. The authorities caught up with Dave Terrell a few days ago in Cartagena."

Tanya brightened up. "Will he be extradited back here for trial?"

"I doubt it. He was dead."

She gasped at the information.

"It looks like as soon as old Dave couldn't move the cocaine anymore, he wasn't needed. I'd be willing to bet he had a big stash of cash somewhere, too, and someone figured out how to get it. Anyway, I finally feel you two are in the clear and this thing is over." The words were barely out of his mouth before he threw Michael a curve "I could use a little help on another matter, though."

Tanya seemed interested, but Michael was wary. The details he revealed were shocking.

"We have a lead in the Slasher case. Michael might be able to confirm something for me."

"I'm listening."

"You probably heard about the attack on the mayor's daughter a few days ago." They nodded. "You can't breathe a word of this. Derek Hunter is our prime suspect."

Tanya blurted out, "Derek Hunter? Impossible."

"Hear me out. We have several pieces of physical evidence pointing to a shop in the San Jose area specializing in Jaguars. We're sure the person who attacked the mayor's daughter was the Slasher, maybe the first time he failed. She said the attacker was wearing a ski mask, but the general build fits Derek. A lot of other evidence fits, too. The kicker was the truck the Slasher used, a Ford Explorer, was discarded less than a mile from his shop in Campbell."

"How do you know the truck was used by the Slasher?" McAllister asked.

"The seats were covered in cocaine and blood. We'll have a definite DNA profile in a few days. We also got a break this time. A local was out walking his dog on the night of the attack and noticed the truck parked a few blocks away from the Stephenson girl's house. People are finally starting to listen to our warnings. He copied down the license number so we know it's the right truck."

"Why don't you just show a photo of Derek to the witnesses you have in Bakersfield?"

"The lead is only a day old. We have him under surveillance but we haven't taken any good close-ups of his face we could show around. We'll get there for sure but in the meantime we'd like to find out all we can."

"You don't have probable cause yet to take DNA?"

"Exactly."

"What do you want from me?"

"He's got your car at his shop. I'd like you to drop by like you're just checking on the progress. While you're there, nose around a little. Look the place over. See if there are cans of virgin solvents and plastic sheeting in the shop, the same stuff we found as evidence. Just sniff around. Maybe you could get a sample of his DNA for us to process."

Michael gave Clark a hard look. "Is that all? Tanya and I are pretty friendly with Derek. I don't like this. I'll go down for one visit and that's it. I'm only going to do it because I'm sure I can clear him."

Detective Clark seemed excited as he left. Michael felt like he was turning on a friend. The whole thing gave him a bad feeling.

Chapter 28

The next day he made a call to Derek. The phone rang quite a few times before he answered.

"Derek, Michael McAllister."

"Michael! How's it going?"

"No complaints. I wanted to check with you about Lucille. Are you making any headway on the repairs?"

"She's starting to look like a car again. I've been busy, though. The Pebble Beach thing has my phone ringing off the hook. I had some rush jobs to fit in. Just too much money to turn down. You two have made me famous."

"That's great. You deserve it. I wondered if I could just come down and see the old girl, even if she's in pieces? I kind of miss her."

"Sure, that would be fine. I've got another rush job going right now. Today is Tuesday. Why don't you come down Friday?"

"Okay, Friday then."

"Bring Tanya with you."

"Tanya?"

"Yeah. Be sure and bring Tanya with you." The phone went dead after the request.

The last statement worried Michael a little. Detective Clark thought it sounded like an odd request, too, when Michael checked in. Could Derek be hatching some kind of plan to get Tanya or maybe even both of them? Clark decided he should go through with the visit, but assured Michael he'd have a team of police nearby at all times. Friday morning came all too soon.

The route to Derek's shop was well known to Tanya because she'd been deeply involved during the restoration process of the cars in Peter's basement. Detective Clark followed closely behind in a car with three additional officers. Michael noticed when he met with them they were well armed. The police officers seemed noticeably on edge, possibly on the verge of cracking the biggest case of their careers.

Before they started, Michael had a request. "You want a DNA sample. Derek doesn't smoke so the best I can hope for is a straw or maybe a paper cup. I need an evidence bag large enough for a cup." An officer quickly retrieved one from the back of the patrol car. "Tanya, I need you to bring a purse large enough to hold this with a cup or something inside." She ran inside and found a slightly informal canvass bag she could throw over her shoulder.

The convoy headed south for over an hour until the city of San Jose loomed with its tall buildings. The shop was located past downtown a few miles south in an industrial area. Michael tried to envision the area at night, a pretty dangerous looking place. Had women been taken there to be tortured and murdered? It seemed possible. Detective Clark beeped his horn as they got close to the shop so he could discuss the final details of the visit. Tanya consulted a map with Clark and they decided on a spot about two blocks away from the destination. Detective Clark and his men would remain at that location. Tanya would receive a call on her cell phone in fifteen minutes. If she didn't answer, they'd rush to the shop. The calls would be repeated every fifteen minutes with Clark posing as a client.

Tanya worked out some code words to denote either they were in trouble or everything was fine. Michael was nervous, but felt they could deal with the situation if Derek was indeed the Slasher.

An open chain link gate offered entry to the shop. The property was surrounded by a very high fence of the same construction, but with barbed wire on the top. The security seemed a little over the top to protect a restoration shop, but maybe it was normal. Considering it was a shop turning out six figure restorations on vintage cars, it didn't seem very fancy to Michael. Two long buildings formed an L shape, one side bordering their entry on the left, the other straight ahead. They parked in front of what seemed like the main building. A door stood open with a vintage Jaguar sign posted on the wall.

Inside the office was furnished with a simple desk, two chairs and a sofa, all of the same vintage as the old Jaguars but none having benefitted from any kind of restoration. Pictures of Derek and his father with various customers adorned the walls. A great shot of Peter and Tanya with the C-type, possibly taken the day it was finished, hung on an adjacent wall. Tanya was slightly younger and so strikingly beautiful Michael stared at the picture until she jabbed him in the ribs. Calls to Derek went unanswered. An investigation of the first building turned up five Jaguars in various states of restoration with parts scattered around like they'd exploded and someone had to figure out how to glue them back together. He couldn't imagine how Derek could make sense of which parts went with each car. He had to have a system. The project with his father on Lucille allowed him some idea of what was going on. Most of the parts were the same.

The far end of the building led to a large open garage. Still no Derek. The door to the other building wasn't locked so they entered. Another call to Derek netted better results.

"Back here."

They glanced at each other for courage. Tanya had her cell phone in hand. Another door led further inside the second building. Would the officers be able to find them if they called for help? When they entered the next room, they breathed a sigh of relief.

Cabinets lined three sides of the pristinely clean room with a double door opening to the outside on the fourth wall. Under the cabinets were all manner of tools and machines capable of performing complicated tasks. In the center of the room Lucille stood as elegantly as if she were a brand new car. Derek was halfway under the car working on something.

"I wanted to surprise you so I've been working like a dog the last few days. She'll be done in ten minutes."

A quick inspection revealed the car to be in better shape than before the wreck.

"How did you manage this in just a few weeks?"

"She really wasn't so bad. These things are built like tanks. I pulled the fenders off and straightened them out and then I decided to paint the whole car over again. No offense to the work done before, but I always think I can paint a car better than anyone else. The windshield was a bitch. The rubber around that thing took me a whole day. I think it turned out pretty good, though."

The paint was so glossy black it looked wet. Derek took a few minutes and pointed out at least twenty things he'd fixed on the car besides the repairs of the damage from the wreck. Michael and his father had done an admirable job on the restoration, but Derek had learned from the master. He'd upgraded the front end with polymer bushings he claimed would make the steering better. He'd repainted the steering wheel which now gleamed in a piano black epoxy like the outside of the car. It seemed he had a never-ending list of upgrades and adjustments he'd done. The only thing that stopped his discussion was the urgent ring of Tanya's phone.

"Excuse me. I've got to take this." She walked back to the other room. Michael assumed she was going to explain to Clark what had happened.

Derek was connecting the master brake cylinder and asked Michael to sit in the car and step on the brake while he bled the air out of the system. After a few minutes the job was accomplished so he could replace the wheels. He gave the spinner hubcaps some mighty whacks with a lead hammer to insure they wouldn't work off while driving. The bonnet latched with a pleasant click and he pulled the jacks from under the car.

"Give her a start and let's see how she does."

Michael turned the key and let the fuel pump prime the motor. When he touched the starter button, the engine sprang to life, running even better than before the wreck.

"The carbs seemed a tiny bit off so I gave them a tweak. I also rebuilt the head. You had a little clatter going on so I reset the valve clearances. I think you'll like the way she runs now."

Tanya returned to see Lucille in all her glory. Derek was spraying a cleaning solution on the body then wiping with a clean rag to remove a few smudges here and there on the paint.

"I can't thank you enough. What do I owe you for all of this?"

"It won't hurt too badly. I'll e-mail you an invoice when I get a chance. Like I said, the news you both made during Pebble Beach has allowed me to raise my rates. You should know, too, that several of my suppliers really stepped up on this car. I had some chroming done and it was returned in three days with no charge. I have several stories from others like that. It seems everyone wants an old Jaguar now, and they want it restored. I've got clients lined up for the next year or more. This has been a windfall for me as well as the others."

A complete shop tour with a short explanation of the work being done on several cars took about a half an hour. Although the shop seemed cluttered no part was out of place. If he'd added a few helpers he could turn out more work but Hunter preferred to do everything himself since his name was written above the shop door. Michael made a split second decision and pushed.

"Can you tell me what virgin solvents are used for? I heard the term the other day."

"You mean what they used to be used for?"

"What do you mean?"

"Follow me."

He led them back through the building to the final room past Lucille. It was antiseptically clean and only used for painting.

"The EPA passed a law a few years back mandating the use of water-based paints. See the paint suit hanging on the wall?" He pointed it out to them. "These new water-based paints are better for the environment but they're deadly while they're being applied. I have to wear a full suit to keep from being poisoned during the painting process. The same mandates apply for solvents. They're all water-based now, too. Any professional painter would use a solvent just before each painting to remove all grease and dirt from the body of the car. The quality of the paint job is only as good as how clean and well prepped you have the car.

"You mentioned virgin solvents. That's the way we used to do it. I still get requests on some of the old cars to paint them in lacquer. I can get the old stuff but it's illegal now. It's not worth the trouble for me to do it. Everything has to be water-based now."

"So virgin solvents aren't used anymore?"

"I didn't say that. I said they weren't legal anymore. There are still shops that paint the old way. My shop is too well known now, but I know a lot of the little shops, even in this area, still do things the old way. It would have to be a very small shop. No high-end clients or possibly only very high-end clients. And, of course, the do-it-yourself guys. They'd probably use virgin solvents and non-water-based paints on homemade jobs."

Derek's wife showed up as Michael was finishing his interrogation. She kept the books for their small operation. They all made a nice spread of lunch on the desk in the main office. Michael and Tanya enjoyed a nice cool soft drink with them while they ate. Derek had a vintage coke machine that charged fifty cents for a drink. Michael decided to buy a round for everyone. As they talked, Michael thought about Derek, his wife and his kids. He admired the niche Derek had carved for himself in the world. Achieving master status at a craft few could learn, supporting his family and remaining totally self-sufficient seemed a dream come true. As far as Michael was concerned the top suspect had just been marked off the Slasher list. The reason Derek had insisted on Tanya tagging along was that he wanted to surprise them with the finished car and wanted them to be able to drive it home. Detective Clark was definitely back to square one.

Derek had been working hard in the shop that morning and downed his Coke quickly. Michael did the same. He looked at the bottle on Derek's desk and then back at Tanya. She got the message. Derek's wife took the cooler she'd brought lunch in back to the car. Michael asked about a client picture on the wall behind Derek. When he turned to look at the picture Michael switched bottles and offered Derek's to Tanya behind his back. He felt it slide into the paper evidence bag. Tanya made an excuse with work so she could leave early. Her job was to hand off the evidence bag to the police for examination. The tests wouldn't be admissible in court but Michael was sure the DNA would eliminate Derek from further investigation.

The drive home was heaven. Lucille felt tighter, steering almost like a modern car. The motor was noticeably smoother and more powerful but she still made some serious noise under the hood when he stepped on the gas.

Chapter 29

The next Saturday Michael and Tanya met her mother at Peter's house for dinner. The occasion was Tanya's birthday, September 12th.

Tanya broached the question of the Waldorf mansion during dessert. "Peter, you said the Waldorf place was mine, so we're ready to move full speed ahead on the renovation. I guess I need to buy it from you or something."

Peter smiled. "Didn't you ever wonder why no one could find the cars after Emma moved?"

"I thought you kept it a secret or something."

"The sale of a house can't be kept a secret. Let me show you something."

He went upstairs for a few minutes and returned with some papers including the bill of sale for the Waldorf house.

"Who's listed as the buyer?"

"T. Stafford. I bought the house?"

"I put it under your name because I knew it would be much more difficult to trace the cars."

"So the house and the cars have been under my name all this time?"

"The cars and all the memorabilia are yours to take when you have the place ready for them. I'm going to be quite busy with my new project so I don't need them anymore. I'll drive the E-type, which is what it needs. It suffers if it doesn't get driven enough."

Tanya's mother seemed quite willing to provide the money for the renovation. Michael was pretty sure Tanya planned to move her mother into the Waldorf place when it was finished, which was fine with him. She was getting too old to be by herself, and they knew they could pamper her if she had a suite in the new house. Everything seemed to be falling into place.

After dessert it was time for Tanya's presents. When she asked what Michael had bought her, he produced an envelope from his jacket pocket. When she opened it, her evil smile appeared and she gave him a big hug.

"What is it?" Peter asked.

Tanya looked at Michael so he answered. "It's a week at the racing school at Laguna Seca. Derek and I have decided Tanya is going to start racing the C-type next year on the vintage circuit. I didn't think you'd mind. She must get certified at the school to compete. Derek is going to be the mechanic, and I'm going to make peanut butter sandwiches and sweep up the trash or something."

Tanya rushed out of the room and returned with an ominously shaped package.

"When is your birthday?" She asked.

"It was in June, just before I made the trip over."

"Well, I'm sorry but I can't wait a whole year to get you something. I found this the other day and have been waiting for the right time to give it to you."

It didn't take much to tear the paper away and reveal a black hard-shell guitar case with a bold Gibson insignia emblazoned on the side. The tomb of King Tut held no greater treasure. The lining of the case was as hot pink as a pimp's casket, setting off the black thin line electric guitar inside. The name Lucille was in script on the headstock.

"This is the most beautiful guitar I've ever seen. I didn't know there was really a B.B. King model. It's brand new. I'm afraid to touch it."

Michael was lying and proved it an instant later. He ran his hands down the finely tuned neck and frets. He turned to her and pulled her close.

"How did you ever find this?"

"I've got connections. One of my clients is a guitar freak. I was telling him about your car and he told me about this. He helped me find one."

Just about that time, Peter dropped a bomb. "Michael, there's a question I've been waiting to ask you until the right time. Exactly what are your intentions concerning my niece?"

He could sense he had the complete attention of everyone in the room as he formulated an answer. He knew Peter said it half in jest and half seriously. He paused a moment to think of just the right thing to say.

"The first thing that concerned me about our relationship was money. I want it to be clear I have no ambitions towards the Stafford fortune. Tanya assured me earlier California law protected her but possibly your lawyers could make sure of that with some kind of document I could sign. Another concern I have is basically at heart I'm just a cowboy from Oklahoma. I didn't grow up in a very sophisticated world. When I had disagreements with my associates we usually just walked out back and knocked out a few teeth until we found common ground. I think there's a good chance Tanya will grow tired of my rather simple outlook on life." He turned to his gorgeous girlfriend and smiled broadly. "I'm not sure what our future holds, but as long as she'll allow it, I don't plan to let her out of my sight." Tanya ran to him and gave him a big hug and kiss. Over her shoulder, Michael could see Peter smiling at her mother. He took that as a sign of approval.

Chapter 30

The next morning Tanya baked a batch of cookies. The aroma filled her town house and Michael was quick to steal a couple, oatmeal raisin, his favorite.

"What's the occasion?"

"I'm going to Los Gatos today to get the permits to start work on the house. I've found some homemade cookies can be helpful in the process."

As usual she was right. The permits weren't difficult for the garage. The house would be more involved. She'd been in business for more than fifteen years now and whipped her crew into action. The upstairs of the racing garage was gutted and the whole structure cleaned to the bare walls the first day on the job.

Michael tagged along every other day or so. A week after the visit to Derek's shop Michael received a call from Detective Clark.

"Don't gloat but you were right about Hunter. The DNA wasn't a match to our known Slasher samples but the blood in the truck was. We're back to square one."

"So what's your next move?"

"We're working our way through the shops around San Jose but we're not exactly hitting any home runs. These shops seem to have very distinctive clients and we're not very good at figuring that out."

"What if I nosed around a little in an unofficial capacity? I think I know a way to find the shop you're looking for."

"Would you mind sharing your idea with me?"

"You might laugh. Why don't you just let me dig a little. I promise I won't get you in any trouble."

As soon as he hung up, he dialed Derek Hunter on his cell phone. He quickly made a lunch date for the following day with a promise of pizza. They gathered in the same old surroundings at the shop filled this time with the aroma of hot Hawaiian pizza.

"I need to get something off my chest." Derek and his wife both stopped eating and gave him quizzed looks. "I'm nosing around a little on the Slasher case, unofficially of course."

"So what's that got to do with us?"

"Three facts point to a Jaguar restoration shop, or at least a paint shop specializing in vintage cars. First, the paint jobs on two of the stolen Fords were done in a Jaguar color, some special red, I think. Secondly, some of the victims were covered with a virgin solvent, something that could be used in a paint shop. Some of the victims were wrapped in a plastic that would normally be used in a shop. Finally, San Jose seems to be about the center of the crimes when they're mapped. The truck used in the murder attempt of the mayor's daughter was dumped close by, too. It makes the police think the shop could be located somewhere around here."

Derek was silent for a minute. "My shop fits all those criteria."

"That's what I wanted to get off my chest. Our visit when you surprised us with Lucille was to eliminate you as a suspect. You even matched the composite sketches done by both witnesses."

"You and Tanya thought I might be the Slasher?" He didn't have a pleasant look on his face.

"No. The police thought you were a match. We wanted to eliminate you immediately, which we did." Michael let him stew another minute. "The cops don't really get the different types of clientele each shop caters to. They don't understand the nuances of the various niches in the restoration market. I thought if I were looking for a shop just like yours, why not ask you? You should know about everything going on in the area."

Derek's wife answered, "Standard Jaguars in Los Gatos."

Derek agreed. "That would definitely be one to check out. It's very much like our shop, a little bigger, a few more employees."

"There's a shop right in Los Gatos?"

"Yes. I can show you on a map. I think the owner's a Swiss guy. Let me think a minute about some other ones you should check out."

They talked for another thirty minutes during Derek's lunch break. When they were finished, Michael had six new potential shops to check out. Two were in San Luis Obispo, probably too far away, but Derek insisted they were worth checking out. Two others were in San Jose and one in San Francisco. The one in Los Gatos seemed like the best possibility.

As he left, Michael asked Derek, "No hard feelings about checking you out on this?"

"No. I guess I understand. Better to check me off the list than waste time. It's kind of interesting, anyway. It's kind of like I'm involved in trying to solve the case."

"I agree. This is the best information I've been given so far. I'll make you a deal. Don't breathe a word about this to anyone, and I'll kind of keep you posted on what's going on."

Derek nodded his agreement.

It was only natural to accompany Tanya to Los Gatos the next day so he could investigate Standard Jaguars. The shop seemed like a very good fit.

Chapter 31

Shortly after arriving at the old Waldorf mansion, which was now in full renovation mode, Michael borrowed Tanya's car and followed the map Derek had given him to locate the Standard Jaguars shop, tucked away on the edge of town. The tension built in his chest as he approached the building but quickly turned to disappointment. The Standard Jaguars sign still hung above the door out front but the building was deserted. Another auto repair shop was located across the street so he walked over to see what he could find out. The owner was under a car.

"Sorry to bother you, but I was hoping to have some work done on my Jag at the shop across the street. It seems to be shut down."

The mechanic didn't even bother to roll out from beneath the car. "Bernard retired a little over a year ago. I think someone is in the process of buying the building but I don't think it's going to be a Jaguar shop anymore."

"Would it be possible to get in touch with him? Is he still in the area?"

"I think he moved down to Los Angeles."

Michael said thanks and goodbye to the legs and returned to the car. It was still theoretically possible the owner might be a suspect but most likely his best lead so far was a dead end. A trip to Los Angeles was the last thing on his mind. The rules from his old case in Tulsa still applied. A little hope each day always seemed to lead to frustration. He'd learned, though, every piece of information had to be evaluated. The smallest detail could be the one that solved the case.

When he returned to the Waldorf estate, Tanya was excited.

"We're going to be able to spend the night in the garage in a few days. After we fix some last minute plumbing issues, we're set."

The garage had been transformed. Metal cabinets across the entire back wall and a peg board system were ready for a complete set of modern tools for working on the Jags. Both walls on the sides housed the original cabinets for the Waldorf trophies but they'd been completely refurbished. Modern electric door openers managed the three sets of garage doors. The floor had some kind of plastic floor tiles connected in an interlocking manner.

Upstairs the décor was even nicer. The suite had been completely modernized with a bathroom on the far end complete with a large glass-enclosed shower. The bedroom was situated in the middle and finally a kitchen and den combo occupied the front. Tanya had furnished it in a rather masculine manner with a leather sofa and the like.

"We'll start moving down next week."

The next day Michael decided he'd better check out the Jag shop in San Francisco if he would be moving south soon. Tanya told him it was the same shop Peter had used for the restoration of his E-type, which in turn initiated a call to Peter.

"Peter, Michael. I've got to check out that shop you used for the E-type. What can you tell me about the owner?"

"In what context do you mean check it out?"

"Detective Clark is trying to eliminate all the shops that could possibly be owned by the Slasher."

"You can mark that one off the list then."

"How can you say that so quickly?"

"Because the owner was killed in a car wreck a couple of years ago. There's no way he could have been the Slasher." Michael found it difficult to argue his logic. His investigation was really piling up the evidence, all of it useless. Michael called it a week and resigned himself to moving the next week. Progress on the case so far was non-existent.

Chapter 32

His world revolved around cocaine, getting it and using it in three and four day binges with a few semi-normal days in between to eat and clean up. A normal person would be ruined by that type of addiction but the Slasher had plenty of time and money.

A new plan hatched one morning in between hits of the coke. By the time he finally managed to proceed, it was after noon. The first step was to steal a Ford Explorer via his normal method. Santa Cruz was his city of choice, mainly because it was close and easy. The bus delivered him to the boardwalk in the afternoon. The closest neighborhood seemed a good place to search for a car even though it was broad daylight. When he found an Explorer the break-in proved a challenge because he realized he'd forgotten his tools, then he noticed the keys were in the truck and it was unlocked. He opened the door, started it up and drove out of the neighborhood. Another car in a discount store parking lot donated a new tag only because he found a crescent wrench in the glove box and quickly switched license plates, again in broad daylight. Luck remained on his side.

Driving north on Highway 17, he pulled up beside a young girl trying to thumb a ride by the corner of a gas station.

"Where are you heading?"

"I need to get to San Jose."

"That's right where I'm heading. It's your lucky day!" He smiled. Nothing could be further from the truth. "I have to stop for gas. I'll be just a minute." He went inside to pay in cash and brought out two Cokes. "I brought you a Coke. If you don't want it, I'll just drink it later."

"Sure. Thanks. It's hot out here today."

She quickly launched into a story about a boyfriend she had met during the summer. He'd returned to school at San Jose State and recently quit calling. A surprise visit seemed to be the best way to find out what was going on.

He let her tell her story and tried to appear only mildly interested. The first time she looked away he poured an entire vile of GHB into her open Coke can as it sat in the holder. Five minutes later, she sat helpless in the passenger seat. The original plan had escaped him by this time, but the new one worked just fine. Fantasies of rape and torture filled his mind on the ride home. At dusk he slowly descended the drive and made the turn into his garage.

Chapter 33

Wednesday was the first morning Michael and Tanya woke up at their new home. As they enjoyed breakfast they watched a doe and fawn walk by on the lawn, totally oblivious to their observation. The noise outside consisted of birds chirping instead of cars honking.

The two leads in San Luis Obispo weighed on McAllister's mind. Was it worth a full day to drive down, investigate and then make the long drive back? So far the answer seemed to be no. He followed Tanya to the main house trying to think of something productive to do for the day.

The house was beginning to take shape. When Tanya had originally described the changes she planned, it was difficult for him to visualize them. Later, after the house was gutted to the bare studs, she took a piece of chalk to show him where the walls would be moved. As they walked through the house now, some walls were gone and others framed in new locations. For the first time, he began to see how it was all going to fit together. He admired her talent.

Plenty of plumbing and wiring still lay ahead but it was certainly easier on her to simply walk up the hill a hundred yards to meet her crew than the drive she'd been making on a regular basis. The workers arrived on the job early, so Tanya quickly got involved with design issues. He wasted the morning watching the work. The only input Michael had suggested was a pool at the back of the house. Tanya liked the idea and added a hot tub on one end and a large koi pond on the other making it a nice spot to spend their evenings. Tanya prepared a late lunch back at the garage. Afterward, she quickly returned to work. Michael stayed behind at the garage. He decided to call Derek Hunter so he'd feel like he was doing something.

"Derek, Michael."

"Hey. How's the detective business?"

"I'm a total failure. I checked out the shops in Los Gatos and San Francisco last week. The guy in Los Gatos sold out some time back and moved to Los Angeles. The guy in San Francisco got killed in a car wreck a couple of years ago."

"I've got something for you, but you have to promise not to laugh at me."

"At this point, I'll listen to anything."

"Well, I'm a little ashamed to admit it but I've taken this detective business quite seriously. I got on the computer last night and did searches on virgin solvents."

"And?"

"I linked virgin solvents and phrases like San Jose and San Francisco but I didn't find anything very useful. I did do a search, though, with virgin solvents and Los Gatos. I got several news stories about some fish kills that had been occurring over the last few years. The locals get real upset about stuff like that. Some thought it was due to palm fronds falling in the water; some real stupid stuff. Anyway, they hired a biologist and ordered some sampling on the dead fish and found out they were contaminated with solvents. That's why I found the stories."

"I'm trying to figure out how this is going to get back to what I'm working on."

"I pulled up a map of the area and it made me remember a guy I did some work for ten or twelve years ago. I would never have thought of him if I hadn't seen the article. He wasn't a professional painter. What I mean by that is he didn't do work for anyone else. He had a real nice hobby car shop at his house and he hired me to come down and paint a car for him. He wanted me to show him what to do so he could do it all himself. He learned really fast and over the years he won a bunch of shows. I used to see him from time to time. His work was very good. The thing was, he only did E-types. I noticed his house was pretty close to the area described in the newspaper articles."

McAllister knew the name before Derek pronounced it. He hung up and called Detective Clark, but got his voice mail. He left a short message about what he'd learned and told him he was going to have a look around. He ran back up to the house and fired up Lucille. He left her idling so she could warm up a minute and went looking for Tanya.

"Tanya, do you have your cell phone with you?"

"Yes, why?"

"I need you to come with me right now."

"Give me two minutes. We've got to work out a problem up here."

Two minutes seemed like hours. When she finally came down he asked her to come with him in the Jag.

"I'm busy. I can't leave the job."

"This is an emergency. Listen to me while I drive."

She reluctantly got in and was surprised when he sprayed gravel as he sped away from the house.

Tanya was upset. "What's this about?"

"Did you ever make any phone calls about Mark Barrow after we visited his house?"

She gave him a quizzical look. "No. He had an alibi. We took him off the list."

"Can you call someone right now and ask a few questions?"

219

"I guess so." She looked up a number on her phone and quickly dialed. "Susan, it's Tanya. How are you doing?"

Tanya made small talk for a minute and then got to the point.

"I'm sorry to be so short, but I have a question. Have you talked with Mark Barrow and his wife lately?"

He could hear the faint sound of a voice going overtime on the other end of the phone. Tanya's eyes widened as she listened.

"Thanks. I can't talk anymore right now. I'll explain all of this to you later." She looked over at him. "Mark's wife left him. He was divorced when we visited him."

"He said she was visiting her sister."

"Maybe he was just embarrassed."

"Remember some of the rooms were missing furniture? He said they were being redone."

"She must have taken a lot of the furniture with her."

"Remember what I said would happen when we found the right guy?"

"The killer will lie when there's no reason to lie. He couldn't have been the killer, though. It was Dave Terrell."

"I'm talking about the Slasher case."

The look in her eyes was pure terror. "You think Mark Barrow is the Slasher?"

"It all fits. He's in the right area. He's got a paint shop in his garage. He only works on Jags."

"That's a long way from proving he's the Slasher. Michael, you've got to be careful. A guy like that will sue you for slander. What do you think you're going to do?"

"I called Detective Clark but got voice mail. I told him to get a search warrant. You and I are just going to go have a look around."

Chapter 34

Detective Clark finally escaped an extremely difficult meeting with the chief of police. The main rule in the police department was that shit rolled down hill. If the chief was getting chewed out by the mayor, Clark was going to get chewed out by the chief. Clark didn't have much to give him. When he turned his cell phone back on, it chimed announcing he'd missed a call. McAllister. What did he want? Maybe he had some news. When he listened to the message he had one brief comment.

"Shit."

He ran back to his office, yelling at a couple of other detectives to follow. He pulled the folder from Tanya's case and removed a picture of Mark Barrow. He ran to the Slasher room and held it up against the two artist's sketches. It was a good match, a very good match. He started barking orders.

"Les, work up a search warrant on Mark Barrow. I'll give you the info in a minute. You've got to find a judge right now. We've got to move on this immediately. Sam, get two patrol cars and three detectives. We're going to do a search down in Los Gatos and maybe an arrest."

He called McAllister. "Michael, I got your message. Whatever you do don't go to the house."

"I'm on my way over there now with Tanya."

"Don't go near that house. We're getting a search warrant ready. You'll screw this up."

"You're cutting out. I can't hear you. I'll call you back later."

The longest hour of his life passed while Clark waited for the search warrant to be signed. The two patrol cars screeched their tires as they sped south. Detective Clark called the police chief in Los Gatos, a guy named Palatine. He'd met him a few times at various training sessions over the years. Without giving him any background he pleaded with him to get a couple of patrol cars near the Barrow house and wait for further instructions. He finally got back around to McAllister and redialed.

"You better pick up."

Chapter 35

The plan was still a work in progress as Michael drove to the Barrow house. His instincts had told him something was wrong with the man when he had met him. The wrong case had produced the right suspect. How could he take a look at Barrow's place without raising suspicion? The creek behind the house offered the solution. Instead of driving to the front of the house, which would give Barrow plenty of warning, he pulled around the end of the block and parked near a small bridge over the stream.

"We've got to make our way along the water to the back of his yard."

Twenty minutes later they were in position. Dusk was near and the trees along the stream were beginning to block out the light. The pipe and drain were invisible from the house but looking back from the bank they were easy to spot. Tests might show the presence of the chemicals reported in the fish kills. He remembered Barrow bragging about how he could wash his cars in the garage and the drain would feed into the stream. It was conceivable solvents had traveled down the pipe and into the water causing the fish kills.

"Okay, detective, now what?" Tanya prodded.

It was a fair question. He didn't have an answer. A minute later he didn't need one. A Ford Explorer turned into the Barrow drive and made its way slowly around to the back. Quickly dropping to the ground, Michael could only hope they hadn't been spotted. Thick vegetation should have obscured them from view. The door to the garage opened automatically and then closed as the truck pulled inside.

A vote was not needed between the newly formed detective team. Images of the little girl drowned in the tub ran through Michael's mind. Immediate action was required if a girl was in the truck. Bushes provided some cover as they made their way along the fence at the edge of the property. Windows across the entire back of the house stared down at them ominously. As they made their way near the side of the garage, the lights came on inside the house, flooding the drive. They risked the clearing to get to the wall of the garage. A side door offered good access, but of course it was locked. Michael worked on it with his small pocketknife. Any minute he expected a maniac to jerk the door open with a giant knife in hand. After an eternity, the lock clicked. Michael gave Tanya a final look, and they each instinctively took in a breath. He opened the door just a hair and peered inside.

The room was dimly lit. He put his arm out to hold Tanya back and listened for a moment. Music blared upstairs, but he couldn't see or hear any movement in the garage. He motioned to Tanya to stay low as they entered. The cars were under fitted covers, offering some protection at the back of the room. They crept along trying to stay out of sight as they made their way toward the main door.

A young naked girl was on their right tied to some kind of metal frame. Her head was drooped down with her chin on her chest and she moaned quietly. What bothered him was that he couldn't see Mark Barrow. What if he'd seen them and was hiding? Maybe he was leading Tanya into a trap. He noticed a pair of work overalls hanging on the wall. He looked at Tanya, motioned to the overalls and then pointed to the girl. She nodded.

It seemed unlikely that Mark had gone upstairs when he had a fresh victim prepared for slaughter, but he remained out of sight. Michael remembered seeing the lights go on in the kitchen area. He decided they'd try to get the girl out, and then wait for the police to arrive. Tanya moved quietly to the victim and put her hand over her mouth. She tried to fight but calmed down when Tanya whispered in her ear. Michael's borrowed pocketknife freed the girl from the tape holding her to the frame. The rescue seemed like it had a chance until his cell phone rang. A fire engine would have been louder, but not by much. Finding it and shutting it off proved a challenge. Suddenly the girl looked up with her eyes wide and her mouth open in a silent scream. Michael turned to see Mark Barrow at the top of the stairs.

"Are we having a party?"

Barrow was wearing a pair of jeans but was bare from the waist up. His red eyes were apparent even from across the room. White powder was splashed over his chin and chest. He looked like he'd been gorging on cocaine. Michael turned to Tanya. She had the girl free, but the overalls were still draped over her arm.

"Get her out of here and call the police."

How could he get Barrow to focus on him while the girls made their escape?

"Why don't you come down here, Mark, so I can knock your dick in the dirt?"

He'd heard a boy say it to another one in Malibu when he was fourteen years old, a sure fire way to start a fight. The ploy worked. Barrow glared at Michael and seemed oblivious to the girls as they left. Michael noticed Barrow brandished a large knife in his right hand. He moved down the stairs with a dreamy smile on his face. Michael searched for a weapon he could use to defend myself. A plastic lid to a trash barrel was the only item within reach. He had to use what he could.

He moved to an open area on his right. When Barrow reached the bottom of the stairs he yelled and charged, swinging the knife wildly. Michael easily used the lid to parry his first two thrusts, but on the third, he tripped over something on the floor, causing them both to go down. As they wrestled on the floor, Michael grabbed the wrist of the hand with the knife so he couldn't cut him. They rolled over a couple of times and then somehow ended up back on their feet. Michael was behind Barrow now, still holding the wrist away with his elbow locked. Michael decided to use a move he'd learned in his police training. With his right hand, he quickly reached between Barrow's legs and grabbed his balls as hard as he could and jerked upward with all his might. Barrow let out a yell and his feet almost came off the ground. They crashed to the cement floor in a heap with Michael on top. When they hit the ground, Barrow immediately went limp. Michael felt a sharp pain in his chin and saw blood streaming down on the back of Barrow's head. Expecting some kind of trick he stayed on top of Barrow, pinning his arms down. Still no movement. After a minute, Barrow didn't even seem to be breathing.

The detective was always surprised at how completely exhausted he became in a scuffle lasting only a minute. He pushed himself up on his hands and finally stood up, keeping an eye on Barrow as he tried to get his breathing back to normal. After a few deep breaths, he observed the motionless man in more detail. The point of the knife was protruding from the back of his neck. Barrow must have fallen on it when they went down. A stream of his blood was working its way down to the drain. In the process, it began to obliterate the large Jaguar head design in the middle of the floor. McAllister touched his chin and could feel an open wound of about an inch. The knife had gone through Barrow's neck and the tip had gouged McAllister in the face. The blood was still flowing out of the cut at an alarming rate. He squeezed on the wound with his hand until he found a cloth he could hold over it. The switch to open the big door hid for quite a while before he finally located it. The police would want easy access when they arrived. He didn't have to wait long. As the door opened, two patrol cars were parked outside with their lights flashing and several officers had their guns trained on him.

They yelled in unison, "Put down your weapon."

Since he didn't have a weapon he simply raised his hands in the air as they surrounded him. Tanya appeared out of nowhere and hugged him in spite of the officers trying to stop her. Eventually they were taken to separate cars and questioned repeatedly about what had happened.

Detective Clark arrived about a half an hour later. The mood seemed to change after he had a long discussion with a large man who seemed to be in charge. Detective Clark finally walked over to the patrol car.

"Ready to get out of here?"

"Am I ever."

"Want me to call an ambulance? That cut looks pretty bad."

Tanya was standing by the car. "I'll take care of him. We want to go home."

Michael and Tanya walked up the drive and along the street to get back to Lucille. Tanya decided they should return to San Francisco to find a specialist to stitch him up as soon as possible. A makeshift bandage provided by one of the officers stopped the blood flow.

A doctor agreed to meet them at the hospital emergency room near Peter's home. Apparently Peter had told him Michael had single handedly solved the Slasher case and it was the least he could do to drive to the hospital in the middle of the night. Using microscopic stitches the doctor assured them the scar would be very slight, which seemed to relieve Tanya. A bed at Peter's house was Michael's only goal for the evening.

Chapter 36

Michael slept late the next morning. He and Tanya made gentle love when they awoke and then took a long shower together. Using his old room at the Stafford house was just like the first time they made love. When they made their way downstairs, they were surprised to find Detective Clark having coffee with Peter.

Clark started with a jab. "Well, the master sleuth finally decides to make an appearance."

Peter motioned to the newspaper opened on the counter. "You're a big star in San Francisco this morning, Michael. The Slasher case is all over the front page."

"I don't want any part of it." He looked at Clark. "Just tell them I was following a lead you gave me."

"It's a little late for that."

"I have a question for you, detective. What started this whole thing? How does a successful businessman married to a very wealthy woman turn into a serial killer?"

"It's funny you ask that. Just yesterday we got a DNA hit on a case in Half Moon Bay from a few years back. They didn't figure it as a homicide so the case took a long time to get into the system. Originally it seemed to be a freak accident but DNA was collected from pubic hairs on the corpse. Turns out they matched the Slasher. We're working our way backwards but it's almost a year before what we thought was our first case. I think eventually we'll put the pieces together and figure out what happened.

"What I've been waiting around all morning to find out is how in the world you figured out Barrow was the Slasher? You didn't have time to explain that to me last night."

"Derek Hunter figured it out."

Now it was Tanya's turn to be surprised. "Derek Hunter?"

"Yes. After we eliminated him as a suspect, I started seeking his advice on which shops I should check out. I figured he'd know better than anyone. He'd been doodling on his computer for a few days looking for leads and last night, I mean the night before, he was checking on virgin solvents. He found some stories about fish kills in the river that happened to be near Barrow's house."

"How in the world would he know where Mark Barrow lived?" Clark asked.

"When Barrow first started restoring Jags, he paid Derek to teach him how to paint. The fish-kill stories jogged his memory of Barrow's shop. Even though it was in his home, it was like a professional shop. He was just the kind of guy who would continue using virgin solvents even though they'd been outlawed because he had a stockpile in his garage. I'm sure you'd have put the pieces together eventually, but it was Derek who saved that woman last night."

Tanya quickly added. "And you."

Michael kissed her on the forehead. "You know what I don't understand, now that I look back on it, is why would he allow us to come to his house to do a story about his Jags?"

Clark thought a minute before he answered. "We found a list in his house of potential victims. I'm sorry to say Tanya's name was included. It was probably why he attended the party at Peter's house in the first place, to look the place over for a possible abduction, or even to just gather information. He might also have allowed you to come over because he thought you might be able to provide some useful information. Maybe he thought it would raise too much suspicion if he didn't allow you to come over. We'll never know. In a way, though, it was a smart move. He had an alibi for that case and we marked him off our list."

He nodded grudgingly. Peter and Clark seemed intent on reliving the action from the night before. Michael didn't want to listen anymore. He found a Diet Dr. Pepper in the fridge and walked out to the koi pond so he could talk to the reclining jaguar. He noticed Tanya looking out the window a couple of times. Finally she came out and sat beside him.

"What's wrong?"

"This big news in the San Francisco paper will undoubtedly get back to Tulsa."

"Yes. So what about it? You're a hero, again."

"Don't you see?"

She stared at him with a puzzled look. "No."

"This will confirm everything my buddies were worried about. Now they'll be sure I'm an assassin. I find the bad guy, and I don't wait for any trial. I hand out my own justice."

"I hadn't thought of it that way."

She sat beside him and stroked his hair for a few minutes. She looked in his eyes and smiled. Her medicine had a strong effect.

"I look at it a different way. You had nightmares for years about the children screaming for help. This time you saved us. You saved my life the first night we met. If you hadn't come down to the garage, if you hadn't come to San Francisco... You saved that girl last night, too. If you hadn't acted immediately, she'd be dead now. She couldn't have had more than an hour to live. This is a happy ending. You should focus on that." She leaned over and kissed him gently on the cheek and went back inside. She seemed to realize he needed a little more time.

Michael eventually got up and walked to the garage. He turned on the overhead lights and looked at Lucille. She stood elegantly in the center of the room where they'd left her. He considered the car. Sure, it was an inanimate object, but she'd already lived three lives. The first was with Jack Waldorf. She'd been banished by his mother because of the tragedy that was his fate. Then she had found his father and helped him win his bride. Again, she found herself banished for years because he had lost Michael's mother. Now, she began a life for a third time with him. She'd led him on a great adventure to California and helped him find his true love. It looked like she was finally going to have a happy ending. Amazingly, and against all odds, she was right back where she had started. She had some interesting stories to tell anyone who would take the time to listen. She would most likely outlive him and find another life with a new owner after he was gone. Her first fifty years had been exciting. He wondered how many more adventures she had in her. He walked along the side of the car with his hand gently running along the sloping line of the body. She wasn't like new cars. She had curves. She demanded respect. Most of all, he thought about how small children loved her. She was like one of their toys come to life. He realized he would never look at an old car the same way again. He would always wonder what stories it had to tell about its previous owners.

What about his future? He wondered if he would ever figure out what had happened to his mother. He doubted he would.

Oklahoma didn't seem like home any more. The ranch was a million miles away. He decided he was beginning to feel like a Californian. Most of all, even though most of San Francisco seemed to think he'd saved Tanya's life, he knew he was the one who had been saved.

THE END

Paul McNabb has written two monthly classic Jaguar columns for many years, The McNabb Report for E-type Magazine (www.e-typeclub.com) and Letter from America for the XK Gazette (www.xkclub.com), providing stories about interesting owners, events and classic cars.

The magazines are published in England and distributed to 55 countries around the world. Recently he was asked by the Jaguar Club of Los Angeles to write a column for the club newsletter, Jaguar Tales, called According to Lucille (www.jcna.com).

The journalistic work provides a rich tapestry of inspiration for his books. He lives on the central coast of California with his wife, Cathy, and their classic Jaguar, Lucille.

Facebook- Paul.McNabb.5
Facebook- The Jaguar Conspiracy
Facebook- Michael McAllister
Visit the official website of Michael McAllister
www.paulmcnabb.com

DISCOVER MORE
FINE FICTION

Visit

www.mitchellmorrispublishing.com

MITCHELL MORRIS is a registered trademark of Celeris Publishing
Group, Inc.
Port Richey, FL

Made in the USA
Charleston, SC
05 November 2012